"I have a pr

The way those had her wishing ng quite different from what he was probably about to suggest. Definitely not that they should get naked and test out her new kitchen counters.

"Yes?" she squeaked out.

"I'll do the work in exchange for being able to rent the spare bedroom from you. This way, I don't have a landlord breathing down my back while I look for another place to live. A win-win for both of us. You're helping me out."

Sarah couldn't speak for a few seconds. She'd never imagined he would suggest living here. With her. But of course, this was no big deal to him. He was not picturing accidentally running into her coming out of the bathroom with only a towel wrapped around her naked body the way she'd been imagining in the few seconds since he'd mentioned the idea.

"This house has one bathroom. One."

He grinned. "I was taught to share."

Dear Reader,

Welcome to the second book in the Heroes of Fortune Valley series. In *Airman to the Rescue*, we get to know Matt Conner, a hero after my own heart. Matt is a single dad trying to reconcile with his troubled teenage son. If you have ever raised a teenager (guilty), you will relate to Matt's struggle. But what he doesn't expect is for Sarah to be the one who will help him understand the depth of a father's love.

While Sarah Mcallister can't resist her simmering attraction to former air force pilot Matt Conner, the road to love is never a smooth one. Have you ever met a man who can "fix" anything? Our hero doesn't just pound nails in his spare time. He also single-handedly manages to restore Sarah's bitter heart.

Welcome to Matt and Sarah's romance. May we always celebrate second chances and the restorative power of love.

I hope you will enjoy!

I love hearing from readers. You can find me on Facebook, Twitter (@heatherlybelle), Instagram (heatherly.bell) and Pinterest (heatherlymbell). Email: Heatherly@HeatherlyBell.com.

Sign up for my newsletter on my website, get all my latest news and updates, plus receive a free novella.

Heatherly Bell

HEATHERLY BELL

Airman to the Rescue

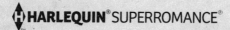

HARLEQUIN® SUPERROMANCE®

Recycling programs
for this product may
not exist in your area.

ISBN-13: 978-0-373-64030-0

Airman to the Rescue

Printed in U.S.A.

Heatherly Bell tackled her first book in 2004 and now the characters that occupy her mind refuse to leave until she writes them a book. She loves all music but confines singing to the shower these days. Heatherly lives in Northern California with her family, including two beagles—one who can say hello and the other a princess who can feel a pea through several pillows.

Books by Heatherly Bell

HARLEQUIN SUPERROMANCE

Breaking Emily's Rules
Airman to the Rescue

Other titles by Heatherly Bell are available
in ebook format.

For James, who can fix anything.

CHAPTER ONE

SARAH MCALLISTER'S EYES fluttered open and her gaze landed on the first items in her line of sight: several exposed wires crawling out of the socket in the ceiling above her bed like a spider's creepy legs.

She hated spiders almost as much as she hated contractors.

Her brand-new ceiling fan and light fixture combination belonged where those wires were, but instead it sat in the as-yet-unopened home improvement store box. She had Gus "should be murdered in his sleep" Hinckle, her hired contractor, to thank for that.

Sarah sighed and rolled over on her side. She startled at the sight of Shackles, her shaggy rescue mutt, sitting on the floor near her bed staring up at her. Unblinking.

A month after adopting Shackles, Sarah and her rescue were still getting used to each other. He'd been through a great deal, she got it, but was it her fault he'd been flown to California by Paws and Pilots only to have his forever family change their mind? In the end, she'd agreed to

adopt Shackles and had given him a name worthy
of their mutual situation. He was unwittingly tied
to her and she was tied to her father's old house
and the small town of Fortune, California, for reasons that didn't seem to make sense any longer.

"Time to get up."

Sarah fought with the white cotton sheets
wound twice around her legs since she'd tossed
and turned throughout the night. In other words,
the usual.

First order of business today was to put in a call
to Gus and ask him for the tenth time this week
when he planned on getting his ass over here to
finish the job she'd hired him to do. Paid him to
do, in fact, with a nice little deposit for his trou-
bles. She stumbled over the unfinished flooring
in the hallway where the hardwood slats were
propped against the wall, waiting.

The last time Gus had been here a week ago,
he'd given her high hopes he might actually finish the job. What he'd done looked promising because, when she could get the man to work, he
knew his stuff. Eventually her father's old house,
a relic of the sixties, would be updated to the
twenty-first century. Then she'd be able to flip
the house for a tidy profit and get out of dodge.
Back to Fort Collins, Colorado, since there was
nothing left for her here in Fortune.

She grabbed her cell phone from the kitchen
counter and hit her speed dial for Satan. As had

occurred every day for the past week, the call went immediately to Gus's voice mail.

Blah blah blah I'm a contractor. Blah blah blah not just a contractor but an artist. Blah blah blah I'll finish your project in time and under budget.

Oh yeah, that last one was hilarious.

"Get your ass over here and finish what you started or I swear I'm calling the cops! And I mean it this time."

As if the cops cared about a shifty contractor. The jails would be overflowing if that were the case. "I'll call the Better Business Bureau and file a complaint! Did I mention my brother is an Air Force pilot? He's big and bad and he'll kick your ass. Get over here!"

She hung up and threw the phone toward her couch. Her brother might be a badass but he was too busy running their late father's flight school, Magnum Aviation, chartering flights through his new company and spending every other moment with the blonde who had tamed him. Sarah wasn't going to ask him for any more help. He'd already done enough by installing the granite countertops after she'd bought him out of his half of the house.

Shackles stared from his empty dog bowl to her and back again. "All right, all right," Sarah said, filling his bowl. Never let it be said he couldn't communicate. In fact, he was better at communication than most men.

On the off chance he'd changed his routine,

that he'd finally begun to trust her a teensy bit, she went back to the counter and started the coffee. But true to his idiosyncrasies, Shackles wouldn't eat with anyone else in the room. He stood, guarding the bowl, less Sarah should suddenly be taken with the desire to start eating kibbles for breakfast. And he had still not touched the food.

"Where's the trust?" Sarah grumbled and headed to hit the shower, grateful Gus had never even started on her bathroom project.

The small south county airport where Sarah worked was bustling with activity when she arrived for her morning shift at the Short Stop Snack Shack. Since her brother had started Mcallister's Charters, he'd managed to infuse the struggling airport with a needed shot of adrenaline. Now they didn't just have the aviation school and an air museum on site, but the Short Stop Snack Shack had been revamped into more of a coffee shop.

Their clients were now not only composed of adrenaline junkies seeking the thrill of skydiving or flying lessons, but Silicon Valley high-tech gurus who worked from home on their sprawling hilltop homes and were occasionally needed in San Francisco and Los Angeles.

Then there were the legal professionals. She'd heard Gerald Firestone was a tyrant in the San Francisco County civil courtroom where he'd recently been made a judge, but he'd never been anything but kind to Sarah. He had a ten-acre farm in Fortune he retreated to every evening, and he chartered a flight from her brother Stone's company every morning and afternoon. She couldn't even imagine how much that would cost a person, but by the looks of his Rolex watch, Judge could afford it.

The Shack was not much more than a counter-top in the middle of the small converted hangar with bar stools circling it and one small makeshift wall. She'd talked the manager into an espresso machine, which made the passengers happy. However, the Shack was definitely still low-tech. But it was either their fresh-brewed coffee and shrink-wrapped pastries or a vending machine.

"How much would it cost to sue someone, Judge?" Sarah asked him, as she poured more coffee.

"That all depends." Judge Firestone glanced at his watch. "Why?"

"Just curious."

Even if it would only cost one hundred dollars to sue Gus—she didn't have the money. She'd worked through most of her savings to buy Stone out, and then taken out a short-term adjustable-rate bank loan to help with renovations. If Gus didn't materialize at some point, Sarah didn't know what she would do. She didn't want her brother to know about any of this. If Stone were to find out about the mess she'd gotten herself into, he'd only remind her he'd never thought it a great idea to remodel the place. No, the whole thing had been her idea and now she had to deal.

But surely Gus would show up. He had a reputation to protect. Besides, she'd recently decided to believe in the goodness of people. She was going to stop being so angry at the world and its inhabitants. Stop being antisocial and learn to be friendlier. *Fake it till you make it.* Judge was a big part of the change, and he made the chit-chat easy. On the other hand, Gus reminded her that no matter what kind of magical fairy dust she wanted to sprinkle all over, people like him turned it into sparkly pollution.

She was a work in progress.

Judge opened his mouth, but the loud speaker squawked and Emily's soft voice called out, "Chartered flight two-oh-three passengers, please come to the tarmac for boarding."

"Guess you better go," Sarah said.

Judge slapped his always excessive tip on the counter and smiled. "Wonder if she's flying me today."

"That happened once."

"A man can dream." He picked up his briefcase and waved to Sarah.

It didn't surprise her that Judge carried a little torch for Emily Parker, soon to be Emily Mcallister. Most men crushed on Emily. And Sarah understood crushes. Unfortunately, she understood them far too well. Crushes didn't go any-where because at heart they were nothing more than fantasies. Judge had to realize he didn't stand a chance with Emily. But the bald, sweet, fifty-something Judge probably loved a gratifying fan-tasy as much as the next person, and as long as the make-believe never converged with reality it was usually a safe and predictable situation.

The door leading to the tarmac opened and the object of *her* personal fantasies strode in, as al-ways seemingly unaware of how he made Sarah break out in a spontaneous sweat. Matt Conner, Stone's Air Force buddy and best friend, carried himself with his usual air of confidence and easy male swagger as he made his way inside, avia-tor shades covering his chocolate-brown eyes. He worked for Stone, one of a handful of pilots on staff. While Matt made his way to Magnum's offices, where he occasionally taught a lesson or two, Sarah forced her gaze away and wiped the countertop. She hated this hyperawareness of him every time he walked into a room. If her eyes were blindfolded, she'd know his presence in the room by the absolute pull of her body in his direction.

Not for the first time and certainly not for the last, she forced herself to get with the program and stop daydreaming. She was here to fix a house, and fix her life if at all possible. Not to lust after a man, no matter how hunky.

"Hey, Sarah. Turn it up, would you?" One of their regulars pointed to the flat-screen TV anchored to the wall behind her.

She usually kept the set on mute, but she now turned up the volume. Yet another car chase broadcasted on national news. California, of course. Not exactly the image she wanted her mother back home in Colorado to see. Mom believed there were earthquakes every day in California, and that everyone was blond and beautiful. Coming out a month ago to meet Emily hadn't done much to dispel that last myth. Now she'd believe car chases were the norm, too.

"Okay, this is ridiculous. Why doesn't he just pull over? He's going to hurt someone," Sarah said as she, too, became entranced. Four police cars were chasing a red convertible Corvette down a closed-off freeway somewhere in San Diego. Someone had a death wish.

"Been a while since we had one of these chases." Jedd straddled a stool. He worked for Stone as a mechanic, and was probably on his break.

The cops surrounded the car from all directions, and when the Corvette tried to pull over, they blocked it in.

"Let me have some coffee? Not your fancy machine. Just the stuff in the pot," Jedd said.

"Coming right up." While her back was turned, there was a little cheer from the small group.

"Yeah! They got him. Look at him surrender-ing like a wimp after putting up such a fight." Jedd stuck out his office mug. "Yeah, that's right, sucker. Hands up in the air."

Sarah poured Jedd's coffee and glanced up at the TV. The man they'd arrested looked an awful lot like… But no. It couldn't be. Everybody had a doppelgänger in the world. Right?

"Ow! Sarah!"

Sarah yanked her attention away from the nightmare occurring on national TV. She'd kept pouring into Jedd's cup and nearly all over his arm. "I'm so sorry. Are you all right?"

"I got a splash, but I'm fine. That coffee's hot."

She'd also spilled all over the counter and down the floor. She grabbed a rag and ran it under cold water. "Here, put this on your hand."

She glanced back up at the screen to see that the man was now on the ground, cops blocking him in on every direction. Maybe she was seeing things. She'd been under so much stress lately, with her father's death and coming out to Fortune to settle his estate, that something like that *could* happen. She might be hallucinating.

"D-did you hear them say what the guy's name is? The one they arrested?"

"Nah, the news probably won't release his name." Jedd used the wet rag she'd given him to mop up the floor instead. "Hey now, Sarah,

you don't need to cry about this. I know it was
an accident."

But Sarah wanted to cry. She also wanted to
scream and curse. The ticker tape across the
screen read "Contractor on the run arrested."
And the man they'd just arrested sure looked an
awful lot like Gus Hinckle.

CHAPTER TWO

MATT CONNER HAD returned from a quick chartered hop to San Francisco and checked back in with Emily and Cassie when he heard a commotion in the converted hangar the airport used for several offices and the Snack Shack. Cheers and a few claps. In other words, not the norm at their quiet south county airport. He stuck his head out the office door, and as usual his gaze focused on Sarah like a laser beam. The waiting passengers were excited and pleased about something or other. Sarah, on the other hand, stood behind the counter of the Snack Shack openly sobbing. Jedd was doing his best to comfort her, his face broadcasting the same pained expression men all over the world wore when they didn't know how to comfort a woman but still had to try.

In seconds, Matt made his way out the door and to the middle of the hangar.

"I don't know what you're so upset about. Everybody makes mistakes. It was just a little coffee," Jedd said as he patted Sarah's shoulder.

"What the hell happened?" Matt barked.

"She spilled some coffee on me and then she…

she just started crying. I'm not hurt, I swear!"
Jedd held up his hands.

"Sarah. Tell me what's wrong," Matt said, his
voice sounding clipped and edgy even to his own
ears. He tried his best to soften his tone, but she
worried him. The passengers were beginning to
stare, too, and she'd hate that.

This had nothing to do with the coffee. He'd
only known her a few months but everything
about Sarah said confident, capable, independent
woman. He'd never seen her give way to her emotions like this, even after losing her estranged father and fighting with Stone over the flight school
and their inheritance. Every instinct in him said
this was much bigger than spilled coffee.

She shook her head, wrapping her arms around
her body like she'd cave in at any minute.

Never one to lack initiative, Matt tugged her
gently from behind the counter and then led her,
hand on the small of her back, toward Magnum's
main office. He opened the door, and when Emily
glanced up from the desk where she sat next to
their office assistant, Cassie, he waved away the
look of concern in her eyes.

"Need a minute." He led Sarah inside Stone's
smaller inner office and shut the door.

"I'm okay." She hiccupped and grabbed a tissue
from the box on Stone's desk. "R-really."

"Yeah, not buying it. Try again."

"Seriously. This isn't your concern. Just give

me a few minutes in here. I'll get myself to-gether." She jerked away from him, but he caught her by the elbow and turned her toward him. The same energy he'd tried to ignore again and again surfaced as it did every time he touched her. A jolt of electricity coursed through him because every time he touched Sarah he got a one-two-punch reminder he was a man. And she was a hot woman. Beautiful. Smart.

But not his.

"Tell me."

Her green eyes, now red-rimmed, found their fire again. "Why? So you can try to fix this for me? I don't need your help."

Good. He had pissed-off, fighting Sarah again. He could deal with her. What he couldn't handle was falling-apart Sarah because she only made him want to haul her into his arms and kiss her until she forgot her name.

"Something happened out there, and it didn't have anything to do with coffee." He leaned back against Stone's desk and folded his arms across his chest.

She slapped her forehead. "Of course it didn't have to do with coffee! This has to do with the fact that I'm an idiot. I trusted a man. I paid him good money, and he didn't deliver!"

At this, he was sure he'd lost a couple of brain cells. He didn't speak for a moment, clearing his throat as he tried with a Herculean effort not to picture Sarah paying for a gigolo's services. But that's exactly what it sounded like even if he knew it couldn't be true. Still, his imagination was enjoying this little side trip. Maybe a little too much.

"Oh my God! Wipe that look off your face. I hired a *contractor*. Somebody up there must really hate me because I picked the loser of contractors. I picked the guy who leads the police on a car chase and gets arrested on national TV!"

Crap. "*That* was your contractor?"

"It's him." She slumped into one of the chairs. "We were all watching. I tried to tell myself it wasn't him, and that it could be someone who looked like him. I don't know what he did, but the man got himself arrested. He hasn't returned my calls and now I know why."

"Great. How much did you pay him?"

"Too much. I gave him a deposit, and there hasn't been much labor. He could never seem to finish a project. Always had to run to the store to get another nail or another stud or God knows what."

"Where did you hear about this guy, anyway?"

"Eloise's List. He had plenty of good reviews so either the people were being blackmailed into leaving them or he's recently changed his work ethic."

There had to be something else, though, or

she wouldn't be this upset. "No worries. I'll find someone else for you. I'll check him out first."

"No."

He cocked his head. "No?"

"You heard me. Unless you know anyone who works for free, I can't afford them."

"You run out of money?"

"You could say that. I planned on selling soon and flipping the house." She groaned and rubbed her temples. "This is so much more complicated than on those home improvement shows."

Those reality shows were filled with so much... fantasy. Find a fixer-upper for two hundred dollars, pour in some "sweat equity" and sell for a cool million. He didn't know where these scenarios happened, but so far as he could tell it wasn't planet Earth. He'd tried, of course, to warn Sarah about buying the house from Stone. To say the house needed a facelift was an understatement. Even Stone had tried to talk her out of the remodeling.

Initially Matt had believed Sarah might stay, but then she'd made it clear she would flip the house and move back to Colorado. So she'd be leaving, and he'd be staying. He only had a few more years left with his son, Hunter, before he turned eighteen. Only a few years to make a difference in his life.

He liked Sarah, but he also didn't need the drama. Especially when she was only here in Fortune a while longer. But he wasn't done torturing himself, nor would he stand by while Sarah lost everything. He squatted down in front of her chair, and put one hand on each of her jean-clad legs.

"I work for free."

"FREE?" SARAH ASKED, distracted by the way his forearms connected powerfully and gracefully to the big hands on her legs. They were great forearms. Great hands, too. Great everything. Damn him. He was balanced on the balls of his feet in front of her, and she couldn't stop thinking about the previous comment she'd made. The one he'd misunderstood so completely.

Or more than likely he was only teasing her with the fully sexual look he'd pinned her with a moment ago. She could almost see the moving frames of the porno movie playing in his mind. Why he continued to play with her like this she'd never understand. Oh yeah, that's right, but she did understand. He was a man.

"I know my way around a hammer. I'll help."

She shook her head. "No. I can't let you do this."

"Yeah, you can."

"No, Matt. You have enough going on in your life."

"And I can handle it."

If she hadn't been trained for her work as a

forensic artist back in Colorado, she might not have noticed the tells of the eyes. Matt's were obvious to her, which made everything between them so confusing. His eyes consistently told her one thing and his words another. Right now the breath-stealing eyes said he was tired, tense, frustrated and something else she couldn't put her finger on. Was it desire? Pity? Oh please, not pity.

Stop it. Stop trying to analyze everyone.

The problem was she knew too much about Matt Conner to believe him right now. When Matt had moved on from the Air Force, Stone offered him a full-time position piloting flights at Mcallister Charters. It had been time, Matt had said, to settle back in his hometown. The teenage son he'd had with a high school girlfriend lived nearby and Matt had been trying to reconnect with Hunter after many years of living abroad. As far as she could tell, the reunion wasn't going well.

She did know a little about teenagers and their anger and resistance to absentee fathers.

Matt also looked in on his father, who had retired early and lived nearby. Then there was the hellish landlord she'd been hearing rumors about lately. Matt was looking for another place to rent in the area, preferably a home where he could have his son visit every other weekend. How could she, in all good conscience, take any more

time away from a man who already had far too
many demands on him?

"Matt," she said slowly, drawing out his name,
and peeling his warm hands off her legs.

"Sarah," he repeated, allowing it, but giving
her a slow and devilish grin that reached into her
heart and gave it a little twist.

"Forget it." She stood up, smoothing down her
jeans and taking a deep and sexually frustrated
breath.

She couldn't have Matt around every day fixing her house. A woman only had so much self-
control around a man like Matt. She figured
within three days of him at the house, working
in a tool belt and no shirt—at least in her fantasies—she'd attack him and make a fool out of
herself. And she'd had enough of that in the past
few months, thank you very much.

"I need to get back to work. Thanks for bringing me in here to calm down. I don't know what
happened out there. I guess I lost it for a minute."
She put her hand on the doorknob and turned to
give him a small attempt at a smile. It felt tight.
Fake.

He was back to leaning against Stone's desk,
his big arms folded across the white button-up
Mcallister Charters shirt. No one wore a shirt
like Matt Conner did. Like Stone and the other
pilots, he wore a type of uniform when he flew.
The white button-up with its logo, usually sleeves

rolled up to his elbows, and black cargo pants filled out in all the right places. The aviator glasses often completed the outfit, making him drool-worthy. She also knew him to be highly intelligent. A pilot. An engineer. A mechanic. Apparently also a carpenter of sorts.

And one hundred percent heartbreaker.

"Hey." His smooth-as-whiskey voice stopped her halfway out the door.

"Yeah?"

"I'm not going to forget it."

She didn't answer, too tired to fight with him anymore, and made her way back to the Snack Shack. Jedd had gone back to work, and the entire coffee mess had been cleaned up as if nothing had happened at all. A couple of customers were waiting patiently, and Sarah apologized to them. Behind the counter, she stayed busy filling coffee orders and warming up pastries in the microwave.

And she tried not to notice when Matt finally emerged from Stone's office a few minutes later, his long, lean body moving through the hangar until he disappeared out the doors to the tarmac.

Tried not to notice. But as usual, she couldn't resist.

CHAPTER THREE

THREE DAYS LATER, Sarah sat in the middle of the floor in the hallway, safety glasses on, a hammer in one hand and a nail in the other. Stone had previously replaced worn, missing and loose panels in the home. She, on the other hand, had decided that she wanted brand-new cherrywood flooring throughout. Now that half of it was done and half not done, she'd need to finish the job herself. And she would make this hardwood floor her bitch. How hard could this be when Satan could do it?

"You can do this. You're an artist. This is just a different medium," she told herself.

This much was true at least. She had a bachelor of liberal arts from Colorado University. Because she hadn't much wanted to starve, she'd wound up working as a forensic artist for the Fort Collins Police Department. Her work had earned her a reputation back home. She'd drawn sketches of alleged suspects worthy of an art gallery, some had said. Of course, she disagreed, but she had a higher standard than most.

Van Gogh. Monet. They were her standard.

She no longer felt satisfied or rewarded by all the hard work she'd done for the PD. No longer happy to simply collect her paycheck and call herself an artist. There was still something to be said for art that simply existed for no other reason than beauty.

But now her father's house would suffer at the hands of an incompetent carpenter. This bothered the artist in her, but maybe her dad deserved it.

She'd read the instructions on the wood slat box. Engineer talk, all of it. Clear as mud. Sounded like they were describing how to build a ship to fly to Mars, so she ignored the stupid instructions and let common sense be her guide.

And now she was short a nail.

She fixed the last nail into a single wood slat, one little tap after another. She'd nearly bruised her lower lip by the time she was done. "There!"

At this rate she should be done in approximately six months.

Shackles came into the hallway, sniffing around her like a Hoover, as if he'd missed a crumb somewhere. When he picked up a nail, Sarah panicked. Had he already swallowed the missing one? If so, why wasn't he lying on the ground convulsing in agony?

"Drop it! Drop it, Shackles."

She pulled his jaw open only to be rewarded with a growl. Finally prying the nail out from between his teeth without getting bitten in the process, she carried him into the spare bedroom and shut the door. He yipped his regret from behind the closed door.

"Too late for apologies. You won't be committing suicide on my watch."

Turning in a circle, air coming in short desperate spurts, Sarah wondered whether she could call 911 for a dog. She finally took in a full breath when she found the missing nail sticking halfway out from under one of the floor slats. So she would now have to rip up this section and try again, but at least her dog wouldn't die.

She had to work faster. Thankfully Gus had left some of his tools and she would be confiscating those as payment for the work not delivered. Maybe a nail gun would be the answer to going faster. Power tools. Great idea. She'd seen Satan fooling with the nail gun, and making good time with it, too. Speaking of Gus, she could no longer leave a message on his phone. Box full. Surprise. Emily had heard from one of her event planners at Fortune Ranch, her family's business, that Gus Hinckle had indeed been arrested. Drug possession was the rumor floating around town. Suddenly the constant runny nose made sense. It was not, as he had claimed, spring allergies.

More importantly, Sarah would never see her money again. Having worked with the police department, she understood felony charges would take priority over anything else. In any case, she had neither the time nor the money to sue him. This was her hot mess, and she'd fix it.

Buying her father's house was supposed to be about a trip down memory lane, and a time for healing. She had a chance to break from her routine life in Colorado and the job that sucked the life out of her soul. A chance to try on a new attitude in a new place. And maybe, if she could make this house her own before she had to say goodbye to it, she might be able to go back home with a renewed purpose. A new beginning. As an added bonus, she'd reconnected with her brother.

Stone had grown up with their father, and Sarah had been raised by their mother. A strange custody arrangement by anyone's standards. Even Stone now agreed, after a difficult period of time during which he hadn't been able to face that the man who'd been his hero had done something wrong. It wasn't like Sarah didn't blame her mother, too. Practically being an only child had tied Sarah to her mother in a kind of guilt bond that had lasted for years. Out here in California, she'd been free from that guilt, even if she still didn't quite belong.

Stop feeling sorry for yourself.

She'd had a goal when she'd come out to Fortune that went beyond hammering out estate problems with her brother. Sarah Mcallister was going to stop being a prickly porcupine. The change hadn't been easy so far. One big mistake—okay, *several* big mistakes in her teenage years—didn't mean that she had to be a nun for the rest of her life. She was going to awaken her inner goddess because life was short, dammit, and she was going to get some.

Yeah, right.

Her doorbell rang. Probably Emily again, who dropped by once a week, with or without Stone. She had to give it to her sister-in-law to be. Emily kept trying her best to make Sarah feel welcome. She'd reached out and made friends, which Sarah appreciated. It wasn't like Stone had thrown out the welcome mat when she'd arrived in town.

But when Sarah opened her front door, it wasn't Emily behind it. Matt stood there in all his male glory. The midday June sunshine pooled through the doorway all around his big body, practically illuminating him. It was as if God was showing off, saying *Behold some of my best work. You are welcome.*

He grinned and whipped off his aviator glasses. "Hey."

Sarah's knees took the hit first. Then her mind followed. Blank. Why, oh why, did she lose several IQ points around the man?

"Are you going to let me in?"

"Oh." Good idea. She should let him in. Why not? How much harm could that do? She moved aside.

He was dressed casually today, in dark jeans and a Giants T-shirt. Mr. Cool.

"How's it going?"

"Great! I just put in some of the flooring in the hallway. There's a little section I might have to redo."

He raised a brow. "You're doing this all yourself?"

"Sure. I can't lie, it's a little challenging, but I figured I'd work with what I have." She followed him into the kitchen, where his gaze studied the cabinets. The doors were all missing. She cleared her throat. "I hope he ordered those. Maybe I'll get a call from the home improvement store that they've come in."

"Yeah. Maybe," he said without an ounce of confidence in his voice. His hand smoothed over the granite countertops. "These came out well."

"Yeah. Well. Stone's handiwork."

"I remember."

Right. Matt had dropped by a lot during the week Stone had been helping her work on the house.

She blew out a breath, and her overgrown bangs flipped out of her eyes. "Matt, what are you doing here?"

"Came to check things out."

"I thought I told you to forget about this."

His dark gaze did a slow slide down the length of her body, and back up to meet her eyes. "And I told you I wouldn't."

"Listen, I'm not being stubborn here."

He snorted. "No, of course not."

"The fact of the matter is I would let you finish the job if I had a prayer of compensating you for your work. Properly." In other words, not in long deep kisses and showers in the new bathroom stall she still didn't have, but in actual money.

"I get that."

"I'm not sure you do."

Ignoring her, he walked toward the hallway. Sarah would have followed him, but humiliation kept her seated at the kitchen table, hands folded in front of her. No point in arguing with the man. She'd let him inspect to his heart's content. Maybe he had a little free time today. She heard him curse when he entered the hallway, and a few more times as he went into each bedroom. Sarah didn't respond. It didn't take an engineer to know her remodel was in trouble.

He walked into the living room and cursed again. Probably at the windows. They were half framed. All the blinds had been removed, and Sarah was currently using sheets for privacy. She stared at the ceiling, trying not to think about the Swiss cheese roof above her. The roof would come later, if at all. She'd planned on giving the new buyers a roof allowance, like the real estate agent had suggested. Roofs were expensive.

A few minutes and several loud curses later, Matt rejoined her in the kitchen. She glanced at him briefly, then looked away when he shoved a hand through his honey-colored hair. She expected him to say *I told you so* or any one of a number of phrases he could have let loose with to prove he'd been right and she'd been wrong.

Instead, he pulled out a chair and sat shoulder to shoulder next to her, stretching his long legs out in front of him. For several minutes he didn't speak, his arms folded across his chest as he stared at the floor.

Finally, she couldn't stand the silence any longer. "How bad?"

His answer was to curse again and shake his head.

That bad. Sarah buried her face in her hands. "I'm screwed."

"No," he said simply. "Not if you're willing to listen to me."

"I already said I'm not—"

"Would you shut up and listen?"

She pursed her lips together and made a show of locking them and throwing away the key. If he had an answer to her predicament, she could at least hear him out. As long as it didn't involve him working for free, she could be flexible.

"I have a proposition for you."

The way those sensual lips said *proposition* had her wishing he were about to say something quite different than what he was probably about to suggest. Definitely not that they should get naked and test out her new kitchen counters.

"Yes?" she squeaked out.

"I'll do the work in exchange for being able to rent the spare bedroom from you. This way, I don't have a landlord breathing down my back while I look for another place to live. A win-win for both of us. You're helping me out."

Sarah couldn't speak for a few seconds. She'd never imagined he would suggest living here. With her. But of course, this was no big deal to him. He was not picturing accidentally running into her coming out of the bathroom with only a towel wrapped around her naked body the way she'd been imagining in the few seconds since he'd mentioned the idea.

"This house has one bathroom. One."

He grinned. "I was taught to share."

"And how long do you think it will take to finish?"

He glanced up at the ceiling, then met her eyes. "Depends on the roof. But I'm thinking a month or two."

"That's about all the time I have left. And I was thinking of skipping the roof anyway."

"We'll discuss it." He studied her. "This could work."

It might work, but she hated the fact Matt was rescuing her again. She'd been an independent woman her entire adult life, but since coming to California this might be the third time Matt had stepped in. Second if she didn't count the coffee incident. When she'd first come out to California a few months ago, after getting the news her father had died, it was Matt who had understood her grief. Not Stone. Matt who had acted as peacemaker between her and Stone. Matt who had listened to her ramble on for hours. Matt who had been such a good friend to her. He was a great guy, and she wished she didn't feel a magnetic attraction to him. Life would be simpler if they could be buddies, and if she would never want anything more than that from him.

Fat chance.

Seated next to her, far too close, he waited for her answer.

"But you'll only get at most two months of free rent before we have to sell the house."

"That's probably all I'll need."

"That doesn't sound like enough for all your efforts. And then there's the materials. The cabinets." She sighed, not wanting to go on with the rest of the list and hear him curse again.

"I've got connections, and I can find a lot of the materials I'll need for less money."

"No."

"Ah, hell, Sarah. Now you're pissing me off."

She smiled, stupid with the satisfaction she could make him feel anything at all. "But I have a counter proposition."

He scowled. "Let's hear it."

She shifted her focus away from him and those piercing eyes to stare at her hands again. "I think you should be a partner with me in this. When I sell the house, I'll give you a percentage of the profits I make."

He studied her. "That sound fair to you?"

"It's the only way I'll do this."

"You've already put too much into this house. Bought Stone out of his half."

"And because of insane valley prices, the house has already appreciated in value since I did."

"I could only take five percent at the most. And that's after all your expenses."

That didn't seem fair, considering all he'd have to put into this. "I'm thinking twenty percent."

He grimaced. "How about ten percent?"

"Fifteen percent, and that's my final offer!"

The chair squeaked across the tile kitchen floor as Matt stood. "You drive a hard bargain. Backward. Fifteen percent, you stubborn woman."

Sarah stood and followed him to the front door.

"I'll clear out one of the bedrooms so you can move in."

"Leave that for me. I'll be by day after tomorrow." He shoved his aviator glasses back on.

And then he was out the door, leaving her to wonder how she'd ever get through the next two months without jumping Matt Conner's bones.

CHAPTER FOUR

THE IDEA OF living with Sarah already pushed boundaries Matt didn't feel comfortable crossing. Taking money from her left him feeling disgusted for accepting her terms. But he knew Sarah would have this no other way.

Later, he'd try to find a way out of their agreement. For now, he'd take one challenge at a time. First challenge: find a way to live in close proximity with Sarah for two months without kissing her—or worse. Second challenge: fix the mess the previous contractor left for him. He was driving down Monterey Road toward his father's house when his third challenge buzzed his cell phone.

Joanne. His ex.

He punched her through to the speaker. "What's up?"

"We have a problem here. Junior has decided he has a new purpose in life. It's called driving his mother to drink."

"What now?"

"He and his friends spray-painted the long wooden fence down from the high school. Security cameras caught the little Einsteins, and now the school wants to have a conference with all the parents before the end of the year. I want you there. I think maybe having his father be an Air Force veteran could help. Can you come in your uniform?"

"Are you *kidding* me?"

"Why not?"

"First, I wouldn't do that if it would get my own father off death row. Second, I'm no longer in the Air Force. I'm not going to put on the uniform to prevent my son from receiving his deserved punishment."

"There you go again, father of the year."

Even now it stung, despite knowing the source. Joanne had never before encouraged his relationship with Hunter. She'd simply wanted the checks sent on time, no matter what part of the country he'd been living in at the time. He'd paid child support faithfully for years, but since he'd separated from the Air Force and settled back in his hometown for good, he wanted a real relationship with fifteen-year-old Hunter. And the kid wanted to hang out with Matt about as much as he wanted to repeat his sophomore year.

"Text me the day and time and I'll be there." He hung up.

Hunter might not want to have anything to do with Matt, but it didn't mean he could give up. He hadn't worked his ass off for most of his life only to be intimidated by a fifteen-year-old kid now.

Matt wanted to be some kind of an influence on his son in the next few years, maybe so the kid wouldn't wind up making some of the same colossal "think with the little head" mistakes Matt had made in his teens.

It also wouldn't hurt to demonstrate to a certain dark-haired beauty that not all estranged fathers were deadbeats. Matt tried to tell himself it had nothing to do with Sarah, but something about her made him care a lot more deeply for her than he wanted to. More than was probably wise. Not that he'd been able to stop. He enjoyed teasing her, playing with her, and while he told himself it was all harmless flirting, he'd have to put a stop to it if they were going to be living together. Because were he being honest with himself, he and Sarah weren't a good idea for many reasons. She planned to leave town after selling her father's house for a tidy profit, and for the first time in years, Matt was determined to be grounded. He'd stay here in Fortune at least until Hunter graduated from high school.

Matt stopped by the local market and stocked up on a few of his father's favorites, and thirty minutes later he arrived at Dad's gated condominium complex in San Jose.

"Hey, Dad," he said as he let himself in the front door with his spare set of keys.

Dad sat in front of the TV watching an old Western. "Did you get my cookies?"

"You think I would forget after you left me ten voice mails in the space of an hour?" Matt set the brown paper bags on the kitchen counter and started unpacking.

Dad wasn't much for cooking any longer, so Matt usually bought frozen and prepackaged meals he could heat in a microwave. The cookies were a treat he didn't think should be in any sixty-six-year-old man's wheelhouse but it was hard to argue with the man. Plus, Matt's special deliveries were about the only time they spent together.

"Did you get the double-stuffs? I don't want those little thin shits they're trying to sell to the health nuts. I want the real deal."

"Got the real deal." Matt lobbed a package of the sugar lard in his Dad's direction and the man caught them one-handed.

"Hear from your son lately?"

"I'm going to be seeing him again next week."

"Good, good. A boy needs his father."

A boy needed his father to show him how to be a man. Matt agreed. But Hunter didn't need Matt to bail him out of jams he'd created for himself. "He's got himself into some trouble and Joanne asked me to come to the meeting at the school."

"What kind of trouble?" Dad ripped open the package of cookies.

"Something about a fence they tagged."

"Stupid kids," Dad muttered. "It's good you're

going over there. Good that Joanne asked you to help. She's a good mother. You lucked out."

Matt supposed this was a dig at his own mother, who'd taken off when he was ten. Dad had been a single father, choosing never to re-marry, and putting Matt first in everything. He'd been a Class A hard-ass, leading Matt to find boot camp a kind of mini-vacation, but he'd kept Matt out of trouble. Mostly. Until Hunter. The re-sulting humiliation at having failed to "keep it in his pants," as his father had repeatedly warned him to do, still hung over Matt.

As the only son of a top-level executive in the high-tech world of Silicon Valley, Matt had been expected and groomed to succeed. And succeed big. With his grades and test scores, he could have made it into an Ivy League school, until one unfortunate night almost sixteen years ago. Shocked and disappointed in Matt, Dad had still offered to pay child support to Joanne so his plans for Matt would not have to be derailed, and had vehemently opposed his idea to join the Air Force. But no way in hell would Matt allow his father to take care of the responsibilities that were rightfully Matt's. It meant that he'd grown up overnight. He'd have been ashamed to be off at college enjoying his freedom while his dad sent regular checks to Joanne. While Joanne struggled to get through business school, living with her parents and raising their child.

Then again, Dad had never understood Matt's draw to service. He'd wanted to join up, as had many of his friends in a post-9/11 world. Plan B had turned out to be the best option for Matt, who'd never much aspired to hang with Ivy Leaguers, top-tier grades or not. The Air Force had been everything to him for years. His friends. His family. His life.

Now he was out and trying to figure out life after the Air Force. Plan C.

"Why don't you take the kid fishing?" Dad now asked between cookie bites. "I hear it's a good way to connect."

Good way to connect? Dad, who had always been about as warm and fuzzy as a missile, suddenly had nothing but fatherly advice for Matt. He would have loved to have gone fishing with his dad. Even once.

"Where do you hear this?"

"Dr. Phil."

Matt couldn't help it. He laughed. A few years ago, Dad would have laughed off TV doctor advice, too. But now that he'd retired and couldn't spend all day on the golf course, he had turned to TV to fill some of his free time.

"All right, if you don't want Dr. Phil's advice, don't ask for it."

"I didn't."

"Listen, Mr. Smart Ass, I'm still your father."

"Dad, I'm thirty-two. I've been lacing my own shoes for a while."

"So I have nothing to add to the conversation?"

Matt cleared his throat. "I'll see if he wants to go fishing. And maybe you could go with us."

"I've never fished in my life. Why would I want to start now when I'm busy working on my golf game? You know what? Forget the fishing. I never took you fishing, and look how well you turned out. Except for that little hiccup, you were a great kid."

Matt's jaw tightened. "You mean Hunter. He's the little hiccup?"

To his father's credit, he wouldn't meet Matt's gaze. "Not him. Joanne was the little hiccup. Told you to keep it in your pants. Just because you have women falling all over you doesn't mean you have to sow your seeds everywhere."

Everywhere? Hardly. That had been only the second time he'd ever been with a girl, and he'd screwed up royally. Then again, his dad had never given much advice beyond his fascination with pants. Near as Matt could recall, the whole event had happened in the backseat of a truck and fast enough that he hadn't even taken his pants off. Since then, he liked to think he'd learned a little bit more how to please a woman, and made wiser choices regarding the women he chose to spend his time with.

The thought brought him back to Sarah. With

the pull she had on him, he wasn't sure how he'd make this new living arrangement work, but he had to try. She needed him, and he wasn't doing anything more than he would for any other good friend.

And he would keep telling himself that until he actually believed it.

Sarah was already dealing with too much. She'd felt cheated out of an opportunity to say goodbye to her father when he'd become ill with cancer and hadn't wanted Stone to notify either his ex-wife or Sarah. James Mcallister hadn't wanted either of them to see him withered away, which both Stone and Matt understood. Sarah, not so much. When she'd first bought the house and not long after decided to flip it for a profit, Matt had convinced himself she was doing it as a way to flip her father off, too. To let him know the house meant nothing more to her than a financial windfall. No sentiment involved. But she'd lingered for months in that old house, even getting a temporary job at the airport to stay a bit longer.

She'd flirted mercilessly with him at the beginning, and he with her if he were being honest. But he wouldn't have a casual fling with his best friend's kid sister. He didn't need the drama or the guilt. Matt would simply bide his time, keep his hands to himself and fix her house. She'd be gone soon enough.

CHAPTER FIVE

HUNTER CONNER WAS about to blow through his next high level on "Call of Duty" when he heard his mother yelling from downstairs. She was so loud that he had to keep turning the volume up but he could still hear her voice screeching in the background. He'd closed his bedroom door and everything. This wouldn't be a problem if he could find his earbuds but at the moment they were MIA.

"Hunter!" His bedroom door swung open.

No knock or anything. It was like living in a damn zoo. He ignored his mother and kept on shooting the terrorists. One down. Two.

"Put that stupid game down. I need to talk to you!"

Abort mission! Abort!

She ripped the controller out of his hands.

"What do you want?" The sooner she got this over with, the sooner he'd get back to killing terrorists. He could kick ass with the best of them. But his mother was all about ruining his life.

"I shouldn't even let you play this game. You're

in trouble, mister. I talked to your father and he's coming to the meeting with us."

"Seriously? Why?" Mom acted like this fence-tagging thing was the end of the world. Who cared? They were talking about a fence! Everyone acted like he'd killed someone.

"Because he's your father and it's about time he did something. With him being a veteran, maybe they'll take pity on you."

Hunter snorted. His dad was no badass veteran. He'd flown fighter jets so it wasn't like he'd gotten his hands dirty or anything. Hunter was going to enlist, too, when he turned eighteen. He hadn't told Mom yet because she might lock him in his bedroom. She treated him like a kid, like he wasn't almost a man. But Hunter would be a Marine or a Navy SEAL. A killer. Not some chair force guy like his stupid Dad.

"Why didn't you ask me first? Maybe I don't want him there."

"Because it's not up to you. It's his duty as your father. Dinner's ready." She slammed his door shut.

Yeah, right. Duty. He didn't need his father anymore. Maybe when he was a little kid he wanted to spend more time with him, back when all they'd had was an occasional weekend when he was home from flying all over the world. He still had those little Air Force toy jets somewhere in the back of his closet. Point being, he wasn't a kid anymore. He didn't need his father. Didn't need his mother, either, but try convincing *her* of that.

All of a sudden this summer, Mom wanted him to spend more time with his dad, so they could "get to know each other" again. She only wanted Hunter to spend more time with Matt so *she* could spend more time with her new boyfriend. He played baseball, a loser who couldn't make the major leagues so now he was trying to break into the minors. If his Mom wanted to follow Chuck the Loser around, she was welcome to it. Hunter could stay alone in his own house. He was too old for a babysitter.

No way, no how would he hang out with Dad and try to be best buddies like he was a little kid again.

Those days were gone.

"THAT'S IT?" SARAH followed Matt to the bedroom he'd be staying in.

The man traveled light. Within a couple of hours he'd moved his few belongings into the spare bedroom. A king-size bed, which took up most of the small bedroom, a dresser, a lamp. His laptop and a flat-screen TV. A few boxes that couldn't contain much of anything.

"You forget I flew fighter jets. Tiny cramped spaces."

"You didn't live in them, did you?"

"Nah, I wish." He grinned. "That would have been cool."

That boyish grin went all the way to her womb.

One of the boxes was open and on top were a few framed photos. She picked one of them up. A fighter jet in the background, Matt and Stone suited up. "You and Stone."

"Yep."

"Where was this taken?"

"Afghanistan."

He didn't smile and didn't elaborate. Of course he wouldn't. She'd already learned from Stone that part of their lives was off-limits to discussion. She picked up another one, a photo of him and Stone and another guy she didn't recognize. "Who's this?"

He glanced over her shoulder. "That's Levi. He's still in."

"Handsome guy."

"Yeah. He thinks so, too."

He didn't hold a candle to Matt in that department, but of course that was only her opinion. She picked up another photo, not done discovering Matt through a journey of a few snapshots. Images, as she realized all too well, told a story. And everyone had a story to tell. She picked up another framed picture of a little boy missing his two front teeth. It was obviously a school photo. His hair was mussed up like he'd just come back from recess, an adorably devilish grin on his face.

"Is this Hunter?"

"Yeah, when he was six. It's probably my favorite picture of him."

"He sure looks like you." She put the photo down on Matt's dresser and cleared her throat. "Okay. Maybe we should discuss, uh, you know, some kind of...*you* know."

"Some kind of...?"

There went the IQ again. "Rules, Matt. Rules."

"I'm not big on rules. You should know this about me."

"G-ground rules." She continued to stammer and sputter like the village idiot. "House rules."

"Ah." Matt winked. "You don't want me to ruin your game."

"*My* game? No, I mean I don't want to ruin *your* game."

He put up a hand. "Wait. Let me see if I understand you. You're saying I can bring a woman over here if I want?"

"Sure." Her hand traced the smooth edge of his dresser. "I don't want you to neglect your... needs. Or anything."

Oh God, was she blushing? *Please let him say he won't bring a woman over.* She'd offered but she didn't want him to accept. Was it too late to take it back?

He quirked an eyebrow. "That's generous of you."

"You're helping me out in a big way." Probably

not in the way she'd prefer, but she didn't want to be greedy. That would be wrong.

"And you're helping me. You should have seen my landlord's face when I told her I wouldn't be renewing my lease."

"Oh, good! Anyway, I don't want you to feel like this isn't your house, too. As long as you're here, this is your house."

"So kick off my shoes and stay awhile?"

She lifted a shoulder. "This is all I'm saying."

"Sounds good. And, Sarah?"

"Yeah?"

"I'm not going to be bringing any women over. But thanks for the offer."

Offer? She hadn't made an offer yet. Had she been handing out offers, she might have asked Matt if he'd consider door number two: Sarah Mcallister, thirty years old, single, no kids. Dark brown hair, green eyes. Five foot eight in stocking feet. Comes with her own toothbrush. Doesn't steal the covers.

"So I guess if you want to see a woman, you'll go over to her place."

His eyes narrowed. "Did you bring waders for this fishing expedition?"

Busted. She had to remember she wasn't dealing with the type of man-child she dated back home in Fort Collins. When she could get a date. Matt was nothing if not direct.

"Uh…"

"For the record, I'm not seeing anyone. How about you?"

She folded her arms across her chest. "I'm not seeing anyone, either."

"That's what I thought, but as long as we're clearing the air..."

"Air cleared!" She waved her arms and moved into the kitchen.

He followed her. "I'm going to get started on those floors in the hallway first. Before one of us trips." Already making himself at home, he reached for a glass from the cupboard.

"Sounds good, and I'll help."

"No worries. I'm going to need to rip up everything you did. Don't take this the wrong way, but carpentry is not your strong suit." He filled his glass with water from the sink.

She laughed like a loon. "I know."

"So, I'm good." He leaned back against the countertop and guzzled water.

She watched as his throat muscles moved and constricted, fascinated. He had a powerful neck, and she watched the way he gripped the glass in his big hand, like it was never getting away from him. She found the way he drank water to be incredibly sexy. Almost sensual. And also, she was probably going to need to visit a psychiatrist soon. She'd never found a man's Adam's apple particularly stimulating but there you go. She was a very sick woman.

She pulled her gaze away from his neck and forced herself to pick up a spoon and pretend she would do something with it. "But I feel like I should help."

"Nah, this is why I'm here." He set the empty glass in the sink and his shoulder bumped hers. "Let me earn my ten percent."

"Fifteen percent, you mean."

He grinned. "Thought I might slip that by you."

She giggled like a schoolgirl, but then she remembered...*underwear*. Shit! She almost ran into Matt trying to race past him to the bathroom.

"What the hell?" He moved out of her way.

Of course today had to be underwear day. She had all her thongs and bras airing out in the bathroom she hadn't had to share with anyone else for weeks. Naturally he was right behind her, probably wondering if she'd accidentally set his fifteen percent of the house on fire. She snatched red push-up bras and satiny black thongs off the towel bars as fast as her two hands could move, but it still wasn't fast enough.

If the unsuccessful way he tried to contain his grin was any indication, he'd seen everything.

"Sorry." She clutched her bras and panties in both hands. "I forgot. I've been living alone for a while."

Matt shook his head slowly, his large body filling the doorway. "That's...not a problem."

"I'll just put these in my bedroom."

She couldn't look at him as she rushed past him. They'd never even kissed and he'd already seen her panties.

An hour later, Matt had set himself up in the hallway and ripped up all of her handiwork. Sarah kept busy by keeping Shackles away from nails and other life-threatening injuries, letting him outside in the backyard and back in again about a hundred times per hour. She needed a dog door, but it was low on her list of priorities. For now, she was Shackles's door woman.

"How long have you had him?" Matt asked.

She'd just let Shackles in again from the backyard and hadn't heard Matt come up behind her. "It's been over a month now. The adoptive family who brought him out with Paws and Pilots changed their mind. Guess their kid turned out to be allergic."

"It was good of you to take him in."

Matt had worked up a sweat and his white T-shirt stuck to him like a second skin. His handyman tool belt hung low on his hips.

"Emily has a way of being pretty persuasive."

"Stone has shared that with me more than once." Matt grinned and squatted down. Shackles came right up to him, sniffing. "I would have taken him except for my old landlord. No pets allowed."

"He likes you." Who wouldn't? She imagined

all pets and children would find him approachable. He looked so safe, so solid and…solid. She swallowed.

"I didn't think you'd want to take him in since you're moving." He scratched between Shackles's ears and her dog melted into Matt, rubbing against his leg.

"We have dogs in Colorado, too."

"Right, of course you do." He gave Shackles one last pat and then straightened to his full height. "And this lucky little guy gets to go back with you."

It had to happen sooner or later and had been the plan all along. She had to go back to Colorado. Even though she'd enjoyed her freedom out here, with Mom safely back home where she'd learned she wouldn't die if her daughter wasn't a thirty-minute drive away. But Sarah was a freelance forensic artist with a nice regular gig in Fort Collins. She was supposed to get back to all that at some point. Back to her life, which, even if it was a little boring, was at least stable. Certain.

When Matt went back to the flooring, Sarah followed Shackles outside again and this time made her way to her father's garden shed. She unlatched the hinge and stepped inside, clicking the overhead lightbulb. Out here, she'd stored all of her father's mementos right alongside the old lawnmower and rusty garden tools. These were all the items she wanted to keep. Maybe

it didn't make sense to anyone else, surely not
to Stone, who'd called most of it junk. And she
had to admit, none of it had been exactly what
she'd been searching for. An old fishing pole, a
worn-out set of skis and poles, a broken snow-
board. Numerous model airplanes. A framed velvet picture of *Dogs Playing Poker*. She smiled,
remembering when Stone had requested to be
able to keep the picture, in front of Emily. The
poor girl's eyes had widened in horror but she'd
smiled and agreed until Stone told her he'd been
joking. Emily was too nice sometimes.

Not like Sarah. Back home, she'd been called
"prickly" and that was the nice word for her. Another more common word rhymed with *witch*. Behind her back, she understood coworkers feared
her, and not just because they were afraid she had
the power to make the likeness of their face ap-
pear on a forensic sketch of a criminal suspect. As
if she would ever be that unprofessional. Please.

The plain truth was that it wouldn't hurt her to
be nicer and more open. Less bitter and prickly.
She was working on it.

Her recent sketch work was in a corner next
to the easel. All she'd worked on in the months
she'd been here. Mostly landscapes, because far
be it from her to get too personal. Anyway, she'd
had her fill of portraits. Wide eyes, narrow eyes,
threatening eyes. Thin lips. Thick lips. Pug nose.
Crooked nose. Shaggy-haired strangers. She was

sick of drawing alleged criminals based on a witness's description. They almost never got the eyes right, which meant Sarah never got them exactly right, either.

Still, she'd been one of the best sketch artists in Fort Collins. Once caught, the suspect's actual photo would be almost a duplicate of her sketch, except for the eyes. So she got criminals almost right time and again. Unlike men in her personal life. Her handful of friends would say it was because she was too picky. Sarah would say it was because she no longer believed in fairy tales. At thirty, all she wanted was a grown-up relationship between two consenting adults who could bring each other a little bit of pleasure. She didn't need long-term.

And, at least for the short time she had left here, she wondered if maybe Matt would be game for a little harmless fun.

CHAPTER SIX

THE NEXT MORNING, Matt made sure to be out of the house as dawn broke over the horizon. He wanted zero chance of running into Sarah in the hallway, half-dressed and stumbling into the bathroom. The underwear had been bad enough. He would have never guessed straitlaced Sarah owned sexy underwear, but thanks to the Pantie Gods she did. Holy crap she did. Barely-there thongs and bras in red, black and pink that he had a good feeling were going to headline a few fantasies in his near future.

The wild look in her eyes as she'd tried to hide them from him had him caught between wanting to laugh and the raw desire to haul her off and kiss her senseless.

Didn't bode well for keeping it friendly.

He arrived at the airport early enough so only Stone was in the office. "Mornin'," he mumbled and helped himself to the coffee in the carafe.

"Hey," Stone said as he looked up from his desk. "I'm filing a few flight plans. What are you doing here? First flight isn't till seven thirty."

"I have to head out of here around noon for a meeting at the high school."

Stone looked over the schedule. "Yeah, that's cool. You should be back by then. Meeting at the high school, huh? Do they want to erect a statue of you?"

"Ha, ha. Good one."

Stone hadn't grown up in the Bay Area, but he knew Matt had. His reputation in their small bedroom-community town went far and wide... which is why Matt had been particularly out-raged when Joanne suggested he wear his ser-vice dress uniform. He'd attended Fortune Valley High School, where most everyone knew he'd joined the Air Force right after graduation. It wasn't something he could hide, nor would he, but he certainly wouldn't use it as an advantage.

"Uh-oh." Stone looked up and met Matt's eyes. "It's about the kid. Isn't it?"

Matt nodded. His kid. His troubled son. It was hard to think about, much less say out loud. Hard not to believe it was somehow all Matt's fault his son was acting out. "Hunter seems to think a brown fence is boring and needs some color."

Stone laughed. "You would have never been caught."

True enough. He had his father to thank, who'd been scarier than any high school principal. When Matt considered his father's example, he realized he had to fall somewhere between his father's hard-ass tough love and Joanne's enabling.

He guzzled the coffee, hoping it would wake him up. He hadn't slept easy last night, thinking of Sarah in the next bedroom. They'd had a light dinner together, and later she'd sweetly come to say good-night to him and thank him again. She apparently had no idea of the effect she had on him, which was good. Meant he'd done a bang-up job of hiding it. He just had to keep it up for another two months. Piece of cake.

"Meant to tell you, too, finally got out of my lease. I have a new address."

"Oh yeah? Where?"

Tread lightly, Matt. Easy does it. "It's temporary. You know the place. Your father's house."

Stone's forehead wrinkled. "With Sarah?"

"I'm sure you heard about her situation."

"Emily mentioned something. Her contractor got arrested on national TV? Why do I always miss all the good shit?"

"Consider yourself lucky. She was a mess."

"Heard that, too."

Matt waited a beat. He wasn't sure how much he should tell Stone, best friend or not. He'd warned Sarah repeatedly not to get in over her head with their father's home, and knowing Stone he too might feel responsible for her situation.

"Doesn't sound much like her." Stone squinted. "Why was she so upset?"

"There's a little more to it than losing one contractor."

Stone covered his face in his hands. "Aw, man. Don't tell me."

"I won't tell you. Just so you know, it's taken care of. Covered."

"Thanks, bro."

"Don't mention it."

"So living with her, huh? What's that about?"

"It was a compromise. She's helping me out of my current situation. My way of getting her to let me work for free."

"Smart. Or not smart, as the case may be."

Matt refused to comment on the grounds his answer might incriminate him.

"Look." Stone threw up his hands. "I don't care what you and my sister do behind closed doors. Between two consenting adults."

Matt held up one hand. "Hey—"

"Don't even try it. I've seen the way you look at her. Like I said, consenting adults. None of my business. Doesn't mean I want to hear about it."

"Understood. But nothing's going to happen. I have no free time. Plus it's my last chance with this kid and he's not making it easy."

Stone stood and went for the coffee. "Don't

blame yourself. It's a tough age. I was a dick. I'm sure you were, too."

While Matt hadn't been the wild kid Stone had reportedly been, he'd hardly been the good kid his father described. Matt had excelled at more than academia. He'd achieved a level of discreetness rarely seen in a teenager. His father didn't know the half of it and never would.

Matt spent the rest of his morning piloting two chartered flights, one a hop to San Francisco to drop off a couple of businessmen and the other for a couple he recognized from the supermarket tabloids. He was to land them at LAX because they'd missed their flight on their equally wealthy friend's private jet. LAX was the kind of airport made for former Air Force pilots. The air traffic was intimidating to most but Matt loved the challenge. However, the turbulence he ran into came from the couple behind him, not the weather.

"If you hadn't been too busy staring between that woman's giant ass and your stupid phone, we wouldn't have missed our flight," the woman said.

"Can I help it if I like a nice ass?"

"No, apparently not. And I obviously like an ass, too, or I wouldn't have married you."

"Funny. Maybe if you stopped your constant yo-yo dieting you'd also have an ass."

"Sure! Let me go ahead and eat like you do so you can just call me fat again."

"You gained forty pounds, and it didn't go to your ass."

"I was *pregnant*!"

Apparently Matt became both deaf and invisible when he put on his headset. This was what he hated about people who possessed no filters. Simply because Mcallister Charters signed nondisclosure agreements, it didn't mean he wanted to hear all this.

He cleared his throat. "Excuse me."

"Yes? Is there a problem?" the man demanded.

Your mouth. Your existence. "There could be."

"You idiot!" the woman whined. "Why did you make me take this little plane? Now there's a problem."

"Shut up," the man said to his woman/wife/verbal whipping post.

"No problem," Stone said with his most authoritative tone of voice. "But there could be. I need absolute silence to land this plane. I have to concentrate."

He could land this plane in his sleep, but after a sharp intake of breath, there was not another sound from either of his passengers the rest of the trip.

By noon, the entitled celebrity couple long out of his mind, Matt sat in the high school's office lobby waiting for Hunter and Joanne. They were both late.

"Matt Conner," said a voice he recognized. It was none other than David Cross, his former Calculus teacher and a good ally should Matt care to have one.

Joanne would love this.

Matt stood up and shook the man's hand. "Good to see you, Mr. Cross."

"And you. We're waiting on Hunter and… and…"

"His mother. Joanne. Joanne Fisher." They'd never been married. Matt had dutifully offered but Joanne had refused him. Didn't want to be a military wife. Lucky him.

Matt followed Mr. Cross into his office. "I'm sure she'll be here any minute." He drew his phone out of his pocket and checked the time. Ten minutes late. Shit.

"I'm glad we have a chance to catch up. I heard you've been overseas for years."

Matt nodded. "True."

"I was shocked to hear you'd enlisted. I never had a chance to tell you how sorry… I mean, after graduation you enlisted so quickly. There wasn't time to…"

The typical awkward stammering happened whenever he ran into someone from his past. Someone who couldn't reconcile Matt Conner from the Principal's Honor Roll with the Matt who had knocked up his girlfriend. Correction, not girlfriend. Date. Matt glanced at his phone again. Had Joanne planned this? He didn't want to rehash the past with Mr. Cross right now.

Hunter's frame darkened the doorway of the office. "They said for me to go in."

"Hunter." Mr. Cross pointed at the seat next to Matt's. "Your father's here on time so we'll just get started."

Hunter grunted and wouldn't make eye contact with Matt, which was fairly typical.

Joanne arrived as Hunter was taking his seat. "I'm sorry I'm late. I'm sure you remember Matt, Hunter's father? Lieutenant Conner, I mean."

"Just Matt," Matt said with a tight jaw.

"He was in the Air Force," she said, sitting between Matt and Hunter. "A veteran."

Hunter rolled his eyes. Mr. Cross smiled. Matt said nothing, but gripped the armrest of his chair tighter.

"As you all know, there was spray-painting done on the fence and our cameras caught Hunter and two of his friends in action."

"And Hunter's so sorry about that," Joanne said.

Matt stared at her, trying to silently communicate that she should let Hunter talk. Helpfully, she then tapped Hunter's shoulder. He gave her a look that could kill and said nothing.

"Where are the other kids and their parents?" Matt asked.

"We met with them earlier in the week, but Mrs., uh… Miss Fisher kept rescheduling. So here we are."

"All I did was paint a fence. It's not like I killed someone," Hunter finally spoke.

Matt had to give it to the kid. When it came to Hunter, what you saw was what you got. No subterfuge whatsoever. If it wasn't for the fact that Hunter was Matt's dead ringer, he'd have to wonder if the kid was his.

Joanne hit his shoulder again. "He doesn't mean it. Actually, I blame myself. He grew up without a father."

"What?" Hunter and Matt spoke at once.

"Let's discuss our options," Mr. Cross said. "We were able to keep this out of the police's jurisdiction. I like to handle these matters, much as possible, in house. The other parents paid for the damages."

Hunter snorted. Joanne tapped him again and then started rifling through her purse. Presumably for the checkbook.

"But someone will have to paint the fence." Matt leaned forward.

"Yes," Mr. Cross said. "We'll hire someone."

"How much?" Joanne already had her checkbook out.

Matt reached out to stay her arm. "Hold on. Why doesn't Hunter paint the fence?"

Mr. Cross didn't speak for a moment. "It would have to be after school is out for the summer."

The kid stared at him, jaw dropped. "Seriously?"

"I'm not sure if…" Joanne said, and then, catching Matt's stop-talking look, stopped talking.

Finally. "I'll supervise," Matt said.

"Actually," Mr. Cross said, "what a good idea. I wish I'd thought of it myself. Of course, the Jacksons go to Europe for the summer, so not all the boys would be available anyway."

"Fortunately, Hunter has no plans," Matt said. "Do you?"

Hunter gave him one of those looks-could-kill scowls but didn't speak.

"Yeah. That's what I thought," Matt said.

CHAPTER SEVEN

"WAS THAT NECESSARY?" Joanne asked. "You're not exactly Mr. Popularity around here."

After the meeting, all three of them had walked to the school parking lot together. Hunter had climbed into Joanne's SUV and slammed the passenger door shut without a word.

"Not interested in winning a contest."

"I know you're trying to be a hard-ass but he already doesn't like you. So ease up on the boot camp stuff and let's see if we can at least get him to want to spend time with you that isn't forced labor."

Shit. Was he being a hard-ass? He hadn't meant to be. He'd reacted in a similar fashion that any of his COs would have to a rookie, to teach him a lesson he wouldn't soon forget. Obviously Matt was still feeling his way around being the father of a hormone-driven teenager.

"I said I'd supervise. More likely, I'll help."

Joanne sighed and leaned against the driver's-side door. "How much longer before he can spend a weekend with you?"

For months he'd been trying to find a suitable

place to rent. At least two bedrooms with a back-yard. Everything he'd located had been rented by the time he called. "No luck so far, but at least the lease is up on my apartment."

"He would have been fine in your apartment. You're so picky."

"It's a one-bedroom."

"He would have been fine on the couch."

"What's the rush, Joanne?"

"Fine. If you must know, Chuck has a chance at the minors this summer."

"Chuck?" That must be the new boyfriend he'd heard about, but let her tell him that.

"We've been seeing each other. Hunter doesn't like him much, but as you can see he doesn't like anyone. Anyway, I want to meet up with Chuck at one of the games, and it's not like Hunter wants to go with me. All he wants to do is hang out with his friends, tag fences and play 'Call of Duty'."

Great. His kid was getting an education in military combat with little if any basis in reality. "I'm working on it."

"Work harder." Joanne slipped into her sedan and they were off.

Matt stood and watched for a moment. These were two people in his life he should somehow feel deeply connected to. He understood why he no longer felt anything for Joanne, but he was supposed to love Hunter. Did love him, in fact, or at least the kid he remembered. The little kid in that framed photo, for starters. But Hunter wasn't a small boy he could please with shiny Air Force toy planes or help guide across the monkey bars. Matt shouldn't have let two years go by between visits, even if Joanne had made it difficult. The last time he'd seen Hunter he'd been thirteen and just on the edge of puberty, his voice squeaking and his feet huge in comparison to the rest of him. But he'd still been at least human.

Fast-forward two short years and Hunter looked like a different kid. He was now nearly as tall as Matt himself, a man-child with an attitude. Not like he didn't know a little bit about them, but the airmen he'd had in his wing weren't children. Hunter was far more child than man, but Matt understood the kid didn't see it that way.

Back at the airport, Matt finished off his day with a onetime flying lesson gifted to a woman on her fiftieth birthday by her Airman First Class son, and a last-minute charter flight to Las Vegas. He was there to pick up a couple of businessmen who'd missed their connecting flight to San Francisco, but when Matt arrived the men had instead hired a private jet minutes after placing the call.

Wonderful.

He waited in line to taxi back down the runway and took off again, fuming. The passengers would be charged, but they'd wasted precious fuel. Stone would be pissed.

Back at the airport, Matt checked out with

Cassie and Emily, gathered his keys and headed to Sarah's, prepared to spend an evening putting in the rest of the hardwood flooring in the hallway. He was tired, irritated as hell and hungry like a lion. The rest of his evening would consist of physical labor and a large dose of sexually charged frustration to boot.

And he couldn't figure out why he looked forward to all of it.

"Honey, I'm home," Matt said as he walked in the front door to Sarah's place.

His place now, too. Or at least fifteen percent his place until he talked the stubborn woman out of their arrangement. Sarah should have beaten him home hours ago, and he'd seen her car outside but didn't find her in the kitchen. Shackles welcomed him instead, wagging his tail double time and leading the way to the sliding glass door. Matt let him out, then went to find Sarah.

Where the hell was she? They had to talk about the roof, and plenty of other decisions that would need to be made about their now joint project. This house was a classic when one got right down to it. A Craftsman built in the early 1960s, it had seen better days, but from the beginning Matt had seen nothing but possibilities. He figured it was the fixer in him, but he'd always admired great craftsmanship.

He headed toward her bedroom when the bathroom door jerked open a few feet away from him.

Sarah emerged. Naked. She took one startled look in his direction and streaked down the hallway toward the bedrooms. Frozen in place, he stood as still as a rock and nearly as hard. Her sweet ass was the last thing he saw before she slammed the door to her bedroom shut.

"You took the last towel!" she screeched from inside.

"Sorry," he called out. *Not sorry.*

If this was what living with her would be like, maybe he should just kill himself right now and make fast work of it. Anything had to be better than letting her kill him slowly like this without any mercy.

He headed back to the kitchen where he stuck his head in the freezer. "Yep. That ought to do it."

Next he reached inside the refrigerator for bottled water and considered whether he should drink the cold water or pour it all over his head. Choosing to drink first, he uncapped it and took a big swallow just as Sarah walked in the kitchen.

"You men are all alike."

He turned to find her standing in the kitchen, arms folded across what he now unfairly knew was one of the greatest racks he'd ever been privileged to see. She wore a blue tank top and loose gray sweats. Was she wearing the red bra or the pink one? Black or red panties?

"I didn't see anything," he lied.

"That's not what I mean. Why is it so hard to

remember to replace a towel? You use one, you put another one back. It's not rocket science."

"You're right."

"I went ahead and put all your towels in the top shelf of the linen closet." Her arms dropped to her sides. "I guess I didn't tell you that."

"Nope," he said, and drained the contents of the water bottle. "But I would have brought you a towel. All you had to do was ask."

She shifted her weight from one leg to another. "I didn't hear you come in."

He scrunched up the water bottle until it was an inch tall, releasing a small amount of tension and pent-up sexual frustration, though not nearly enough. "Easy mistake. Don't worry. We're both grown-ups here."

"Okay," she said, sitting down at the kitchen table. "It's just that…well, first the underwear and now the naked thing. I don't want to scare you off."

"Scare me off?" Was she seriously worried about this? Did she not notice his tongue practically hanging out, mouth salivating? Or maybe that was the problem. She didn't appreciate the salivating.

She stared at her hands. "I need your help, as you know."

"And you've got it." He took a seat next to her.

She met his eyes and a tiny smile curved her lips. "Have I said thank you enough?"

"You have." He forced himself to relax and unkink his shoulders. "Now, about the roof—"

"You said we'd talk about it, but honestly, the Realtor I talked to said we can just give the new owners a roof allowance. Roofs are expensive, they—"

"Unless you have a roofer in your pocket."

He smiled, because now they were in his territory. Fixing inanimate objects, whether it be a broken sink, jammed window or bad electrical wiring. Planes, cars, bicycles, vacuum cleaners; you name it, he could damn well fix it when it broke. As long as it didn't talk back to him.

Sarah was staring at him. "Is there anything you *can't* do?"

"Yeah. I'm a lousy cook."

"I'm not half-bad, so I'll cook for both of us."

"You don't have to do that."

"I know I don't have to, but I want to." The way she gazed at him with her pouty bottom lip made him think about the panties again.

He wondered if electroshock would help him with this little problem. He got up. "Sure, but nothing fancy. I better get to work."

"Me too," Sarah said, rising from her chair.

He winced. "What are you going to do?"

"Don't you give me that look."

"What look?"

"The girl-needs-to-stay-out-of-my-way look."

Check him out, male chauvinist pig of the

year. "Of course you can help. What do you want to do?"

She smiled, and she might as well have cold-cocked him for the way it temporarily stunned him. "I'm going to put the baseboards back on in the living room. Stone already painted in there, but I bought new boards. They have cool edging to them."

So she'd picked out fancy baseboards but didn't want a new roof. Okay, he'd let her have that one. Not going to judge. "Do you know how to use a nail gun?"

If he wasn't mistaken she blinked twice as if to signal *help me* but her lips didn't move to say those words and the hell if he'd be accused of being a chauvinist.

She nodded. "Yep. I watched Satan use it."

While that didn't mean she could use it herself, Matt went over to the nail gun he'd brought over and handed it to Sarah. He reminded himself that while trust didn't always come easily to him, he did trust Sarah. Mostly. The rest of it he was working on.

"Thanks. I'll just go get dressed in my construction outfit first."

He almost asked, but thought better of it. If she had a special outfit she wanted to wear that was probably a good idea. Maybe some steel-toed boots or something that could protect her from catastrophic injury. He was on board with protecting her from injury. A few minutes later, he was going through his tools when she emerged from her room wearing what surely was from a page in a fashion catalog. And sue him if he still thought she looked blazing hot in khaki carpenter pants, a light-colored blouse, boots and protective eyewear. Nice touch with the protective eyewear. He felt better already. She carried with her a small toolbox in one hand and the nail gun he'd given her in the other.

"Okay. I'm ready."

"So you are." He felt a grin coming on. "Sometimes I wear old clothes, but what you're wearing is good, too."

"Everything was on sale," she said as though this explained everything. "Forty percent off with free shipping."

She walked away from him and while he considered getting her set up, that might look like he didn't have enough faith in her, so he hung back and let her do it all herself.

Have a little faith. Trust, Matt, trust.

Yeah. Still working on it.

Trust issues and him went way back, so it was no wonder that even with good friends he still occasionally wound up verifying. It had cost him a relationship or two in his past, but after Joanne his trust when it came to women had been compromised almost permanently.

A half an hour later, he still hadn't heard the

sounds of nail gunning in the living room so maybe Sarah was still lining up the boards. Or possibly trying to figure out a way out of this while saving face. He tacked in the last wood floor slat and determined he'd go in and pretend he only wanted to check out her great progress, then underhandedly find a way to assist her before she impaled herself.

He heard a strange whirring sound, immediately followed by the sounds of a nail gun…being operated at the rapid-fire rate of a machine gun.

Shit. *Not* good.

He dropped everything and ran to the living room, where he found Sarah on the ground, wearing her safety glasses, legs spread out, holding the nail gun away from herself as it shot nails out like it was possessed by the demonic soul of an assault rifle.

Fuck. Heart pounding in his ears, he yanked the electrical plug from its socket then dropped down next to her, worried because she looked shell-shocked. "Are you okay?"

"I'm s-sorry."

"Don't be sorry. Explain what the hell happened." He took the nail gun from her.

"I don't really know. Maybe it jammed? Everything was going well, and then…and then…" Her safety glasses slightly askew, she pushed them up with her finger.

Thank God for the safety glasses. "Doesn't matter. Just please tell me you're okay."

"Fine, but a little humiliated. This looked so easy. I read all the instructions. Well. Most of them."

He let out an uneven breath, and took a good long look at the wall. The wall Stone had painted not long ago with a shade of brown had nails all over it in interesting random patterns.

"You killed the wall."

She covered her face with her hands. "Oh, crap."

Yeah. It was okay, he told himself over and over again. She wasn't hurt, and that was the main thing. Instinctively and possibly without much thought, he pulled Sarah's back to his chest. They both sat on the ground of the living room floor staring at the massacred wall for several silent minutes. Finally, she leaned her head back and told him she was sorry another dozen times.

"Maybe you should stay away from power tools for now."

She nodded slowly.

This would be an interesting couple of months, if they each lived to tell about it.

"HONESTLY, MATT, YOU look exhausted. Let me help," Sarah said. "Please."

"I'm good," he said from the top of the ladder

where he was fiddling with the wiring coming out of her bedroom ceiling.

Good. He was always good.

The man had run himself ragged all week long, working at the airport most of the daylight hours, helping his son paint a fence—she didn't ask because Matt didn't look happy about it—and working on her numerous home improvement projects. Being forever banned from using power tools meant that she couldn't help him much anymore. But no sooner would he finish one house project than another issue would present itself. Either it was a wiring problem or a plumbing problem. Rather than the list getting shorter, it got longer. Just like the summer days.

And Matt got sexier every day. Each time he recited the complex reasoning behind why the house's electrical wiring had "issues" she'd stare at him, appreciating that he understood her to be intelligent enough to follow was the single most attractive quality about him.

Of course, his most attractive quality changed from moment to moment and depending on what the man was doing. Sometimes his forearms were the single most attractive quality about him. Sometimes his eyes, beautifully dark and edgy. She had to face it—she had a large menu to choose from.

And now tonight he'd finally put in her ceiling fan, and those tentacles falling out of her ceiling would be covered up and stop giving her spider nightmares. She'd run the fan tonight and cool down from the suddenly hot summer nights. They were having a small heat wave.

Unless that was all Matt.

She was still feeling her way around this whole friends-and-roommates thing, thinking up ways to get Matt's attention other than leaving all her underwear out, flashing him or scaring him with her appalling lack of carpentry skills. So far she'd accomplished all of those without even breaking a sweat.

He stood now on the ladder just under the wires, balancing his weight on the second highest rung. Her only job was to keep Shackles away from him, since her dog now had a serious case of hero worship for Matt and followed him around the sometimes-dangerous house. The evening sky had begun to darken and little slits of light were all that was left of the daylight coming through the bedroom window blinds he'd replaced for her. She walked to the window, still holding on to Shackles's collar, to open them further and give Matt more light while he worked.

An enormous spark popped out of the ceiling, and Matt cursed as he fell from the ladder. Letting go of the dog, she lunged for the ladder to steady him, but he grabbed it and took it with him, presumably to keep from falling on them. Shackles yelped and ran out of the bedroom. Somehow Matt managed to topple onto her bed, at the last minute throwing the ladder away from them both. It landed with a crash against the far wall.

Matt lay on his back on her bed, staring up at the ceiling. "That wasn't supposed to happen."

Recovering from her small heart attack, Sarah rushed to him. "Matt! Oh my God, Matt, are you okay?"

"I'm good," he said, wincing.

She climbed on the bed with him. "If you say you're good one more time I'm seriously going to have to kill you."

He groaned his response.

"What can I do? Do you need me to call 911? Should I get you a cold wet rag? How about a warm one? Talk to me!"

It took her a minute to realize that in her panic she'd crossed a dangerous line. She was pretty much straddling his hips. Not exactly how she'd pictured winding up in this position, with all her clothes still on, but damned if she would move now. She had a perfectly good excuse to be hovering over him, in care and concern over whether he'd managed to electrocute himself trying to fix her money pit of a house.

"I'm okay."

"What happened?"

"It's worse than I thought." He looked at the wiring above them, then at her. "I'm not sure I can move my legs."

Sarah drew in a sharp breath. What had she done? Why, oh why, had she let him help her? "You…you can't m-move your legs?"

He didn't answer, but in one swift move he flipped her and now she lay under him.

"How about that? Guess I can move them. Just needed a little motivation is all."

She pushed on his chest, marveling at how quickly he'd switched gears. "Not funny, Matt! You scared me."

But his eyes were serious now, incredibly so, as he braced himself above her. She shivered when one hand skimmed down her arm until he came to her wrist and cuffed it. Sarah didn't breathe. Didn't move. Letting go of her wrist, Matt's hand went to her hair clip and he removed it. He made an innately male sound as her hair tumbled down around her shoulders, loose. His finger traced the edge of her jawline and he followed with his lips. *Oh boy.* She'd wanted this for so long that the moment they were both caught in seemed surreal. But these were her hands moving under his shirt to touch the solid planes of his muscular chest, luxuriating in how warm and hard and positively male he was. This would finally happen. Happen now. Any minute he'd kiss her senseless, unless she kissed him first. Any time now.

The doorbell rang.

Shackles yipped and barked, doing his job and

sounding the alarm. *People! People! Hurry and let them in so I can sniff them!*

Matt removed his hand from her ass. "You expecting anyone?"

"No." She tried to tug him down by his powerful neck while she prayed silently that whoever was at the door would give up and go away. Fast. But Matt wasn't giving an inch.

The doorbell rang again. Shackles became hysterical with the barking. Matt moved off the bed. And Sarah decided whoever was at the door would be dead in two minutes flat.

"Okay." She rose from the bed and smoothed back her hair. Licked her unkissed lips. "I'll go see who that is."

But no one was dying tonight, because behind her front door stood Emily and Stone.

CHAPTER EIGHT

SARAH RELUCTANTLY OPENED the door because Emily and Stone had already seen her through the front paned window. All she had hanging there was a mostly see-through white cotton sheet. Besides, she should let her brother inside. He was blood and all that.

"Hi!" Emily said. "We thought we'd come by to help."

"Hey," Stone said to Sarah. "I don't want to be here."

Sarah smiled at her brother's honesty and waved them both inside.

"It will go faster if Matt has some help." Emily squatted as Shackles yipped and yapped his welcome.

"He doesn't want my help," Stone protested. "I'm telling you, his exact words were 'I'm good.'"

"I brought some beer, too." Emily held up a six-pack. "As a reward for when the guys are done."

"That's not what I want as a reward and you know it," Stone said to Emily. Then he caught sight of Matt coming out of the bedroom. "What's up?"

"Electrical," Matt said and they both disappeared back into Sarah's bedroom.

"How's it going around here?" Emily handed Sarah the six-pack.

"Super." She'd just been in Matt's arms and about to kiss him. It was the best thing that had happened all year, hands down. Sarah opened the fridge and set the beers inside.

"Boy. You look...flushed," Emily said as she studied her.

"This is hard work. And Matt got zapped."

"Uh-oh."

"He's good, though." Now *she* was adopting Matt's pat phrase. "But I'm guessing my electrical isn't."

She was back to thinking about the house's many problems when she would have preferred to still be wondering whether Matt wore boxers or briefs. She might even have been about to find out.

Shackles trotted to the sliding glass door leading to their backyard and Sarah followed, Emily behind her. Sarah stopped at the edge of the lawn and turned west to watch the sun begin its slow sink over the horizon. The painted skyline over the hills was awash in red and gold tonight and woke her up a little bit. She'd been about to cross a line with Matt, maybe even two or three, and somehow this should bother her. Worry her.

Only it didn't. She'd wanted to cross lines with

him for a long time. Erase them, if she were being honest. He'd been the one constantly holding back. Flirting but only to the edge and no further. But something had changed tonight. She hoped it had nothing to do with an electrical shock.

"You guys didn't need to come over, you know."

"Why? Did we interrupt something?" Emily grinned.

"Uh…no. It's just… Stone has done enough. He put in the kitchen counters, and he basically sold me his half of the house for below market value. I don't think he realizes I know."

It was better, too, not to admit she'd figured it out. When she'd first come out to California, Fort Collins real estate prices were all she had to compare with. Bay Area prices for the oldest and smallest houses had been like a jolt of ice water on a cold winter day.

"You didn't answer my question."

Sarah toed the edge of the lawn with one bare foot. "Okay, yes. Nothing happened. Something… almost happened. Am I that obvious?"

"It took you a while to get to the door, and once you did…your face. It's flushed but in a nice way. And your hair. It looks good down like that. You look great, by the way."

Her hair clip. Sarah's hand went self-consciously to her wild and crazy mane of hair. It was so un-ruly she always kept it in a bun. "Well, as long as

I *look* great. I don't know what I'm doing, actually. Pretty sure he's clueless, too."

Emily gave the look of a woman who knew about these things. "Oh, I can guarantee you that."

"Matt has a lot going on right now. All I did was become one more item on his list."

"I don't think so. I think he likes you."

"I know that he probably doesn't want to hurt me. That's just who he is."

"Who says he's going to hurt you? Maybe you'll be the one to hurt him."

She shook her head. "I'm not going to hurt him. I couldn't do that."

"When you leave."

It was difficult to believe. Matt was such a confident, assured man. But it occurred to Sarah that she'd never spent much time thinking about how her leaving might affect him. Maybe it was why he'd kept a healthy space between them, despite the occasional flirting. A space which had taken a bit of a hit tonight. She understood he didn't want a fling with his best friend's sister. But if she was leaving eventually, and no one but the two of them had to know, why did it matter?

As a light came on inside, Emily turned toward the house, then met Sarah's eyes. "I'm sorry. I just think that Matt really needs someone. He doesn't act like he does, sure, but he's lonely."

"Emily, he could have anyone he wanted. If he's lonely, it's by choice."

"Or maybe he just hasn't had the best luck with women. Might have some abandonment issues, even. His mom left them when he was ten and he hasn't heard from her in years. There's really no relationship there. And then his ex Joanne. She never made it easy for him to see Hunter."

Sarah had wondered about Matt's past but beyond light conversation they hadn't delved deep. They'd been too busy talking about her problems. Her grief. But she wanted to go deeper with him. Hear all of his secrets and painful mistakes. The kind of private, personal matters only lovers knew about each other. But in order to have that level of intimacy, she might have to tell him her biggest regret, and she wasn't quite ready for that.

"Have you found anything else about your dad?" Emily nudged her chin toward the shed. "Anything important?"

"Nothing."

It was too late now. He was gone and Sarah had to move on. Sell the house and go back home to Colorado and her life back there. The change she'd wanted, the one that could only happen from the inside out, hadn't happened. She wanted to feel alive again. She'd traded her pantsuits for jeans and tank tops. Her framed glasses for contacts. But still nothing. Those were all external changes, and she had to work on her heart. It had to be more open…or something.

"I'm sorry." Emily squeezed Sarah's shoulder. "I had hoped maybe there was something in this old house."

"Besides memories and a bunch of junk? Probably not."

Shackles, done with sniffing every square inch of his territory, joined them on the patio. He whimpered at Emily's feet until she bent down to scratch behind his ears. "Sometimes we just have to find a way to lick our own wounds. Huh, Shackles?"

Sarah was familiar with being her own hero. She'd done that for most of her life. Each time she had felt a little more dead inside as she proved over and over again that she didn't need anyone. For once she'd wanted something, someone, to rescue her so she could stop being so tough and strong all the time. But that had been a mistake. There would be no rescue for her. She'd do her own saving again.

Emily straightened. "One thing you should know about Matt. He feels like a total screw-up."

"Why?" Not Matt Conner. Air Force pilot Matt? Mechanic? Engineer? Single father? He'd already done so much with his life.

Perhaps that was why she'd been so drawn to him from the start—because it took a screw-up to see a screw-up. She didn't see a screw-up, though. She saw someone who'd made mistakes and lived with the consequences. It was quite possibly the most attractive quality about him. Maybe because she'd been struggling to do the same for years.

"Matt was raised by a single father. Mr. Conner was tough. He was a top-level executive in Silicon Valley for years. And he expected a lot out of Matt. More than the Air Force, that's for sure."

"What's wrong with the Air Force?"

"Nothing, but when you've been groomed to go to an Ivy League school, I guess it can be seen as a step down. At least it did to Matt's father. And probably most of his teachers. Matt was on the Principal's Honor Roll every semester. His SAT and ACT scores were near perfect. He was supposed to do better."

"But then Hunter came along."

The screen door opened and both Stone and Matt joined them on the patio. Within seconds Stone had drawn Emily into his arms like the two of them were magnets.

"Are you guys already done?" Emily asked.

Stone, who had his head partially buried in Emily's neck, could barely be heard. "More than we can fix tonight. Babe, I need to go home. Come with me."

Emily turned in his arms. "Of course I'm coming with you, silly."

"Score."

Oh, sigh. Those two were so adorable, and yes, at times irritatingly so. Sarah turned away because no matter what those two did, even if it was simply holding each other's hands, it carried with it an air of jolting intimacy. She glanced toward Matt, assuming he too would be smiling at the display, but instead caught him studying her, his head cocked. He didn't look away but his head straightened and his gaze slid up to meet her eyes. He had a beer in his hand and took a pull of it without breaking eye contact.

Sarah swallowed and wanted to get Stone and Emily out of her house even faster than they were moving. "Gosh, thanks so much for coming by. I'm getting tired, too. Early day tomorrow and all."

"Oh yeah," Emily said. "We should go."

"This is what I'm saying." Stone took Emily's hand and led her through the house.

Matt said good-night and Sarah followed them to the front door. But Emily wanted to talk wedding plans, and so Sarah followed them out to the truck where she stood next to Emily's rolled-down passenger-side window. She listened for ten or more minutes to talk of tulle, lace and satin, and whether or not it was a good idea or not to have Emily's almost two-year-old niece Sierra be a flower girl. Listened as Emily considered whether they should be married outside at her family's ranch, or perhaps the Methodist church, or maybe someplace completely different. She listened until Stone turned on his truck and began to slowly inch away from the curb while Emily kept talking.

She finally laughed and waved. "We'll talk later."

At last! Sarah practically ran back inside where Matt would be waiting. Hopefully to finish what they'd started. He wasn't in the backyard, nor was he in her bedroom. Not in the bathroom. No, instead he was lying on his roomy bed, faceup. Eyes closed. Breathing slow and regular.

Dammit. She couldn't catch a break when it came to Matt, but the poor guy was firing on all cylinders lately. Getting up at the crack of dawn. Staying up late working on the house. She turned to leave when she heard his voice, sounding deep and gravelly from sleep.

"Sarah."

She faced him again, and boy was that a mistake. He rose up on his elbows, a lock of his dark blond hair falling over one eye. She'd never seen put-together Matt look so comfortable. Huggable. Vulnerable.

"I didn't mean to bother you. You must be exhausted. Go back to sleep."

"I'd rather you not sleep in your bedroom tonight. I want to look at the electrical tomorrow when I have daylight."

"Oh, okay. Where should I sleep?" Because she had some pretty good ideas, but she couldn't assume Matt was on the same wavelength.

"Right here." He patted his bed.

Oh boy! Jackpot! Home run! Touchdown! Her heart slammed into her rib cage and she smiled at all that sexy. It was a bit of a leap to go straight from the almost-kiss into his bed, but she could take this jump with him. Only him.

"And I'll sleep on the couch." He grabbed a pillow and climbed off the bed.

Screech! Crash! Boom! "No, Matt! Are you kidding me? I can't have you sleeping on my couch."

"Why not?"

"It's…it's uncomfortable and I don't want to kick you out of your bed."

"You're not. If anything, I'm giving the bedroom back to you. Temporarily."

"But fifteen percent of this house is yours."

He moved past her to the doorway. "And tonight my fifteen percent is in the living room. The couch is fine with me. I've slept on worse."

Sarah opened her mouth to speak, but Matt gently closed the door.

"What just happened?" she asked Matt's bed.

It didn't answer.

She had *not* imagined all the heat in her bedroom earlier, and none of it had been caused by the faulty wiring. For months they'd been dancing around each other. She'd take two steps forward and he'd take a step back. They could just keep up this routine where he flirted and then backed off. She could let him.

But not this time.

CHAPTER NINE

SARAH STUMBLED INTO the now dark living room, and found Matt lying on the couch, Shackles curled up at his feet. Through the sliver of moonlight shining through the window, she could make out that he had his shirt off, a pillow over his face. As if she'd given him a headache.

Wait until she got going. "Matt."

Under his pillow, she heard him groan.

"What's going on here?" She stood hands on hips and then decided that looked too accusatory for seduction, so she relaxed her arms at her sides.

"Go to sleep, Sarah."

"No."

He lifted the pillow from his face, one eye open. "I don't want to argue with you."

"I don't want to argue, either. I just want you to tell me what happened tonight."

"Guess if you don't know, I must not have done it right."

"You did everything right." Her voice softened. Now that she faced this—thing—between them her mouth was parched and dry. But she couldn't lose her nerve now. "The only thing you did wrong was stop."

"Wasn't my choice."

"But now it is."

He didn't move. "Go to sleep. Please."

"Well, since you said please."

"Seriously? That's all it takes?"

"No. I lied. I'll go to sleep, but not until you hear me out. I might be Stone's sister, but I'm also a grown woman and I know what I want."

"What *do* you want? Because I thought you wanted to fix this house and flip it. Sell it so you can get back to Colorado."

Couldn't a woman want more than one thing? "I want you, Matt. That's what I want."

"Do you? Be careful what you're asking for. Maybe you don't know me as well as you think you do."

"I know enough. I know you're one of the good guys."

He snorted. "Yeah."

"Do you think I'm going to fall in love with you? Is that it? Because that's not an issue. I don't believe in love."

At that he removed the pillow from his head. "You don't believe in love."

"Does that shock you? Why should it? I grew up as the child of a broken home and I've seen more divorces around me than I care to remember. You of all people should understand."

"*Me* of all people?"

"You're also from a broken home. And…you're a single father."

"That doesn't mean I don't believe in love. And I think it's pretty messed up that you don't, Sarah."

"Okay. What do *you* want? Is it me at all? Because a couple of hours ago you had me pretty well convinced, so if you've changed your mind you need to tell me now."

There. She couldn't believe she'd let all her thoughts spill out at last. Everything she'd intended to tell him for months had come pouring out of her lips, like the semidark of the room had given her added courage. In the ensuing quiet Sarah didn't think he would answer her at all. Worse, in the dark of the room she couldn't take a cue from his usually expressive eyes.

"I want you, Sarah." He finally spoke, the sound of his voice so naked and raw that Sarah's knees went boneless.

Easily enough, she took a seat next to him on the couch. Shackles growled at her. "Was it so hard to say?"

"Yes. Because you can do better."

"I don't care. I want you." She put her trembling hand on his bare chest and felt the muscles tighten under her touch.

"Sarah, look at me." He met her eyes. "This thing between us? It can't happen."

"Wh-why not?"

"You're leaving, for one thing."

"Not right this minute."

"I'm not going to have a fling with my best friend's sister."

"Why not? Who's going to know?"

"I would." He met her eyes. "And you don't really want this."

Pissed off, she drew her hand back. "Don't you tell me what I want and don't want!"

He didn't respond, but simply groaned. "Go back to my bed before I carry you there."

"No! I'm sleeping on the couch. Not you." She pushed on his large frame which, of course, didn't budge.

"Damn," he growled. "Why are you so stubborn?"

"I'm *not* stubborn."

"Yeah, right."

"You're the stubborn one. You want to kiss me. You almost did."

"What I want doesn't matter right now. Get that through your head."

"And you say I'm stubborn!" *Universe, please save me from obstinate men!* "Go back to your bed and stop being such a baby."

"I'm not going anywhere." Matt settled deeper into the couch.

Two could play this game. Sarah lay her body down lengthwise in the small space left next to his, spoon-like. No way could he sleep like this, her ass scrunched up against him, her hair in his face. He'd move now.

Or maybe he wouldn't. She decided that she could live with either one of the possible two outcomes.

He cursed under his breath. "Settle in then, if this is what you want. I should warn you that I snore."

"I can take a little snoring. As long as you can take a little talking in my sleep."

He didn't say another word, but shoved the pillow back over his head. The man was going to sleep cramped next to her all night long rather than give in.

And so, apparently, would she.

CHAPTER TEN

HUNTER HAD DISCOVERED his teachers were full of crap and child slave labor hadn't been abolished in this country. Neither was cruel and inhuman punishment. It was probably a thousand degrees outside today and he and Matt had finally finished the boring fence. It was brown again. Hunter hoped everyone would be very happy.

Most of his friends were inside their houses right now, enjoying their central air-conditioning or swimming in the family pool. He was stuck here with Matt. Matt was cleaning and gathering up the tools, handing Hunter crap and expecting him to put it in the back of the truck even if his arms were about to fall off at the sockets.

"It's a good feeling being done, isn't it?" Matt asked.

"Yeah, Matt. It's cool being done." Hunter was calling him Matt from now on. He didn't deserve to be called his dad.

Too bad it didn't seem to bother Matt to be called by his first name. Hunter thought about the one time he'd called Mom "Joanne" and she'd acted like he'd called her a ho or something. Joanne was her name, so why couldn't he use it?

"It's pretty hot today. Want some ice cream?"

He wasn't a little kid anymore, but he still liked ice cream. Ice cream was a kind of ageless thing so he said yes because he was no idiot. Free ice cream? The way he figured, Matt kind of owed him.

"Sure."

A few minutes later they were down at the Lick n Spoon. Cones were for little kids, so he ordered a chocolate milk shake like a man. So did Matt.

They sat at the booth in silence for a few minutes until Matt asked Hunter about his grades for the last semester. Typical parent stuff. School was out for the summer but it was like no one would let him relax for a nanosecond.

"They're all right. I don't have to make up any credits."

Matt nodded. "So your mom wants you to start spending weekends with me. What do you think about that?"

"It's because of her new boyfriend. She wants to follow him around like a fucking groupie."

Matt didn't even blink. Hunter couldn't figure him out. He was a hard-ass who would force Hunter to paint a fence instead of letting his mom pay for the damages, but didn't mind if he cussed or called him by his first name. Go figure.

"Do you want to spend weekends with me?"

"Do I have a choice?"

Matt met his eyes. "Put it this way. I'd like it to be your choice, but your mom is kind of forcing the issue."

"Yeah, she would." Hunter had just invited Matt to rag on Joanne, if he wanted to. Why not? She complained about him all the time.

"I'm looking for a house with enough room for both of us. You'd have your own bedroom."

Huh. Matt didn't take the bait. "I don't see why I can't stay at the house on my own. I'm almost a man."

"For one thing, it's against the law. We're responsible for you until you're eighteen. The second thing is that you're also my son, and maybe you should live with me a little while before you go to college. Just see how it is."

"I guess." He lifted a shoulder.

He didn't want to admit he did wonder sometimes what it would have been like to live with Matt all these years instead of his mom. To travel around the world and see Germany and Saudi Arabia, and some of those faraway places where he'd received Matt's postcards from. It had to be boring as shit for him to be back in Fortune where if you weren't a techie guru you'd eventually work for one. That's why Hunter wanted to get out of the Bay Area. He wanted to go overseas and be a badass Marine. Or a Navy SEAL.

"Do you have any friends who were Marines or Navy SEALs?" Hunter asked.

"One of my high school friends was a Marine. Is that what you want to do?"

"Yeah." He got ready for Matt to tell him how he should join the Air Force instead.

"Good choice. Fine organization."

Matt wasn't going to warn Hunter that he might put his eye out or something? One good thing he could say about Matt was he didn't have a whole lot of experience in the father department, and so far this was beginning to weigh in Hunter's favor.

Matt dropped him off at his mom's house a while later, and Hunter rushed in the door and passed his mother in the kitchen.

"How was it? Did you two have fun?"

"Sure, it was really fun painting a fence in a heat wave." He grabbed an apple from the fruit basket and ran up the stairs to his bedroom. "Can't wait to do it again."

"Good news! Chuck's team won another—"

He didn't hear the rest because he slammed his bedroom door shut. What did he care about stupid Chuck and his minor-league team? They could win every game they played and it still wouldn't improve their loser status. They were major-league losers stuck in the minors and nothing more. Hunter whipped on his no-longer-MIA earbuds and logged in to his online account to

play "Call of Duty". Trent and most of his friends
were already logged in and kicking Nazi ass. He'd
already be doing the same if it weren't for the
fence. Most of his online friends still couldn't believe Matt had made him paint the fence, except
for one friend, someone Hunter suspected might
be older than he pretended to be.

StarWarz: Is your mom still dating the loser?

Jarhead2018: Yeah, and they won some game.
Super excited about being losers. Grown-ups are
so sad.

Hunter killed a Nazi. Then another. Booyah!

StarWarz: Check out Twitter. I've got your mom's
boyfriend there.

Hunter grabbed his phone and checked his
Twitter app, and there he saw an obviously Photoshopped picture of Chuck Johnson next to Wade
Hopkins of the San Francisco Rockets. In big
bold letters that were coming cartoon-like from
a bubble above Chuck: Los Angeles Jumpers are
losers!
    This could be a problem for Chuck, since he was
currently a second string pitcher with the Jumpers.

Jarhead2018: Did you make that meme?

StarWarz: You're welcome. ROFLMAO!

Hunter retweeted the photo and hashtagged it a few times. His friends did, too. Let Chuck try to catch this fastball.

He was still laughing his ass off when Mom called him to lunch.

CHAPTER ELEVEN

MATT HAD BEEN in a hell of a foul mood come morning, which might have had something to do with the fact that at 5:00 a.m., when his internal clock woke him from a fitful night's sleep, he had his arms full of a gorgeous woman. Sarah. Fully clothed. The stubborn woman had slept in the small space beside him all night long rather than give in. He thought for certain she'd have moved sometime during the night but no.

Instead, her sweet ass had been flush against his dick when he woke. Slaying him. He'd woken with his body asking, *Oh yeah, where do we sign up for this?* Mornings were torture on a single man like him, with his body reminding him what it was made for, and his big head arguing he wasn't a caveman. He had to stay the hell away from Sarah and so far, it was going about as well as he might have expected.

She had been so soft in his arms. So beautiful with her hair down. So damn fucking sweet. It was all he could do not to haul her back to his bed with him and finish what he'd started with her.

She didn't believe in love, which shouldn't surprise him. *Bitter* and *angry* had been two of the best words to describe Sarah when she'd come out to Fortune to settle her father's estate. Still, he'd never imagined that she was so messed up as to have given up completely. Love hadn't worked out too well for him, either, but he couldn't say he'd given up. Just put it on a long hiatus. But frankly, all that meant was that he was likely even more stubborn than Sarah.

Matt rarely wound up on the flight schedule on a Saturday, and so he and Hunter had finished the fence. Considering the sweltering heat and the fact that Matt had barely made it up in time himself, he would consider it a win. He and Hunter had painted side by side in relative silence, and Matt later took Hunter for ice cream in a lame attempt to connect with the kid. Matt had tentatively started the talk about weekends, and Hunter, while in relative denial about his level of maturity, didn't seem to hate the idea completely. Matt had dropped Hunter off at Joanne's around lunchtime.

His arms were killing him, and not just from the painting. These arms had wrapped around Sarah all night long. Why, again, had he done that to himself? Oh yeah, because she'd refused to take his bed instead of the couch and both of them were too pigheaded to give in. Which made them both idiots.

This morning, when he'd disentangled himself from her long legs gently so as not to wake her, she'd mumbled something in her sleep which he couldn't make out so he had moved closer. Big mistake. Her long dark hair had fallen in waves around her face, a few strands stuck over her lips. It was beautiful and wild, like a lion's mane. She wore it up in a bun all the time, so it was a little like seeing her naked for the first time. He'd been...not at all disappointed. He'd brushed the hairs aside, and it'd turned out she'd had a tiny smile there, her face relaxed and empty of the stress lines he'd seen there over the past few weeks.

She's so beautiful.

A no-longer-so-small part of him wanted to put the smile on her face. And a whole lot more than a smile. He wanted to see her gasping and writhing beneath him. Or on top of him.

But reality hit him front and center. Love was not on the menu. It wasn't for Sarah, and it shouldn't be for him. He had his hands full with Hunter. Unfortunately, his son was at that awkward shift between little monster and fledging human being. Matt saw the promise in him, and wasn't about to give up, but he couldn't expect that from Sarah.

When he got back to Sarah's in the afternoon, he planned on fixing what he feared could be a serious electrical problem. Last night, he and Stone had discovered at least two generations of wiring behind the walls. They'd both wondered how the entire place hadn't burned down before this. It was why he hadn't wanted Sarah sleeping in the bedroom and why he'd slept fitfully and on semialert status all night long. That, and Sarah being up close and personal with his favorite organ.

Sarah's car was in the driveway, but inside, his only greeting was from Shackles, who jumped on his hind legs and acted like Matt had been gone for a year. No. A decade.

"Calm down." Matt picked up the scruffy guy, who immediately licked his ear. "Okay, a little too intimate for me."

He set Shackles down and let him out in the yard, where he noticed the garden shed's doors were open. Shackles trotted to the shed, stopping once to look back as if to say *This way, idiot.* Matt followed Shackles into the shed and was rewarded with a beautiful sight. Sarah stood at an easel, her back to him, presumably so involved in her sketching that she didn't hear him come up behind her. Then he realized she had earbuds in and couldn't hear him. He had a few minutes to enjoy the moment, listening to her hum slightly off-key to "Beautiful Day" by U2.

She wore an old worn pair of jeans with paint smeared on…interesting places. Her hair was back up in that bun again, though wisps of it fell out, reminding Matt far too much of last night.

Her hand moved over the canvas, shading a charcoal sketch of a hill he recognized. El Toro, the fourteen-hundred-foot-tall hill rated as a moderate to expert hike. A few of the personal things he knew about Sarah—she liked to hike and draw.

He had a feeling there was a lot more for him to discover about her, like why she gave him the uncanny feeling she could see right through him. On the other hand, maybe he didn't want to know.

As if she'd heard his thoughts, she turned to him and jumped. "I didn't hear you come in."

He nodded at the sketch. "I like it."

She took her earbuds out and stood in front of the sketch like she wanted to block his view. "It's nothing. Just something I fool around with when I'm bored."

"Is that El Toro?" he asked.

She turned to glance at it again. "Yes."

"Have you hiked it yet?"

"Not yet. I wanted to, but I missed the citywide hike last month."

Because the land was partially on private property, the city hosted a sanctioned hike once a year. The Boy Scouts hung ropes for those who couldn't make the climb without assistance. And if you made it to the top and back down again, you could get a certificate from the city of Fortune saying you'd climbed El Toro. With the kind of mountains they had in Colorado, he was surprised Sarah hadn't poked fun at the size of the hills in their valley.

"I'll take you. I know another way."

"A secret way?" She smiled, and while it didn't look as relaxed and honest as the one he'd seen on her this morning, he'd take it.

"The local's way." He stepped closer to the easel and she moved aside.

"I've been experimenting with landscapes, but I don't know. Something's missing."

"People?"

She hit his shoulder and laughed. "Then it wouldn't be a true landscape."

"Yeah. I don't know that much about art."

"No, you wouldn't. You're an engineer."

"But I can appreciate beautiful things. I've got twenty-twenty vision." He slid her a look full of obvious. She was the beautiful thing to him. *Hello, lame.* "What if you put some people here at the bottom, ready to go up the hill?"

She sighed. "But then—"

"I know. It wouldn't be a landscape. It would be something else."

"Maybe I got tired of people."

"I'll try hard not to take that personally."

"*Drawing* people. And I'm only tired of criminals. Not…not you." Her hand went back to the sketch and she shaded in more at the bottom of the hill.

"Good to know. Think you can sketch me?

I'd be your model any day of the week. But not naked. I'm shy."

Her eyes narrowed. "Of course you are. But I don't do nudes. Particularly not you. I wouldn't get any sketching done."

"No, I agree. Don't get me wrong, I support the arts, but it would be a damn waste to spend your time sketching me nude. Wouldn't want to tease you." He grinned, thinking he was doing exactly that. Teasing, when he'd been the one to shut her down.

Stop it.

She looked at the ground. "Matt. About last night…"

"Yeah?"

"You were right."

He nodded. "You should have let me have the couch."

"Maybe. Okay, fine. But that's not what I meant. I'm sorry if I was a little too direct. It's just… I know what I want. Just because I don't believe in love doesn't mean I can't have a little fun."

His phone buzzed in his pocket and he ignored it. "You'll have to find your fun with someone else. I'm not playing."

"That's interesting. Because the way you look at me makes me feel like you're very much interested in playing."

"True enough. I'm human." His phone buzzed again. "Not a saint."

He withdrew it, spotted Joanne's caller ID and decided he'd deal with her later. Realizing he and Sarah stood a little too close for two people who were apparently not in any imminent danger of getting it on, he stepped back.

"You're definitely no saint. I could feel that this morning." She smiled and caught his gaze, then looked away.

For once glad his body had spoken for him, Matt fought a grin. "I can see why it would be hard not to notice that. Very hard."

She laughed. "You're good at that, you know?"

"Getting hard? Yes, thank you. I am."

"Verbal foreplay." She threw her pencil down and passed him on the way out of the shed.

"You're no slouch in that department." He followed her out.

In the yard, Shackles sniffed around a peach tree, then barked and chased after the bird that flew out of it.

Sarah locked up the shed. "I'll try to do better."

"We can do this. Even if we're both physically attracted to each other, we can live here together without getting intimate."

"Sure we can."

He would have to stop wanting her. Stop flirting with her. He'd forget that almost-kiss and the way she looked in his arms with her hair down. Her lips parted. Waiting.

She turned to him and her palm pressed against his chest. "We're good. I'm good. Are you good?"

"I'm good," he lied.

He was completely screwed.

CHAPTER TWELVE

WHILE MATT WORKED on the electrical the rest of the afternoon, Sarah busied herself with the second spare bedroom. Matt had already framed the windows in there and all she had to do was paint. This was her sweet spot anyway. She'd chosen a dull shade of brown because the Realtor had advised to paint in neutral shades. For boring people, she guessed. While she hated the thought of a boring person buying her father's house, those were the breaks. Point being, she supposed, beige and every shade of brown in the color wheel matched everything.

Sarah would have chosen green had she been making her own choices. But she'd keep the bright colors on her easel. Today's project had been charcoal sketches, but Sarah had recently issued herself a challenge. It was time, long past time, to paint in colors again. Sure, the charcoal pencil sketches were what she'd become accustomed to in her line of work. But she'd never improve her craft if she didn't branch back into acrylics. Oils. Watercolors.

Her cell phone rang with Gloria Gaynor's "I

Will Survive." Mom again, and why not? Sarah hadn't spoken to her since this morning, an entire six hours ago.

"Hey, Mom." Sarah picked up on the third ring.

"I'm sorry to bother you."

Sarah rolled her eyes. "No bother."

"What are you doing?"

"I'm painting the spare bedroom." She tried to sound upbeat, cheery. Sarah found that her mother was easily influenced by tone of voice.

"Wonderful. Progress. How much longer do you think?"

"Before I'm back home, you mean."

"In Colorado where you belong."

Yes, after all, Mom had decided that Colorado would be her home many years ago when she'd entered into the ridiculous custody arrangement with Sarah's father. Her family had lived there, and so she'd hauled Sarah thousands of miles away from her father, not even considering how difficult that would make it to ever see him. But neither one of her parents had asked where she wanted to live, or with whom.

Sarah pushed the roll down the wall with a respectable amount of force. "It won't be long now." Naturally, Sarah couldn't tell Mom about the latest development, as that would only upset her.

Mom sighed deeply. "If I had a nickel."

"It's an old house. It needs some repairs."

"Yes, I saw that when I visited. I think you should have listened to your brother and sold as-is. You could still buy two houses in Fort Collins for the price of that one."

Sarah was painfully aware of that fact and so was her bank account. She rolled some more of the dull beige paint on the roll. "We already talked about this."

"I'm sorry. I hate to sound like a broken record. Oh, I do have some news. I saw Hank last week. He asked about you."

Sarah's stomach dropped at the memory of one of the most painful and difficult times in her life. Hank had been the one guy, a good friend, who'd done his best to protect her.

"Far be it from me to say, honey, but you didn't have to go from one extreme to the other. Men aren't all bad. We have some of the best ones here in Colorado. It's the mountain air." Mom paused for a breath. "And maybe you can't be picky at your age."

Sarah ignored that, because hell yes, she could. She could be extremely picky and choosy if she wanted to be. Sarah rolled the paint down the wall so hard that it drooled out the sides of the roller. Great. She took her rag and wiped it up.

"Because of the eggs," Mom said.

Here we go. Sooner or later, it always came down to the eggs. "Mom, please. For the love of—"

"They have a short shelf life, honey. It's not my fault. Blame science. If you want children, you need to get started soon. You've got a few more good years while the eggs are ripe and ready. Before they rot inside of you."

Sarah closed her eyes. What a beautiful, lovely image. Exactly what Sarah needed right now. This is what she'd been missing all these months: a picture of eggs rotting inside of her body.

"Thanks, Mom. I could have gone all year without hearing that."

"You have time! They're not rotting yet."

Gah! "Good to know."

Far be it from Sarah to break it to Mom and start that ball rolling, but she'd thought for some time now that maybe adoption would be a good idea. She didn't want her fabulous Mcallister genes propagating the world right now. But telling Mom that right now would be akin to elder abuse. Besides, maybe someday Sarah would change her mind. She wouldn't rule it out. And as long as her eggs hadn't rotted inside of her by then, maybe she'd have a baby one day. She wasn't going to rush it.

Matt popped his head into the bedroom. He had a pizza in his hands and a sexy grin on his face.

"Mom, I've got to go. It's dinnertime. Say hi to Hank for me."

"I won't see him for another four thousand miles. You'll be back by then and can say hi yourself."

Sarah hung up with her mother and followed the glorious smells of fresh baked bread, cheese, meat and sauce into the kitchen. By the time she spotted Matt in the kitchen setting up paper plates on the table, she'd forgotten all about the shelf life of her eggs.

"You ordered dinner. I could have cooked." The box was from her favorite pizza place in town, Pizza My Heart.

"Please tell me you didn't want gluten-free."

"Don't you know me at all?" She grabbed paper towels and sat down with him at the kitchen table.

"Great, because it has extra gluten. Special request."

Sarah eyeballed him. "There's no such thing."

He gave her a devastating grin, then glanced at his phone. The grin slid off his face. "I have to take this."

Sarah watched as the expression in his eyes flipped from relaxed to guarded mode. His voice sounded clipped and professional. The airport? Did Stone have a last-minute job for him? Chartered flights were an unpredictable business and the pilots were often called in if needed for a last-minute flight. If a deep-pockets client had the funds to call up a pilot for their disposal at any time of the day or night, Stone and his company did not usually turn them away.

But that didn't make sense, either, because suddenly Matt had moved to the front door with a scowl on his face. "You're here? *Now?*"

Sarah stayed seated, no longer enjoying the spicy taste of pepperoni and cheese lingering on her taste buds. Something was wrong, and she could feel it. It was in Matt's suddenly rigid movements. And in the fact that in the next second, he was out the front door without a word to Sarah.

She moved to the kitchen window that faced the house's front lawn. A dark sedan was in her driveway, and Matt had put his phone away. This was obviously who he'd been speaking with. The petite blonde woman who got out of the driver's side of the car had an expression on her face dialed to angry ex-girlfriend. Uh-oh. Did Matt have an ex who wasn't happy about his living arrangement with Sarah? She could see why it wouldn't look good. Then again, he'd just told her over a week ago that he wasn't seeing anyone. So either this was someone who couldn't let go, or Matt had lied to her. Wait. Unless…

It wasn't long before Sarah had an answer. A tall and lanky boy climbed out of the back passenger-side seat. From here, several feet away and inside her home, he appeared to be the image of Matt. *Hunter.* He grabbed—was that a *suitcase?*—from

the trunk, and a backpack. Matt waved him toward
the house and Hunter moved at the pace of a glacier
in that direction. Matt and the blonde—who had
to be Joanne, Hunter's mother—continued to talk
animatedly. Or rather, she waved her arms around
while Matt stood still enough to be made out of concrete and listened. Sarah eavesdropped for several
moments, catching snatches of the conversation.

"I've had it… Your turn… Be back… Mess to
fix… Your son…"

Sarah tore her gaze away from the two as she
heard sounds of heavy steps on the small porch
entryway.

She met Hunter at the screen door. "Hi there.
You must be Hunter."

He didn't say a word, just grunted his agreement.

From here she could see clearly that he had
Matt's brown eyes, full lips and the same dark
blond hair. Hunter wore his short, crew-cut style.
She thought it made him look a little older than
his fifteen years. Like Matt, he was headed to be
tall. As she opened the door and he stepped inside, she noticed he was already taller than her.

"We were about to have some pizza."

Pizza she no longer wanted. She'd lost her appe-
tite at this turn of events. Hunter had done something to seriously upset his mother. One didn't
have to be a psychic to see that. Sarah wondered
what he could have done to upset his mother

enough to drop him off here as if he would stay awhile.

Because surely she wasn't abandoning her son.

Hunter didn't say anything, but threw a look of teenage-boy longing at the pie.

"Would you like some?" She led him toward the kitchen.

Leaving his suitcase and backpack in the living room, he sat down at the table and helped himself. "Dude, don't worry. I won't be here long."

He speaks! "Oh, I wasn't worried."

"Joanne's just got a bug up her right now."

"You call your mom Joanne?"

"Now I do." He shrugged. "And I call my dad Matt. Those are their names."

"Sure. Right."

He finished chewing, wiped at his lips and narrowed his eyes. "Are you Matt's girlfriend?"

"No!"

Dear Lord, had she just shouted at the poor kid? No need to protest so strongly. She took a deep breath and spoke softly. "Your dad and I… Matt and I are just good friends. He works for my brother."

He seemed to accept that, nodding and going back to the pizza.

What luck that they were having pizza tonight and not, for instance, Indian food, one of her favorites, too. Pizza and teenagers were made for each other, were they not? Then again, what did she know about teenagers anymore? She'd been one once, about a decade ago. That was the sum of her experience.

Finally, a car door slammed outside. Matt walked inside the house, mouthed *sorry* to Sarah and turned to Hunter, who was now enjoying his third slice. "Seriously?"

He stopped eating long enough to glance up at Matt. "It was a joke."

"*Not* a funny one."

"Joanne is crazy. It *was* funny. You should have seen it." He smirked a little.

Matt shoved a hand through his hair. She now recognized this as his completely frustrated and pissed-off look. She'd been on the other end of that expression a couple of times herself. Now she only wished she understood what either Matt or Hunter was talking about. On the other hand, this was clearly a family situation and she didn't have a place in it.

"I'll leave you two alone." Sarah moved down the hall and toward her bedroom so they could have some privacy.

She just hadn't expected that Matt would follow her in there.

CHAPTER THIRTEEN

MATT STILL COULDN'T believe it. Joanne had shown up, unannounced, and dropped Hunter off for an entire week. Sure, Hunter had made an idiotic decision, but bonehead move or not, this wasn't the way to handle it. Matt wished he'd answered his phone earlier when she'd called and maybe he could have calmed her down. But by the time she'd pulled up in front of Sarah's house, she'd reached a point of no return. There had been no talking her out of her decision.

Now Matt followed Sarah into her bedroom, where he'd spent all afternoon fixing the electrical. He shut the door. "Sorry about this."

"What happened?"

"Hunter decided it would be a good idea to retweet a photo of Joanne's boyfriend. A photo that one of his friends had Photoshopped."

"What kind of Photoshopping did they do?"

Matt winced, wishing like hell he didn't have to answer that question. "He's on a minor-league team and I guess it was a photo of him with someone from the San Francisco rival team. Words coming from Chuck, implying that he believes his current team are losers. Joanne said his contract is up for renewal, too. Lousy timing and the thing went viral."

Sarah's hand flew up to her mouth and a little squeak came out.

Yeah. This was bad. And a great way to introduce her to Hunter. "Joanne's going to fly down to Los Angeles where they're playing to help him do damage control with his teammates."

"It's that bad?"

"No idea. She seems to think so."

"Still, I can't believe this." Sarah lowered her voice. "He should be grounded. Have his phone privileges taken away. But dropping him off like this? I kind of feel sorry for him."

Funny thing was, Matt did, too. He didn't know where that had come from, but looking at Sarah's expression now, he had the relief of realizing that it wasn't just him who thought Joanne had overreacted. Then again, she really seemed to like Chuck and from the little Matt had heard, he was a decent guy.

"She'll be gone till next Saturday. She's been pushing for Hunter to spend weekends with me, and I've been working toward that, but this…"

Sarah didn't say a word, just stared at him wide-eyed.

"I'll go get us a motel room. We'll be out of your hair in a couple of hours." Matt opened the door.

He felt Sarah's hand immediately come up against his back. "Wait. You're leaving?"

"Well, we can't stay here."

"And why not?"

"It's too much, Sarah. This wasn't part of our deal."

"It's one week. I think I can handle that."

"And every weekend from here on out this summer. She's not waiting anymore."

"Oh."

Yep. Hello, beautiful. Meet single dad of teenage boy. Not so interested anymore, are you?

"Yeah." He moved to the door.

"But that's okay. We have another bedroom, and I just finished painting it. Hunter can stay there. There isn't a bed right now but maybe he'd be okay with a good sleeping bag for now?"

Matt thought sleeping on the floor was the least that Hunter deserved for pulling this stunt. Sarah appeared to be sincere. Given that she hadn't always given him the idea that she was particularly warm to strangers, he could see this would be a stretch for her.

"It's a whole week with a teenager who's not in a good place." He met her eyes, wanting to get across just how bad this could get.

"I understand."

Matt didn't like this at all. He hated to impose. But the cost of a hotel room also weighed heavy on his mind, and he'd already made plans for a good chunk of his change going to buy materials to finish the remodeling. "It's not fair to ask you to take both me and Hunter on."

"You're not asking. I'm offering." She pulled on his arm.

"You sure?"

"Of course. Remember what I said. This is your house, too." Her lips tugged in a half smile.

As if he would forget anytime soon that she'd forced him into accepting fifteen percent of the house. But right now, her quiet assurance and genuine acceptance had switched his disgusted mood in a way he hadn't expected. His body no longer felt coiled up tight with frustration. Sarah had him relaxed again. Comfortable.

Unfortunately, she also had a way of reminding him he was a flesh-and-blood man first and foremost. Not just a father, but a man with a crazy and intense attraction to his best friend's sister.

He nodded his agreement and didn't say another word, because he was afraid if he opened his mouth it would be to kiss her.

HOLY SHIT, THIS pizza was good. Hunter had this kind of pizza before at his friend Mike's house. Joanne never ordered from Pizza My Heart. She said it was too unhealthy and Hunter was a "growing boy" so it wouldn't hurt to develop good eating habits now. His mom was about as fun as a swimming pool filled with concrete.

He'd already almost inhaled the pizza whole when he decided he should slow down. Maybe Matt and his girlfriend might want some.

As usual, Joanne had overreacted. The tweet had traveled fast and one of Chuck's teammates had seen it. Probably laughed his ass off too, but then the teammate told Chuck about it. When Joanne had practically broken his bedroom door down to ask him if he knew anything about it, Hunter had lied through his teeth. It hadn't worked. She'd wrestled the phone out of his hands and told him she'd already checked his Twitter account. It had become hard to argue with her after that, not that she'd been listening to him or anything.

He hadn't made the damn meme, he'd just retweeted it. Was it his fault that the tweet had started to trend before someone pulled it down? It was a little bit of fun, if only *someone* would grow a sense of humor. Still, Hunter wished he'd thought about it more. He hadn't expected she would just take off for an entire week and leave him here with Matt. Hunter didn't even really *know* Matt anymore.

Hunter used to see his dad once a year, but the last time he'd seen him before he left the Air Force months ago had been two years ago when he'd been thirteen. A little kid. Things were different then.

Matt walked back into the kitchen without

Sarah. Hunter reconsidered taking another pizza slice and put it down. He'd left two slices for Matt and his non-girlfriend. Grown-ups had to watch their cholesterol, anyway.

"Sorry about interrupting your Saturday night."

"That's not your fault," Matt said and took a seat.

"Maybe, but tell your girlfriend I'm sorry anyway."

"She's not my girlfriend."

"For *real*?" Sarah wasn't lying to him?

"She's a good friend and I'm helping her renovate this house. She's from Colorado and she'll be going back when she sells the house."

Matt didn't seem to be lying. *In-te-res-ting.*

"I can always stay with a friend. Joanne wouldn't listen to me, but she wouldn't have to know about it."

"No." Matt ran a hand down his face, like he was kind of PO'd.

Probably at Hunter, when Matt should rightfully be pissed at Joanne. "Joanne only left me here because she's pissed. It isn't because she thinks you're such a great dad."

Matt seemed to ignore that. "Why are you calling her Joanne all of a sudden?"

"I call you Matt." He shrugged.

"Your mom said she'll call you tomorrow. When she's cooled off."

"On what phone?" Grown-ups were so stupid.

"On mine."

"So I'm going to be with you 24/7?"

"We're talking about a week."

Might as well be forever, but yeah. "Could I at least text my friends and let them know I'm offline for a while? She wouldn't even let me do that."

"Make it quick." Matt handed over his phone. "Why did you do it?"

Hunter looked up from the group text he was writing to all his friends. Joanne hadn't even asked him that. Fact was, Hunter didn't really know. "Why not? It was hella funny."

"To mess with Chuck's career?"

"Again, it wasn't my tweet. It was my friend's. I thought it was funny." Hunter realized that he didn't have any of his friend's phone numbers memorized. Never had to. He went to Twitter and instead sent a direct message to Trent. Best he could do.

Matt shoved a hand through his hair again. It was kind of long. Hunter wondered if girls liked long hair better than short. He kept his short to look like a badass. Maybe that wasn't working for Hunter.

"Look, I realize you might not like having Chuck in your mom's life, but she seems to like Chuck a lot."

"I don't care that she has a boyfriend."

"Even if you feel ignored?"

"I wish." Hunter pointed to the pizza slices left. "Are you going to eat that?"

"Go ahead," Matt said, leaning back in his chair, arms crossed.

Hunter didn't waste any time, picking up another slice. "What about your girl—?"

She came in the kitchen hauling a sleeping bag and a pillow with her. "I found a nice comfy sleeping bag. And you can have one of my pillows, too."

Hunter stared at her. She'd changed out of the clothes she wore earlier when it looked like she'd been painting. Now she had on a short dress like the kind Joanne wore when she wanted to impress a guy.

Not Matt's girlfriend my ass.

Matt stood up and took the sleeping bag and pillow from her. "Your room's in here."

Hunter wiped his hands on a paper towel, grabbed his bags and followed Matt down the short hallway. "Here?"

The room was brown. First the fence and now this. It seemed like this color would follow him everywhere this summer. Probably straight into his nightmares.

"There's no bed, so I figured you could sleep on the floor for now. Kind of like camping." Sarah smiled at him. "I just finished painting in here."

"It's brown," Hunter said.

"Beige."

Funny, she didn't look happy about that, either.

Matt was cleaning up the paint trays and brushes against the far wall. "I'll take the tape down tomorrow."

"Oh, I'll do that," Sarah said and gave Matt a look like he was one of those actors Joanne was always drooling over.

Yeah, sure. Not his girlfriend. Like he would believe that. Again, grown-ups?

Stupid.

CHAPTER FOURTEEN

SUNDAY MORNING SARAH woke to the soft thrumming sound of her ceiling fan. Matt had finished putting it up yesterday. After thirty minutes of tossing and turning, she'd finally fallen asleep in the cool night air.

And dreamed of her father. He'd been about to board a plane and urged her to come along with him. She'd refused because she'd never much liked flying. Ironic since lately she was surrounded by people who loved to fly—Stone, Emily and Matt. Even her favorite customer, the Judge.

She wondered what the dream really meant. Her father, beckoning her to the plane. Planes meant fun and adventure to her father. But she had resisted. Was she still angry at him, or simply hurt she'd never been able to see him one last time? Either way, she wanted to get past the memories. It was time to move on.

She rolled over. No Shackles staring at her this morning. There were sounds coming from the kitchen. Matt had to be awake. He'd probably already fed Shackles and let him out a dozen times. Hopefully Hunter liked dogs. He hadn't seemed too fond of Shackles last night, but then again he'd been a little preoccupied after being abandoned.

Because that's exactly what Hunter's mother had done, in Sarah's opinion. What kind of mother chose a man over her son? *Maybe a lonely one.* Not like she didn't know a little about lonely. She'd been single and alone for the past five years. But Sarah didn't care what Hunter had done, he didn't deserve his mother dropping him off with no warning. And Matt? If possible, Sarah felt even sorrier for him. Both he and Hunter had just learned how to swim and been thrown into the deep end of the pool. She couldn't let Matt do this alone. Couldn't send him off to a motel room so they'd both be out of her house. Because she didn't want that. No, she wanted them both here with her. Why, she wasn't entirely sure. They had one bathroom. She was supposed to share a bathroom with Matt and a teenage boy for a week.

What had she been thinking? And it wasn't as though she'd spent much time around kids. But the way Hunter had gone for that pizza last night brought back memories of her old boyfriends back in high school. Teenage boys tended to eat huge quantities. She'd go to the store today and load up on snacks he might like. Maybe then he'd crack a real smile. Surely he could survive without his phone.

What did teenage boys like these days, anyway? She didn't know, but she'd find out. Sarah swung her legs out of bed and proceeded to get fully dressed so she could go take a shower. Fortunately she already had the panties-and-bras and running-naked-out-of-the-shower disasters in her rearview mirror. The night before, she'd carried a stack of towels into the bathroom and put them under the cabinet and on every available surface. Just to be on the safe side.

When she walked into the kitchen, Matt had his back to her. He wore jeans and a dark blue loose shirt, but she could still see the muscles in his back bunch up as he worked over the stove. The smell of pancakes, bacon and coffee teased her stomach. Hunter sat at the table bent over a stack of pancakes. When she walked into the room he glanced up for only a second. Odd. Didn't teenage boys sleep till at least noon?

"Morning," Sarah said, going for the coffee carafe.

She poured coffee, and out of the corner of her eye caught Hunter slip Shackles a piece of bacon. Of course, Shackles left the room with his bounty.

"Do you also want some of my famous coconut pancakes?" Matt asked.

He hadn't shaved yet, and those dark bristles on his jawline and chin made something ping low in her belly. Then he grinned and the ping became a pang.

"Sure." Safe answer. Not *Sure, meet me in the shower.* Just plain, safe *Sure.*

She grabbed her coffee mug and took a seat next to Matt's progeny. "How'd you sleep?"

"Yeah, great. Until six o'clock when Matt woke me up." Hunter scowled at his father.

"The floor was too hard, anyway." Matt slid a plate of pancakes in front of Sarah. "Might as well get up. Right, Hunter?"

"We should search this house for an inflatable mattress. I think there might be one somewhere around here. My father was a bit of a pack rat," Sarah offered by way of explanation. "No telling what we'll find around here."

They'd hauled away a lot of junk but she was still finding things that surprised her. Once, she'd found a coffee can of receipts so old the ink had worn off them. Some things were easy to throw away. Others, not so much.

"I'm cool," Hunter said. "I don't mind the floor."

Shackles had returned to beg for more. Hunter picked up another piece of bacon, then looked to Sarah as if asking her permission.

She nodded and made an effort at a smile. Shackles left the room with his food. "He usually doesn't eat when someone is watching."

"Weird," Hunter said and took another mouthful of pancakes.

Not a problem he shared with Shackles, obviously.

"I'll get you one of those throwaway phones today," Matt said to Hunter.

"Like the kind the drug dealers have?"

"Like the kind with no internet access." Matt went back to the stove, the irritation heavy in his tone.

"Looks beautiful outside. What is everyone doing today?" Sarah tried for a bright and cheery tone. Well, it worked with her mother.

"I don't know," Hunter said. "I'm what you'd call a slave, so I don't make my own decisions."

Matt ignored the sarcastic comment. "We're going to work on the window framing today. Hunter is my assistant. Unless you need help painting. Hunter likes to paint."

Hunter grunted.

"I'd love help painting. Maybe we could start in my room today, since you already framed the windows in there."

LATER THAT MORNING Sarah pulled the tape off the walls in Hunter's room, then proceeded to show him how to tape before they painted in her room. She remembered to soften her edges and ask instead of demand. Despite his obvious reluctance, Hunter did everything he was supposed to do.

They were in the middle of painting one wall when she asked him, "How long have you liked painting?"

"I hate painting. Painting sucks."

"Oh." So much for finding a kindred spirit.

Sarah wasn't sure she could find much in common with someone who didn't appreciate color.

Well, except for the abandonment thing. There was that.

Of course, it had been different for Sarah. After the last summer she'd visited her father and both he and Stone had been so unhappy to have her around, she'd decided not to come back. Her father hadn't pressed the issue. Technically it wasn't the same, even if she'd still been the one to feel abandoned. The point was neither one of them had wanted her around.

"Do you like school?"

"Nah, school sucks." He dipped his roll into the tray. "Why do you like brown so much?"

"I don't. My favorite color is green. And after that, definitely blue."

Hunter stared at her. "Then why are you painting everything brown?"

"Actually, this is beige. The reason is that most people like neutral colors, according to the real estate agent who's going to sell my house. And since I don't know who's buying it yet I have to go with something that is sort of…pleasant to most people? Does that make sense?"

Hunter nodded. "That sucks."

Okay, favorite word registered. "I guess it kind of does."

"Why do you live in Colorado?"

"That's where I live. I have a job there and I

own a condo I'm subletting. My mom doesn't live too far away, either. We're pretty close." Suffocatingly close. Best not to add that tidbit.

"What kind of a job? Are you former Air Force, too?"

Sarah laughed. "Oh, no. That's funny. I don't even like to fly. I'm a forensic artist."

"For real? So you, like, meet the criminals and shit like that?"

Hunter had a serious vocabulary limitation. Unless this was all teenagers.

"Actually, no. I just paint the criminals. The 'alleged' criminals, er, suspects, I mean. I talk to the witness. Sometimes they're also the victim so I have to be sensitive. In order to get a good description, it's all about asking the right questions."

"Dude. That is wicked cool."

"Yeah?" Imagine that. She, Sarah Mcallister, was cool.

Matt popped his head in the doorway. "Everything okay in here?"

"Great," Sarah said.

When she turned back to the wall, Hunter was studying her. Eyes narrowed slightly. Lips a straight line. Suspicion. *Oh my God, he knows. He knows I've got the hots for his father.* Was she that obvious? Yes, she'd worked her entire adult life toward studying human expressions. But she'd never become an expert at schooling her own. And didn't all kids secretly want their parents back together? Maybe that's what this whole rebellion of Hunter's was about. Sarah mentally slapped her forehead. Of *course* he didn't want Joanne dating the ball player. He wanted his mom and dad back together again. And what better way of doing this than throwing them together for a common goal? Save Hunter from being a juvenile delinquent.

"I'm seriously not your dad's girlfriend."

"I know. That's what he said."

"H-he did? When did he say that?"

"Sorry, dude. I thought you were lying to me."

"I wouldn't lie to you."

"Everybody lies. And I know you're not his girlfriend, but he wants you to be."

Hunter's voice was so matter-of-fact, but she couldn't help but wonder if this was his sneaky way of drawing information out of her. He couldn't possibly know that about Matt. But if she argued with him, she'd be protesting too loudly. If she agreed, he might not like that, either.

She decided her best response was to keep quiet.

"I DON'T LIKE THIS," Sarah said.

"Don't worry, I've done this before. Plenty of times," Matt said.

"Shouldn't we call an expert?"

"We will if we need one."

Sarah closed her eyes and held on tight, hoping it would all be over quickly.

Late in the afternoon, Matt had insisted he would take a look at the roof. She held the ladder steady and in place while Matt clambered up to the roof. It wasn't that she didn't trust he could handle a routine roof inspection, but the shingles were old and not the safest place for him to walk. But if she were being forced to put up with Matt climbing her roof and walking around on it, at least she could enjoy the view on his way up.

Enjoy it she did, appreciating every muscle that bunched in his arms and muscular back. He wore a lightweight T-shirt that left little to the imagination and a pair of board shorts that had her staring at his ass.

But seriously. Pilot, engineer, mechanic, carpenter and roofer. Would the overachieving never end?

When he reached the roof and started walking around it, she didn't like the sounds he made. Curse words were interspersed with the sounds of his footsteps as he walked and squatted, walked and squatted some more. It was much cheaper to offer the new buyer a roof allowance, according to the Realtor. But Matt had insisted he could repair it all himself.

The Saturday sun bathed them in its midmorning heat, though not yet with the oppressive are-you-kidding-me temperatures expected to melt them all into puddles of flesh today. Hunter was in his bedroom, presumably sulking and staring at the four walls because Matt wouldn't let him go up on the roof, too.

"How's it going up there?" she asked hopefully. Maybe *good* would be the next word out of his mouth. Maybe the roof would survive.

A grunt. No answer.

"Please say something." *Anything.*

She pressed her forehead against a rung of the ladder and pictured happy thoughts. Finally getting to kiss Matt. Taking his shirt off and running her hands from his pecs down to those delicious abs. She would lick in a straight line from his abs down to the gorgeous V and follow the line of hairs leading to his happy place. Then she would…

"Well, crap!" Matt muttered and a shingle flew off the roof and landed in the yard.

"Matt! Please! Is it really that bad?"

He crept to the edge and looked down at her, not smiling, his aviator shades hiding his eyes. "It could be worse."

Sarah moaned and pressed her forehead against the rung of the ladder. *It could be worse* was not exactly what she'd been hoping for, but she'd take it. She did not want Matt spending any more of his hard-earned money on her father's house. And until they sold this house, she couldn't pay him back, so she had to hurry up and get on with the selling, too.

Matt came back down the ladder. "I'm going to need to go inside and climb up in the attic."

"There's an attic?" Why didn't she know that?

"It's just a crawlspace attic. Probably no more than a few feet high. I want to check and see how bad the damage is. There are rotted shingles just over the space." He carried the outside ladder to the side of the house where he propped it.

Sarah followed him inside and down the hallway, wringing her hands. "There's going to be spiders in there."

Matt stopped in his tracks and turned to her, his lips curving slightly. "And I'm bigger than they are. Why? Would you like to do the honors? Because I wouldn't mind spotting *you* on the ladder. I can stare at your ass and return the favor."

Busted! He had her dialed, didn't he?

"Oh, no. Not a good idea. There's also... There might be...mice."

"Also bigger than them." Matt carried the smaller inside ladder with him and stood it in the middle of the hallway.

Sarah looked up, and sure enough there seemed to be an almost unnoticeable gap in the ceiling panel. Matt pushed on it slightly and it lifted up like a lid. He climbed through, and Sarah, her curiosity getting the best of her, followed one step behind him on the ladder rung. She stopped only when her head had an acceptable view of the attic space.

"What's all this?" Matt shone his small pocket flashlight, lighting up the dark spaces.

No one could miss the cardboard boxes stacked one on top of the other in a line against the far wall.

"More of his junk. We should get rid of it." By now she doubted she'd find anything that would matter.

The best so far were the three photo albums, which Stone had let her have. She understood fathers weren't usually the ones who kept the family history of birthdays and vacations, so she should have been happy that some photos included her. And she had been. It just somehow didn't work out to be enough.

"Looks like old clothes." Matt opened one box and rifled through it, holding the flashlight between his teeth.

He slowly began to hand one cardboard box after another to Sarah, and she carefully backed down the ladder and set it down. One by one he did this, until in the end there were no less than five cardboard boxes in the hallway. Great. Did the man ever throw anything away?

While Matt continued to crawl around in the attic, Sarah opened one of the boxes. They were indeed clothes, as Matt had said.

She just hadn't expected that they would be *hers*.

The old jeans she wore holes in the summer she'd been about ten and they'd gone fishing nearly every day. She'd never caught a thing, happy enough to thread the bobs with the squirmy disgusting worms for him. T-shirts she hadn't seen in years. Tennis shoes, a light Windbreaker, all in different sizes. Nothing too girly in here. They were all the comfortable clothes of a tomboy. And why on earth had he kept them?

She remembered that although she always brought a suitcase or two full of clothes for the summer, her father always wound up buying her more. The stuff Mom had packed for her were dresses and nicer clothes. Dad had said she needed to wear stuff she wouldn't mind getting dirty. Those new clothes tended to stay all year in her room at her dad's house.

He hadn't given them away, but it didn't make sense to have kept them, either. Unless you were talking about a man who had a hard time letting go of his possessions.

Or maybe this was about something deeper. Something she hadn't allowed herself to consider often enough.

Maybe she'd been the one to abandon her father.

She was so caught up in rifling through her old clothes, each piece eliciting a memory that played like a video in her mind, that she hadn't noticed Matt climb down the ladder until he spoke.

"Girl clothes?"

"They're my old clothes. He kept them."

"This box says 'Sarah's room.' Check it out."

Indeed, her father's familiar scrawl was all over the box in black lettering.

"Sarah." Matt had opened up another box.

Inside that box were drawings. Hers. She flipped through them, her agitation increasing as she studied all her childlike drawings and sketches from the time she'd been small and could barely hold a crayon. Her mother had boxes of her drawings she also kept, but Sarah never had any idea her father had these. Of course, they were his. Special drawings she'd obviously created for him. Father's Day drawings and cards, a day which she'd spent with him since it fell during summertime. Letters, still in the opened envelopes, she'd sent him throughout the year. A Christmas card in her childish writing.

"He kept all this?" She flipped through dozens of envelopes in faded ink. "Why?"

"It's pretty obvious, isn't it? He never let go. It's hard to do that with your own flesh and blood."

Matt would know, wouldn't he? "It would have been nice if he'd said something. All those years he never picked up the phone."

"Did you?"

Her head whipped up and her gaze met Matt's.

His dark eyes were soft and tender and she absolutely hated that about him right now. She wanted to fight. Throw things. Get messy and real and raw.

"I was a *child*. It was up to him to tell me that he missed me. Ask me to come and visit again. Not just stand by and accept it."

"It's a little more complicated than that."

"It's not complicated!" She threw an envelope back in the box and shut it, her jerky movements swift and irate.

"No matter what a father wants, he's always going to do what's best for his child. It's always got to be about the kid first."

"Don't defend him!" *You're supposed to be on my side!* she wanted to scream.

"I'm only trying to help you understand."

"No, Matt. There's no comparison. I know what you're trying to do. You're also a single father, but you care about Hunter. You want to see him."

"I'm glad to be a part of his life. But it wasn't always easy."

"There's no comparison. You're not just allowing Hunter to drop out of your life."

Matt looked at the ground, then met Sarah's gaze. "If that's what I thought he wanted, maybe I would."

"But sometimes kids don't even know what they want or need. They shouldn't be allowed to make those choices. Not when they're so young and self-centered that they don't even realize they've…hurt someone…they don't even…"

Great, she was crying again, unable to finish her sentence.

"C'mere." Matt pulled her into his arms.

She folded into him, such a rock-hard and warm assurance encircling her. His arms were tight around her, holding her close. She never wanted to go anywhere else. Just stay right here where Matt made it all bearable. And she was getting addicted to the friendship she had with him.

Addicted to him.

She'd been such a ridiculous wreck since she'd arrived in Fortune. Trying to be strong, holding it all inside even while still grieving over her father. She'd tried to find something, anything that could give her some comfort. And then Matt. Sexy as sin, sweet and gorgeous Matt. He managed to wreck her all over again in brand-new ways.

"I'm sorry," she sniffed against his beautiful, powerful neck, getting it wet with her stupid tears. "I think I've cried as much in these past two weeks as I have in my entire life."

"I'll try also to not take that personally." He tugged her in tighter still, his hand moving down her spine to the small of her back and back up again in soothing strokes.

She laughed a little at that, still against his neck, trying hard to catch her breath. If he'd brought the emotions out of her, it was only because he made her feel so much. Thoughts and sensations she'd stuffed down for years. Both hating men and loving them too much, wanting to fill an overwhelming gap in her life for years. She'd basically shut down. Tried to tell herself that none of it mattered, that she was a competent and take-charge woman of the world who didn't need a man, and certainly didn't need her father.

Except that in the back of her mind, she'd entertained the notion that someday, as a grown-up, she would reconcile with her father. Stone would get married and have a child, or she would, and the next generation would reach out to be a bridge. She'd never been in a hurry about any of it, charging through her life like she had a million days in front of her. Like time was insignificant and never in short supply. Now it was far too late for grandchildren or connections, or hope. He was gone.

She'd never even had a chance to say goodbye. Because if she'd had half a chance, she'd have told him she was sorry. And maybe that was the hardest pill of all to swallow.

Matt had her face framed between his hands and his thumbs wiped away her tears. He studied her carefully, his gaze shifting from worry and concern to a more heated look that she understood all too well.

And just like a switch had been flipped, she came alive again. "Matt—"

Then she was hauled up by her elbows to the tips of her toes and he lowered his lips to hers.

"Hey."

It sounded like…everything stopped as Sarah turned to follow the sound and found Hunter standing in the hallway just outside his bedroom door. He stood, hands stuffed in his pants pockets, trying hard to look anywhere else. His eyes were unnaturally fixated on the ceiling.

CHAPTER FIFTEEN

SHE WAS KILLING HIM.

When Sarah clung to him, every inch of space between them wiped away, he wanted to haul her into the nearest bedroom. He'd make her feel good, at least for a little while. They could both get lost in each other and forget everything and everyone else. Fighting this attraction for her was turning out to be the toughest thing he'd ever done. And now Hunter had practically caught them in the act.

"Is Sarah okay?" Hunter asked the minute Sarah stepped into the bathroom.

"Yeah." Matt took a seat on the couch. "Why?"

"Because she looked like she'd been crying?" Hunter said this with almost exaggerated patience.

"She's having a hard time." Matt wondered how much he could tell Hunter without violating Sarah's confidence. He quickly decided on nothing. "If she's upset, it's not because of you."

"Why would it be me? I figured it was something *you* said to her."

If Matt wasn't mistaken, Hunter sounded almost accusatory. Defensive.

Of Sarah.

A surge of pride kicked Matt hard in the chest. This was his son, his boy, and he felt protective about Sarah already. Not bad. Maybe he and his son were more alike than he'd realized, going beyond the obvious physical likeness.

Matt shook his head, fighting a grin. "I didn't say anything. Not this time, anyway."

"Huh."

If Matt wasn't mistaken, Hunter wasn't buying it. "Look, I should probably explain what just happened there."

"You don't have to."

"See, Sarah and I—"

"I know. You're just good friends."

Matt cleared his throat. "It's not what you think. Well, it's *probably* not what you think. She's... See, the thing is..."

"You like her. Anyone would."

"What do you mean *anyone* would?"

"Uh, hello? Take a look at her."

"Yeah, but here's the thing—I don't just like her because of the way she looks. That would be wrong."

"Why?" Hunter looked completely puzzled.

No wonder, since Matt was clearly talking out of his own ass. "What I'm trying to say is there's a lot more than her looks I like. And that's how it should be. When it's…right."

Hunter squinted at him. "But what else is there?"

A trickle of sweat rolled down Matt's back. "When you like a girl it should be for who she is. She's someone you can talk to, feel comfortable with and spend time with."

"And you like her."

"I do like her. But she's going back to Colorado. She and I have decided we'll just stay good friends."

Hunter nodded. "Seems to be going well."

"Yeah." Matt sighed, catching his son's deep sarcasm.

So well.

He had a feeling he was supposed to impart some more Dad-like wisdom to his son here. Something deep and profound. Wise. But he had zip. How was he supposed to resist a woman who fired him up the way Sarah did? A woman who challenged him, made him laugh, made his heart hurt for her and drove him bat-shit crazy with her stubborn streak. She made him want to slay her dragons. Fix everything in her way. Except that some things couldn't be fixed, and he knew that better than most people did.

Minutes later, Sarah came out of the bathroom, a smile plastered on. She looked fresh-faced, like she'd taken some time to clean up.

"Boy, those allergies are getting to me! Summertime, right?"

Matt and Hunter exchanged a look. In a few short seconds, they had an entire conversation, and in that conversation they'd both decided to play along with Sarah.

Because that's how much they both liked her.

"You should take some antihistamines," Hunter said. "That's what I always take."

"Good idea!" Sarah said, her fake enthusiasm full tilt and coming close to overkill.

"Hey, Hunter," Matt said, standing. "Help me move these boxes into Sarah's bedroom."

"What's in these?" Hunter asked, picking up a box and carrying it into the room.

"Lots of junk I need to go through," Sarah said. "I told you my father was a pack rat. He kept everything."

The statement spoke volumes. When Matt had first helped Stone clear out the bedrooms after Mr. Mcallister's death, they'd both been surprised at how much the old man had accumulated over the years. Matt had held his tongue, but wondered with a small amount of judgment why, if Mr. Mcallister was the saving kind, there hadn't been anything of Sarah's lying around. He'd told himself it was the move Mr. Mcallister had made to Fortune after Sarah had stopped visiting him. Still, he'd thought a father should have some memory of his daughter. There had been boatloads of Stone as a new Air Force recruit and throughout his career, and a few scattered photos in frames of Sarah and Stone when they'd been small. None of Sarah older, and certainly not grown.

Matt realized it had bothered Sarah to discover that, but now he wondered if Mr. Mcallister had ever had any recent photos of her sent to him. The discovery of the hidden boxes made one thing clear to Matt: Sarah's father had never been able to part with the memories he had of her. As a single father, Matt understood making tough and raw choices. He'd never liked the idea of sharing custody of a kid, forcing them to live three days of the week with one parent and the rest with the other.

It wasn't because, as Joanne had often accused, he wanted weekends so he could be "fun and carefree Dad" and never experience parenthood in the trenches. Matt thought he might have been the only single father in California to feel this way, but he wasn't interested in tearing his son in half.

Now Matt began to wonder if he and Mr. Mcallister might have had a lot in common.

SARAH TURNED FROM the "throw away" bag to the "keep" pile. In the "throw away" plastic garbage bag were all the moth-eaten, spider- and rodent-trampled clothes and toys from her childhood. Sentiment aside, she would have to let those go.

But there were still too many items in her "keep" pile.

Too many old and faded drawings of the past. She forced herself to crumple up a childish drawing of a red barn that held no special meaning she could discern. The stick figure drawings of her fishing side by side with her father, scribbles that they were, would remain.

And so it went.

She'd been at this exercise for a couple of hours, avoiding the inevitable. She would have to call Mom. Having already missed three text messages from her between last night and this morning, it was time. Not to mention long past the stage for the two of them to have a difficult conversation.

Sarah didn't want to put the blame on anyone else. She'd done that for far too long and it hadn't done anything but make her miserable and angry. Walking through her life only half-alive. Unable to love and be loved. Shifting the blame from her father to her mother would accomplish nothing, other than the simple fact that she would have someone still alive and present with whom she could discuss the most painful parts of her past.

Sarah picked up the phone lying on her bed. It was dinnertime, which would make it early evening in Colorado. Matt and Hunter had gone out to get dinner. She would have several uninterrupted minutes, so she dialed Mom.

"Hi, honey," she said. "Do you have your flight scheduled yet? I'd like to make plans to take the day off work and pick you up."

"No." Sarah took in a deep breath. "I haven't bought a ticket yet."

"You're so busy. Maybe I should do that for you."

"That's okay. I don't have a date yet."

"I see. You don't want to make a firm commitment to leaving with a commercial plane reservation that might lock you into a date."

"Don't—"

"Make you face the truth? You don't want to come home, honey. Admit it."

"It's not that I don't want to come home. I mean, I have to—"

"Have to, or want to?"

Have to. My life is there.

"Why are you even asking me this? You know I have to come home. I have a condo, a job and a life in Fort Collins."

"That's true. You can't just abandon it."

Or abandon *her*. She'd been there for Sarah. Been there for those awful teenage years in which Sarah had been scarcely human. She'd colored her already dark hair a shocking shade of black, painted her fingernails in alternating colors of black and bloodred, and listened to loud, head-banging heavy metal music. Gone temporarily insane and boy-crazy, broken her curfew and lied to her mother every chance she'd had.

They were tough years during which Sarah earned a reputation with boys. One that had been nasty and hurtful. She'd been seeking love and not just sex. Even so many years later, she still felt disgust for having missed the mark so badly. Yes, she'd gotten part of what she'd wanted from boys—plenty of attention. But eventually she'd wound up feeling even more dead inside than when she'd started.

It was Mom who'd said that Sarah could choose to start over while away at college. Wipe the slate clean. She could reinvent herself and leave the past behind where it belonged. Exactly what Sarah had done. She'd dropped the wild and crazy hair for a neat librarian's bun. Gone from contacts back to her glasses and dressed conservatively every day of her college career.

Funny how everyone still believed she was the frigid prickly porcupine she'd dressed like on the outside, and never quite seen the real her. Except for Matt. From the moment he'd first laid eyes on her it felt like he'd seen right through her. He'd noticed that the outside didn't quite match the inside of her.

"Sarah?"

"I'm still here."

During all those rough-and-tumble years, Mom

had never given up on Sarah. How could Sarah give up on Mom now? She thought she needed Sarah in Fort Collins, for whatever misguided reason she believed. Sarah didn't always understand why. Mom had her tight-knit group of girlfriends and though she'd never remarried, Sarah knew she'd tried the speed dating thing a time or two. Laughed about it and said one day she'd write a book about her experiences.

"I found more boxes in the attic," Sarah said.

"Not surprised." Mom snorted. "Your father put the 'rat' in pack rat."

Sarah ignored that. "This time they were mine. My old drawings and cards, even my old clothes. He kept everything."

More silence, and then Mom spoke. "That's good. Isn't it?"

"It means a lot to me. Did he ever ask you why I wouldn't come to see him again? I never asked before and I'm sorry to ask you now, but I really need to know."

"Why? What's wrong?"

"What's wrong is that I just realized everything that happened between Dad and me was my choice. I used to think he didn't want me around, but the truth is that maybe he loved me the right way. Without conditions. He just wanted to give me what I wanted. He wasn't going to force me to visit him if I didn't want to. He tried to do his best, and he probably thought eventually I'd come around."

"Is that what you think? That your father was being noble?"

"Matt seems to think so."

"Matt Conner?"

Mom had met Matt when she'd come out to visit a month ago. "Yes. Do I know any other Matts?"

"You tell me something first. Is Matt the real reason you're still there?"

Sarah sucked in another breath of what little hot air remained in this room. She'd never been good at lying to Mom. "Maybe a little? But also there's Stone. He and Emily are getting married. They'll probably have children before long."

"Who you can visit."

It wouldn't be the same. Matt would move on, and so would everyone else. He'd eventually find a nice woman that wasn't his best friend's sister. Someone who wasn't leaving town. Someone who believed in love. Life in Fortune would resume its natural rhythm without her, something she'd always realized on some level. She didn't understand why that bothered her so much now.

It took a minute for Sarah to realize that Mom had skillfully diverted her question about her father. "You didn't give me an answer."

Mom sighed. "Of course your father wanted to know if he'd done anything wrong. So did I when Stone didn't want to visit me anymore. But we decided to leave our children out of grown-up matters. We didn't want either of you to feel torn or forced to spend your summers away from the friends you had. At some point we understood it would be your choice. Stone had a job the summer he stopped. Probably a girlfriend or two."

"But that's not why I stopped visiting."

And God how it hurt right now, thinking of her father asking whether he'd done anything wrong.

That last summer, Sarah had felt left out. The third and unneeded wheel. She'd been excited to see Stone and hoped he'd build her a fort again, out of blankets and chairs where she could sit and draw for hours. He'd been too busy with his job and his friends, and she'd been the tag-along little sister always in the way. Suddenly that summer fishing hadn't held the same attraction, and neither had the slimy, disgusting worms. Plus, Dad had started aviation lessons in his spare time and talked nonstop about airplanes and the kind of mechanical stuff that made Sarah glance out the window and daydream. She hadn't come to California to meet new people, not that any kids her age seemed to have any interest in her. She'd come to see Stone and her father and that summer neither one of them had any idea what to do with her.

"It was me. I abandoned him, and not the other way around."

"Oh, honey, no. Don't blame yourself. You were just a kid."

Right, right. Sixteen-year-old Matt hadn't planned on Hunter, either, but at least he'd had many days since then to make it up to his son. And he was a wonderful father too, the kind who loved his son unconditionally. No expectations.

Just like James Mcallister had loved.

CHAPTER SIXTEEN

By Monday morning, Sarah was back for her shift at the airport and serving Judge his coffee as he read his paper. When she'd left this morning, Matt and Hunter were already gone. She had no idea what Matt's plan was for Hunter, but he hadn't left him alone at the house. Then again, she assumed that would have had to involve a certain amount of trust and she could see why it would be in short supply.

She was still trying to process the knowledge of the boxes. Not to mention still working through the fact that Matt had almost kissed her. Again. But the almost kisses had to stop. They were either going to do this, or they were not. But as wonderful and drop-dead sexy as Matt had been all weekend, Sarah had to wonder if he was attracted to her or her *mess*. He had a clear case of white knight syndrome and she had to face it; since the day she arrived in Fortune, she'd given him plenty of material.

"I heard your contractor was arrested," Judge said. "Is that why you asked about suing someone?"

"Sort of." Sarah poured coffee grounds into an empty filter. "It's been taken care of, though."

"Excellent."

"I do have a question for you. You have teenage sons, don't you?"

"Three of them, thanks." Judge sighed. "And don't get me started."

"What do teenage boys like these days? Besides their iPhones."

Judge looked up from his paper. "Teenage girls. Some things never change."

Sarah laughed. "I was thinking something more along the lines of skateboarding."

She wished she could think of something to redirect Hunter's energy. On the one hand, maybe she should just stay out of it and let Matt handle it. It's just that she'd noticed the tight lines of tension around his mouth whenever he spoke to or about Hunter. Not that she had spent an inordinate amount of time studying Matt's mouth, but okay, yes. She had.

After Judge had left on his chartered flight with Stone, and they were experiencing their midday lull, Sarah closed up and went to the Magnum Aviation office suites to check in with Emily and Cassie. This was her second job at the airport. Sarah helped by checking weather patterns for the following week, making copies of flight plans, following up on fuel tags that Jedd brought in and filing.

Now that Emily had more than her sport pilot's license she was taking more flights. Since Cassie kept threatening to retire at any moment, someone needed to keep up with most of the administration. And there was a comfort for Sarah to be part of her father's old business. His stamp was still everywhere, from the old-fashioned fishing pole that hung on the wall to the framed photo of "Captain James" posing near his prized Cessna.

"Ah, there she is." Cassie smiled when Sarah walked in. "Our resident angel."

Cassie was Emily and Stone's right-hand admin, and had been the backbone of the flight school when her father, James Mcallister, had owned and operated it. She was close to retirement, but had agreed to stay on until Stone and Emily had fully transitioned the business from a small and unimpressive flight school to the charter company they'd formed.

Sarah wasn't sure there would ever be a time when she'd be ready to say goodbye to Cassie. In some ways the woman had understood James Mcallister better than even Stone had. She called Sarah and Stone's father an old fart without the slightest tinge of regret in her voice and often mused out loud about his ridiculous filing system. But it seemed clear, in every nuanced word and memory of James Mcallister, that she'd loved and respected the man.

"Why am I an angel?"

"We heard." This was from Emily, sitting at the desk next to Cassie's. "About Hunter."

"Matt was in this morning and mentioned it before his flight," Cassie said. "We had to pull it out of him but, well, this is what we do. He finally confessed. You didn't just take our Matt in—you took in his teenage son."

"Not a problem." Sarah smiled. She enjoyed Cassie's praise, even if this instance of it wasn't well deserved. "Any one of you would have done the same in my position."

"Sure," Emily agreed.

She would have, too. Sarah believed it. Cassie she felt less certain about.

"Hmm," Cassie said by way of an answer.

Sarah would go ahead and guess that was a big fat *Hell, no.* "Where is he, by the way? They both left early this morning."

"Matt dropped Hunter off at his father's apartment complex. He thought the two of them could get better acquainted." Emily opened up a laptop. "And Matt had a chartered flight this morning to Arizona. He should be back soon. They hired him to wait until it was time to come back."

More deep pockets. They seemed to be all over Silicon Valley.

"So what do you think of Hunter so far?" Emily asked.

"He looks just like Matt. It's uncanny. But Hunter has a limited vocabulary."

"Funny, so does my grandson," Cassie said.

"I'm sure he's pretty angry at his mom, not that he didn't deserve to be punished," Emily said.

Cassie cleared her throat and raised a brow. "You think?"

A small plane took off on the tarmac and Sarah listened to the chatter of the pilot communicating, announcing his position and plan. On a clear day like today there weren't just chartered flights and flight lessons but private pilots who flew their own planes for fun. The airport didn't have a traffic control tower, but they had the CPAF, a Common Party Advisory Frequency to communicate position and intention between all pilots taking off and landing. It wasn't unusual to hear one pilot telling another one a smart-ass joke interspersed with their information, presumably after all passengers had been delivered. Sarah loved listening to them. Particularly Matt's voice, which sounded smooth and sexy over the system.

"I just wonder if Hunter is trying to get his parents back together by being so difficult." Sarah threw this out, an idea which had continued to brew on its own all night long. Maybe all she wanted was for someone to tell her she was dead wrong. She waited.

Emily frowned. "Yeah?"

"Entirely possible," Cassie said as she stuck a file in the cabinet.

Not what Sarah wanted to hear. "He's certainly got them working together for a common goal now."

"Only it sounds like it's not so much together. It's more like 'your turn now.' Not quite fair if you ask me. Not that anyone did." This was from Cassie, who, if at all possible, was even more over the moon for Matt than Sarah.

Of course, Sarah was *not* over the moon. She had a wild crush on the man. Nothing more.

Matt's voice came over the intercom.

"Oh my goodness." Cassie fanned herself, then threw a significant look in Sarah's direction. "That man. I swear if I were only thirty—I mean twenty years younger… Well, I certainly wouldn't waste any time."

Sarah let that comment slide off her back. He'd made it clear he didn't want to hop into bed with her. And she wasn't going to beg the man. Not yet, anyway.

A few minutes later Matt and Jedd walked into the office laughing.

"Hey, Sarah," Jedd said. "Sorry about your contractor. You should have told me that was him on the TV."

"No worries."

She glanced at Matt, to find him looking in her direction, smiling. He still had his aviator shades on, so she couldn't see what his eyes were telling her. *Thank you? How are you? Did you have lunch yet? Let's get naked?* All right, that last one was wishful thinking.

"Can I talk to you for a minute, Matt?" Sarah asked.

"Sure." He whipped off his shades and led her to an office suite. This one was his office. It was a little smaller than Stone's and farther down the hall, but Matt was the only other pilot on staff with an office of his own.

Matt shut the door. "I'm glad you wanted to talk. I wanted to thank you for putting up with Hunter."

"Matt, it's been two days." True, Hunter had been sarcastic in his comments and limited in his word choices, but so far she couldn't say she disliked Hunter Conner. Not even a little bit.

"Again. Thank you."

"I've been thinking. Maybe Hunter is misbehaving to…to try to get his parents' attention."

"It's working. I've never seen his mother so upset."

"Right. And now you're both working together toward a common goal. Fixing Hunter. Keeping him out of trouble."

Matt nodded. "I can see that."

He wasn't going to make this easy, was he? "I guess what I'm trying to say, Matt, is that I took some psychology courses after I started freelancing for the police department. And every child of divorce secretly wants their parents back together."

His eyes narrowed. "But Hunter isn't exactly a child—"

"Even so."

"Damn. I feel even worse for Hunter now. Because that's never going to happen."

"Are you sure?"

"Joanne doesn't love me and hey, I don't love her. It's not going to happen. But I think Hunter knows that. And would it really be such a great thing for him to see his parents together, barely tolerating each other? What do your psychology books have to say about that?"

She didn't remember. Probably wasn't even covered in class. "I'd have to look that up."

"Look it up. I think Hunter would like it if his parents were happy. Or eventually he will, when he becomes human again, which I have it on good authority will happen in the next couple of years."

Sarah took a step toward Matt. She wanted to get a better look in his eyes. There was no other reason. Was he lying to protect her feelings? Telling her what she wanted to hear? What he thought she wanted to hear? His pupils were definitely dilated, not always easy to appreciate in a dark-eyed gaze, but Sarah reminded herself that dilated pupils were not always an indication of sexual desire. Pupils would also dilate in a somewhat dark room. She reached behind her and flipped the light switch on. His office had only one window and she couldn't have his big pupils lying to her.

He reached behind her and shut the light off again. Then he leaned in close. Much better indicator of sexual desire. Mystery solved. Her throat was so dry she couldn't swallow.

"What are you doing?" He had better not almost kiss her again because she couldn't take that.

His hand palmed the nape of her neck. "Getting ready to kiss you."

In the next moment, he did just that, pulling her toward him the rest of the way. His kiss was long, deep, with blazing heat that rocked her world. It felt as if his warmth would slice right through her. His kiss was rough and insistent, but also a little like taking a stroll on a summer day. As if he didn't want to rush anything, but take his time and see the sights. Pick every flower and touch each soft petal. And funny, she began to feel the same way. Like maybe this was the place she'd like to stay, all day if she could, taking her time to taste and explore every inch of his beautiful mouth and tongue.

She was breathless, but didn't want the most incredible kiss of her life to stop anytime soon.

When he finally broke off, it was to simply study her intently. His hand skimmed down her spine to rest on the small of her back. She watched him carefully, too, because something had changed. Whatever this thing was between them had shifted into something frighteningly... real.

"Sorry," Matt said, his thumb on her lower lip. "I probably shouldn't have done that."

"Don't you dare say you're sorry."

"But—"

She wanted to argue, but decided she wanted to kiss him again more than she wanted to debate with him, so she rose to her tiptoes and kissed him. Hard. He didn't mind, clearly, and he tugged her even closer so that she could feel every inch of his big hard body. When his hand roamed under her blouse and pushed aside her bra to tweak her nipple, a soft moan tore from her lips.

He became fascinated with the column of her neck, licking and teasing her with small and tender bites followed by open-mouth kisses. So she moved her neck to give him better access.

Sarah thought she heard footsteps outside coming closer, but Matt had just sunk his teeth into her earlobe. The whole building could go up in flames all around her but she wouldn't be the one to stop him. No. Not her. Not stopping.

"Hey, Matt. You in there?" Stone's voice called out. "McWilliams wants you."

Oh Lord. She pulled away. The last thing she wanted was for Stone to walk in on them. Not like this. Matt didn't answer, and he also didn't stop touching and exploring. His talented hands were now squeezing her ass and his tongue was licking down the column of her neck.

"Um…" Sarah's voice trailed off. Some kind of word or thought came after that but damned if she could think of it right now.

Stone knocked again and tried opening the door. Sarah startled, but the door was apparently locked.

Matt had locked it.

Oh boy.

"Shhh," Matt whispered near her ear. "Don't worry, he'll go away."

Sarah opened her mouth to disagree, but then Matt tugged on her earlobe and she forgot everything. Even words.

"Ah, dammit," Stone said. "Emily, you're wrong. He's not in his office. Someone find him."

Then there was precious silence. Ecstatic that Matt had the foresight to lock his door, and turned on beyond belief by that fact, Sarah pulled him toward his chair. He sank down in it and she straddled him, making fast work of untucking his white button-down. Her hands drifted up to roam the hard planes of his chest and down his back. Wasting no time, either, Matt pulled off her top. Sarah slapped a mental high-five with herself for having chosen the uncomfortable demi plunging bra this morning. It was red satin and possibly the sexiest thing she owned.

Matt's gaze said he agreed with the sexy part. "Damn, girl."

His teeth guided one bra strap down. When his mouth suckled one nipple, Sarah thought she would go out of her mind with lust. Her fingers dug into his back and she grinded into him.

"Hey, Matt?" Came Emily's soft voice. "I know you're not in there, but when you get a chance we have a last-minute flight. Mr. McWilliams asked for you specifically. You *know* how he is."

Matt groaned and everything stopped. He cleared his throat. "I'll be right there."

"Thanks, and also, I'm sorry," Emily said, and then there was more silence.

Sarah's breathing pattern had been more or less shocked back into normalcy but she couldn't say the same thing about Matt's. Then again, her hand had somehow found its way just inside the waistband of his pants, which might have something to do with the problem. She slowly removed her hand and pressed her forehead to his.

"Too bad you're so popular." Sarah climbed off his lap and put her top back on. "I should get back to work, too. This isn't going to get me Employee of the Month status."

"Right." Matt stood and started shoving his shirt back into his pants. Pants with an impressive bulge in them. "And you should probably stop staring. It's only making it bigger."

"Sorry!" She forced her eyes away.

"I'd like to say I'm sorry too, but I'd be lying." Matt pulled her into his arms and placed a chaste kiss on her lips.

"Maybe I'll stay in here for a few minutes after you leave and that way…" Her voice drifted off. What? Emily and Cassie would think Matt and Sarah had been in his office behind a locked door playing charades?

His hand was on the doorknob. "Babe, we're not fooling anyone. Least of all ourselves." With that, he was out the door.

CHAPTER SEVENTEEN

MATT APPRECIATED A special request as much as any private pilot would, particularly since it meant more money for the chartered flight. Roger McWilliams was a regular flier with them, an altruistic and philanthropic businessman who actually did a lot of good for the community. It was a pleasure to fly him all over the country on most days.

Except for today. Today he'd had Sarah half-naked and in his arms. He was done with shutting her down. Done with being sorry for feeling the way he did about her. All he had left to do was make one thing clear to her. Neither one of them were ever going to regret this thing between them.

Stone had already filed the flight plan to Las Vegas and all Matt had to do was fly McWilliams and wait for him at the airport until his business was concluded. The way these things went, it was usually a two-hour wait so Matt figured he'd be back to Fortune around three o'clock at the latest.

But at two o'clock, Matt received a phone call from McWilliams saying that the McWilliams

Legacy Center meeting had run late. No problem. Tired of the slot machines and people watching, Matt phoned his father to see how the day with Hunter had progressed.

"Everything okay over there?" Matt asked his father.

"Super," his father said. "Hunter is a pretty smart kid, you know? Figure it runs in the family on the male side."

Matt let that one slide. An insult both to his mother and Joanne. "What are you two doing?"

"Taking apart my old Apple. Hunter called it a dinosaur."

"Remember what I said about letting him online."

"Sure, sure. But I think you and Joanne are going overboard. You can trust this kid. Believe me."

What had happened to the man Matt had grown up with? He'd grown as soft as a peach in November. "I need to respect Joanne's wishes."

Matt hung up and paced the length of the airport once. Twice. Looked at his phone. Considered calling Sarah, but what he wanted to tell her had to be said in person. He'd never been one to examine his thoughts about a woman and get all caught up in the feels. But Sarah reminded him that at one time in his life he'd longed to trust someone again. He believed in love, but trust was the real challenge. It was different with Sarah. After all, she'd been his good friend first, at a time when he'd decided she was "hands off" both for him and any other bozo. He'd witnessed firsthand the small changes in her and he'd been a witness to how hard she'd tried.

He glanced up from his phone to spy a woman obviously traveling alone, struggling with an infant carrier seat and too many bags. Fresh guilt poured into him again, the knowledge that this might have once been his child and his child's mother. He hadn't been there for either one of them.

When the woman struggled toward the escalator leading to check-in, Matt stood up and walked over to help.

"I'll carry this for you," he said, grabbing all her bags.

"Thank you!" She gave him a huge smile and stepped onto the escalator, carrying the baby seat with both hands. "You so rarely meet a real gentleman."

Yeah, that was him. An officer and a gentleman. He'd fooled most people, though he might have not fooled Hunter or Joanne. Maybe they could see the real him. The man who'd run from his child instead of toward him. He helped the woman get to baggage check-in and had to accept another big smile and thanks. Even a hug.

What he'd done to help the woman was such a small part of a father's role. The hard work day in and day out was what being a father was about. It was about much more than financial support and he realized it now. But he hadn't been around for Hunter, except as a part-time father. Clearly, Hunter resented the hell out of him. Now they'd been thrown together and Matt had a chance to make things right.

But to further complicate his life, a certain green-eyed brunette was slowly turning him inside out. Nothing about them was simple, not like he wanted it to be.

She was still not a good idea for him, but one thing was abundantly clear to him now. Everything felt easy with her. Familiar. Comfortable. And this scared the crap out of him. Sarah had no room in her life for him or his teenage son.

So much had changed since the night he'd first met her at the Airborne Bar & Grill. She'd worn a black all-business pantsuit to a bar in which mostly Air Force guys hung out. Her hair up in a tight bun and wearing black-rimmed glasses instead of the contacts she wore more often now, she'd looked like his hot librarian fantasies come to life. He'd taken one look at her and decided if she was game, then hell's bells, he was game, too. Anywhere, anytime. Then she'd introduced herself as Stone's sister.

Game changer.

That evening he'd crossed her off his one-night fantasies list. They'd become good friends as he tried to ignore the spark between them. Had tried to squelch it, beat it down and snuff it out. There was no more ignoring it now, not while she kept walking around, sharing oxygen with him and looking like the woman who would headline all his most erotic fantasies.

Matt pulled out his phone and played solitaire. Just because he had a suspicious nature at heart, he signed on to Twitter and looked up Joanne's boyfriend. Seemed that the photo had been taken down at least. Maybe the whole thing would calm down soon enough. Kids today had it rough, Matt had to admit. There was a camera or device everywhere at the ready to document their sheer teenage stupidity. He looked at his watch. Now he would be late to pick Hunter up, so he dialed him on the throwaway flip phone he'd bought him. "Hey, I'm running late. Wanted to let you know."

"Where are you?"

Hunter sounded frustrated, and Matt got that. But seriously, the man Hunter was dealing with today was a damned pussycat compared to the man who had raised Matt.

"Las Vegas, waiting for a client."

"Yeah." He sighed. "Okay."

"That bad, huh?"

"Sucks."

Would be nice if the kid had at least one other word in his arsenal. "Talk soon."

But it wasn't until an hour later that McWilliams finally finished with his meeting. "Wish you guys took tips. You deserve it."

Matt wouldn't argue. He understood most commercial pilots had to handle layovers, but the charter company didn't usually do this kind of thing. It was far too expensive for most customers.

"Don't worry. The bill will reflect my time."

By the time they arrived at the airport back in Fortune, only Stone and Emily were left and the two of them were only waiting for him to close up shop.

"Long delay, huh?" Stone asked. "I know you hate that."

He hated wasting time. If he had to run this kind of flight too often, he'd have to find a hobby. Learn how to sleep on his feet again. Or something. "The man does good work."

Emily and Stone brought up the rear and all three of them left the airport and closed it down. Matt had just started toward San Jose when his cell phone buzzed. It was Sarah's number.

"Hey."

"Don't worry about picking me up," said Hunter. "I'm already at the house. Your girl—I mean, Sarah picked me up."

"She did?"

"I called the airport, and she said she'd pick me up. No drama."

"Did you thank her?"

"Like a hundred times." Hunter sounded as though he'd moved the phone away from his mouth. "Hey, Sarah. Thanks for picking me up. Happy?"

"Yeah." Matt grunted. "Should I get dinner?"

"Nah, Sarah got more of that pizza you had the other night. I think there's some left for you. Better hurry, though."

"Uh, yeah. Thanks." Matt hung up, a little dazed.

Okay, what just happened?

Hunter had sounded human for the first time in a while. Matt supposed pizza could do that to a teenage boy, but then again it might also be Sarah. If she had even half the effect on Hunter that she had on Matt, it could happen. When he pulled up to the house, the lights were on in the kitchen and he could see Sarah through the window. Her head was bent over the sink. She turned around for a second, and when she turned back she was laughing. Then she must have seen his headlights because she looked outside, caught his eye and smiled. Her smile had a certain amount of heat to it, but what floored him was the something else he caught in that smile...her heart.

It had the double-edged-sword effect of making him hard and scaring him shitless. He couldn't do this with her. It was too big with too much potential for massive damage. He couldn't screw up. Not with her. Eventually he'd disappoint her and he couldn't live with that outcome. He couldn't lose her friendship and nothing would be the same after a breakup, no matter what they told each other. As much as he wanted her, the fact was he didn't deserve her, so he was going to have to back off.

He shut off the truck and his cell phone buzzed. Joanne. "What's up?"

"Just got done with damage control and it's the first chance I had to call. How's Hunter?"

"He's okay. Insists he had nothing to do with that tweet."

"His best friend did, and I can't imagine why he would do that other than for Hunter. So stop defending him. Plus he had a part in it."

"Still don't think this was the right way to handle it."

"What's wrong, Matt? Did we disturb your little love shack plans this weekend?"

He stopped himself from swearing. "No."

"I know about the girl. I hope you're not letting her run around the house in next to nothing. Hunter is a teenage boy on hormone overload, so keep that in mind."

This time, Matt did swear under his breath. "Not that this is any of your business, but that woman is my friend. Sarah Mcallister. And she doesn't run around in anything but a T-shirt and jeans. Practically wears an overcoat on her way to the shower in the morning."

Good thing Matt had long ago learned how to control his temper. He was long past giving a damn what Joanne thought, but he also couldn't have her talking about Sarah.

"And another thing. I noticed he's started to call you 'Matt.' He tried that with me once, too."

"I don't mind."

"You shouldn't let him call you by your first name. It's a sign of disrespect. Or distance. But maybe that's what you still want, no matter what you tell yourself."

Matt shoved his response down. "Anything else?"

It was true that sometimes Matt resented that Joanne would forever be a part of his life based on one single mistake of his youth, but then immediate guilt would press down, accompanying the thought, then segue right back into anger at the situation. Same place he'd been in for years. Guilt, anger, guilt. It pushed down on him, and try as he might he couldn't forgive himself. Joanne had rooted him to this spot for years.

You owe me. I had your child.

"That's it. Now let me talk to my son."

"Hold on. I'll see if he's available," Matt said in his most annoying tone and opened the front door. "Hunter, it's your mom on the phone."

He was spread out on the couch in front of the television, remote in hand. "Huh."

Matt threw the phone in Hunter's direction. "Give her your new number."

Hunter caught the phone in midair. "Not sure she makes clearance."

"Smart-ass." He stepped out of the room to give Hunter some privacy and found Sarah in the kitchen.

The cabinets missing their doors did their work of pissing him off all over again. He wanted to wring that contractor's neck. But that reminded him he had to follow up with his connection this week. He would take Sarah to a warehouse where she could choose some new ones.

"Hey."

Sarah shut the refrigerator door and turned to him. "Hey yourself. Your son eats like a race-horse."

"Yeah? How much does a racehorse eat? More than a regular one?"

"I don't know. A lot?" Her hand ran along the length of the countertop. "About today…"

They were going to talk about this afternoon, when he'd had his tongue down her throat and she'd had her hand down his pants. She wouldn't want him to be sorry, and try as he might, he couldn't say those two words to her. He was sorry for nothing that had happened this afternoon, as crazy as it seemed.

"Yeah."

"I was hoping we could maybe resume—" She

wouldn't even look at him now, following her finger on the counter, glancing at the floor. "Sometime."

He cracked a smile because he'd had his mouth on her nipple and she couldn't look at him. "Maybe that's not such a good idea."

That did it. She met his gaze, heat flaring in her green eyes. "You're sorry?"

"Hell, no."

Her eyes softened. "Neither am I."

"It will change everything."

And, dammit, there'd been women in his past, women he liked just fine. Just six months ago, he'd been excited about a beautiful woman whose name he could barely remember now. But there was only one Sarah. Stone's sister. His good friend. Only one woman he found he couldn't resist, even while his mind told him he should.

The question was how much was he willing to risk? Because if things went south, as they often did for him, they might never salvage their friendship.

"I don't know about you, but I'm ready for a change," Sarah said.

"Hey, Sarah, do you have HBO On Demand? What channel is it?" Hunter yelled from the living room. "I might as well get caught up on *Game of Thrones* while I'm here."

"I'll be right there," Sarah called back.

As she passed by him on the way to the living room, Matt squeezed her hand. She squeezed back, giving him a heartbreaking smile.

An evening of watching cable TV with his son and Sarah lay ahead of him, even if he would rather finish what he'd started with Sarah this afternoon.

CHAPTER EIGHTEEN

JUST WHEN HUNTER thought he'd seen enough stupid and sad adults to last the rest of his life, he had to spend another day with the saddest one of all: Grandpa.

Hunter saw Grandpa Conner about once a year at Christmastime, even when Matt hadn't been around. Joanne would bring him over, or he'd come over to their house. When he was little, Grandpa Conner was always the kind to bring the "good gifts." No clothes or new underwear, for instance, like he always got from his other grandparents. No, he brought cool shit like remote-controlled airplanes and monster trucks, PlayStation and all the other expensive stuff. He also always brought a big check in an envelope and made a big show of giving it to Joanne "for the college fund." Of course, Joanne was all over it. But Christmas was the only time he really saw the man.

But holy crap, this guy was depressing now. He spent all his time in his super-exclusive condo or playing golf. The condo was pretty cool but mostly because there were all kinds of awesome gadgets in really weird places. Yesterday, when Hunter had found an old Apple computer in the closet, he figured he could take it apart and put it back together. *That* was how bored he was.

"What are you doing over there?" Grandpa asked from his favorite chair.

He was watching a soap opera. A soap opera!

"Looking for a screwdriver."

"In the kitchen?"

"The junk drawer." Joanne kept all the tools, the few she had, in one.

So far Grandpa had gum and loose change in his junk drawer.

Grandpa got up. "You'll find a screwdriver in the toolbox, where it belongs."

He shuffled over to a utility closet and brought out a big yellow toolbox. "Every man needs one of these."

"Thanks," Hunter said and went back to taking the thing apart.

"Back to that again, huh?" Grandpa was still standing here.

"What else am I going to do all day?" He had a phone like something from an '80s movie. It had no texting. Who talked on the phone anymore? His friends would laugh at him.

"What's wrong with you, kid? Don't you like Windows? I've got a PC."

"Yeah, but—" But nothing. There were advantages to hanging out with an old man, after all.

Once he had his password, Hunter hopped on Grandpa's computer and brought up Twitter. He sent Trent a private message. When he didn't reply, Hunter sent a message to Caleb, and a few minutes he'd replied back that Trent had been grounded, too. Which, come on, was only fair since he'd been the one to get Hunter into this mess. Hunter couldn't find the meme, either, which was a good thing. He didn't want any more trouble coming to him this summer. There was a chance that when Joanne got back from seeing Chuck she'd be in such a good mood she'd forget the whole thing.

Already he could see he was a big fat imposition on Matt and Sarah, who had been making goo-goo eyes at each other last night while pretending to watch *Game of Thrones*. Which meant that both of them had lied to him. He didn't see what the big deal was that his dad had a girlfriend, or why no one thought it was okay to tell him. Sarah was cool and Hunter liked her. Anyone would. Plus she had a supercool job.

Maybe she wouldn't move back to Colorado after all. Maybe she and Matt would get married and Matt could go focus on being husband of the year instead of father of the year. Hunter thought she'd be a great stepmother and would help get everyone else off his back. But hell, it probably wasn't going to happen. Joanne had been engaged three times and never once been married. From

time to time she said that she should have married Matt when she had the chance. She didn't
know Hunter could hear her talking to her mom
late at night on the phone, but he could. Still, he
couldn't imagine two people on earth who would
be worse together.

Hunter switched to Facebook and went into the
"Call of Duty" group he belonged to.

Hey, I heard what happened.

It was a PM from Megan Miller, who had to be
the prettiest girl at his school. Hunter didn't even
know she was in the group. Usually Megan didn't
give him the time of day, so what now?

Sucks, but I'm at my grandpa's and he doesn't
mind me getting online.

Actually, I was going to go dark for a while myself.
I thought it was cool you were doing that, too.

Why?

It's a challenge. Haven't you ever heard of a challenge?

Duh. I challenge myself every day.

Oh yeah. You want to be a Marine so you probably work out all the time.

Word.

He was going to get started on that this summer. But he needed a membership to Gold's Gym
and the way things looked right now it wasn't
about to happen.

When are you starting this challenge of yours? Coz
you're online right now.

So are you.

Yeah, going dark wasn't my choice.

Okay. But would you do it with me?

What was the catch here? One of the prettiest
girls at his high school wanted to go dark with
him? How exactly were they going to go dark *together* anyway? How would Hunter know if she
was really offline unless he was online to check
up on her? He was no techie genius but he could
already see a lot of holes in this plan.

That doesn't make sense.

Sure it does. We can meet at the library every morning it's open.

Yeah, and they have computers there to get online.

There's a long line for them. And don't you have any self-control?

Dude, who's asking for help going dark? I've been doing it for four days now on my own.

Too bad, you broke your streak.

If I hadn't, would we be having this conversation?

Good point.

"What would you like for lunch?" Grandpa asked from the kitchen. "Is a tuna sandwich all right?"

"Sure."

We could always go to The Drip and hang out. They don't even have Wi-Fi.

Good idea. I need to bring my phone in case my mom wants to get ahold of me.

I have a flip phone now. Like the kind the drug dealers have.

???

Never mind. See you there tomorrow. Nine o'clock.

Hunter logged off the computer and went to have lunch with Grandpa. Tomorrow he'd ask Matt to drop him off at The Drip in the morning, or if worse came to worst he'd walk over there himself. It was only a mile. Because one thing was for sure—he wanted to know why anyone would choose to go offline.

SARAH STARED AT the giant warehouse. It looked like a large barn from the outside, but inside, the rafters were up to forty feet or higher. There were displays everywhere of wood, window frames, doors and cabinets. And yes, even kitchen sinks.

"The mother ship," Matt said as he strode inside. "Best-kept secret in Fortune. Jack used to be a contractor, one of the best in the business. But he retired a few years ago. Now he owns this discount outlet for contractors and opens it up to friends and family, too."

Sarah wondered if Satan had been in here to get materials recently. Had he stiffed Jack, too?

"Have I told you how sorry I am that I didn't ask you to help me with the remodel in the first place?"

"Believe me, I'm sorry, too." He pulled off his shades and slid her a look that said she'd been silly not to assume he was an expert in…everything.

She melted a little bit from the heat in those eyes. "How was I to know you were a jack of all trades?"

"Ask around." He quirked a brow.

Too late now. She'd already seen his work firsthand, and without a doubt Matt knew what he was doing. It might take him longer to get the work done, between all his other obligations like working, and raising a teenager and, oh yes, sleeping, but he'd do it. What's more, he'd do it with class if she let him. His tastes often ran on the expensive side, but while she wasn't footing the bill she didn't want him to waste any more of his money.

"What do you think of these cabinets?" Matt tugged on her hand, taking her down the aisle.

What she thought was that this place was like the local home improvement store but without all the charm. There were piles of sawdust everywhere. A sawhorse sat in the corner of the aisle.

"Those look too expensive."

Matt had pointed to cherrywood cabinets. She'd priced those out once before and discount or not, she understood they were more expensive than a simple oak finish.

"Price is not an issue. Quality is."

Except Sarah would beg to differ on that point. They were running out of time and her father's house would have to be fixed to the lowest common denominator. And yes, the artist in her was cringing at that statement.

"We don't need quality. We're on a budget and on a timeline." She kept moving down the aisle until she found serviceable, sturdy, plain oak-finished cabinets. "What about these?"

Matt scowled, then pulled Sarah to the side and spun her toward him, one hand on each hip. "Let me explain something to you. Your father's house is a *Craftsman*. Do you know what that means?"

She squinted. "It's old?"

"Try again."

She threw up her hands. "I give up! What does it mean?"

"It was built at a time when people cared about quality. When a builder put his heart and soul into the house. No skimping. No cutting corners to save a dollar here or there. Quality."

She snorted. "And I'll bet milk was twenty-five cents a gallon."

"These homes are unique. Special. One of a kind."

She didn't speak, too entranced with how passionately he'd just spoken about a house. He kissed just as passionately. Of course, she'd wondered often how many other random things he did with equal passion as he'd kissed her. Because if she ever got to find out, she might spontaneously combust from the heat before all was said and done.

"If you're worried about money, don't be. I'm—"

She placed her hand over his mouth. "Do *not* say 'good,' Matt."

He grinned and lightly bit her finger before she drew it away. "I've got this."

"You know how I feel. It was hard enough for me to let you do this in the first place. Now you want to overspend. I guess I could see doing that if I was staying." She didn't like to bring the unhappy fact of her departure up, but it was true.

Why spend money on a perfect house, suited for her in every way, when she would have to let it go?

Matt didn't say a word, but walked back down to the cherry cabinets and waited for her to join him. "Tell me honestly. Do you like them?"

Truthfully? She lusted after those cherry cabinets. Would probably dream about them tonight. They'd actually go well with the current oak cabinets, which she'd painted black for effect. Dammit. They were a beautiful deep chocolate brown with a million red highlights in every groove. The perfect marriage of color. Both the brown and the red seemed to complement each other and bring out the best in each shade. Different but the same.

Confession time. "Yes. I love them."

Matt didn't waste any time. For the next few minutes he conferred with a clerk, checked measurements and finally moved toward the cashier.

He pulled out his wallet. "No second thoughts allowed."

She opened her mouth. Closed it. Too bad she was already having second thoughts. How was she supposed to let the house go if Matt seemed determined to make it everything she'd ever wanted? Not to mention the fact that he was driving her crazy with the sexy sideways grins. She wanted to be back in that office with him again, only this time with no interruption.

After Matt and a warehouse helper had loaded up the cabinet doors into the back of his truck, they drove back to the house and proceeded to unload them.

Sarah picked up one heavy cabinet door. She started carrying it up the few steps to the house and nearly dropped it.

"Let me do that," Matt said, wincing.

So now she was not only banished from power tools but from lifting anything she might drop. "I can handle it."

Even if "handling it" meant she mainly half carried, half slid the wide cabinet door inside. Worried she'd scuff the doors, she stood back and let Matt do the rest. She rather enjoyed observing him as he made use of those strong arm and back muscles. Would it be possible to talk him into a massage after such an exertion? Preferably naked.

Matt settled the last cabinet door with the rest of the stack just outside the kitchen. He hadn't even broken a sweat. He peeled off his work gloves and threw them on the ground.

"I could get started on these this Friday after Hunter leaves. It won't take long."

He took a step toward her as if he'd only now realized she stood, waiting, for something from him. A signal, anything that showed what had happened in his office meant as much to him as it did to her. Everything around them seemed different now, the air charged with a different level of electricity that felt far more intimate. She'd had her hand down his pants, for crying out loud. She didn't do that kind of thing with every man she met and liked enough to kiss. Or at least, not for a very long time. Maybe she should tell him that.

"Matt—"

As if taking advantage of her mouth being open, he covered it with a kiss. She felt herself being tugged to him, closer than close. Her hands slid up his back, feeling all the strength there, all those taut muscles tensing under her touch. He deepened the kiss, and she got lost in the sensation of his tongue teasing hers over and over again. She craved him completely, his kiss and his taste. Every single cell of him. More than she'd wanted or needed any other man in her life.

His hand slid down her spine to the small of her back and he broke off the kiss. "I'm not sure what you're doing to me, but I think I need to stop kissing you."

"I'm not sure I agree with you."

"You don't agree with me? Shock." He pressed his forehead against hers, his hand palming the back of her neck. "I have to leave in a few minutes anyway."

Sarah's knees went boneless and she clung to Matt so he couldn't get away. "Yeah? Why? How much time would you need?"

His eyes lit with humor. "For what?"

"For…more kissing and…um, whatever else might develop."

"I'd rather not put a time limit on it if it's all the same to you." His lips teased her jawline and he nuzzled her neck.

"No. That sounds…um, good."

He looked down at her and grinned. *"Good?"*

"Isn't that your favorite word?" She teased.

"Not even close."

"What is it, then?"

His eyes shifted right once. "Harder."

"Your favorite word is *harder*?"

"For now." He gave her a devilishly sexy grin as he pulled away.

She swallowed. "Okay. Then I'll try to remember that."

"See that you do." He picked up his keys and grabbed his cell phone, moving toward the door.

Sarah watched him go. *Harder.* Now to find the perfect opportunity to use his favorite word.

CHAPTER NINETEEN

THIS AFTERNOON SARAH would meet Joanne for the first time. Joanne, who was the mother of Matt's only child—who, despite the fact that they seemed to only tolerate each other, probably knew Matt a whole lot better than Sarah did.

Sarah took off early from work, rushing home to straighten up as much as possible. She thought Joanne might want to come inside and if she did, she'd want to find that her son had spent the week in a clean house. Matt would come later, stopping first to pick up Hunter, who'd spent part of the day with Matt's father again.

Sarah cleaned up the dishes in the sink from this morning, swept the floor and tried her best to arrange the stacked and waiting cabinet doors. Hopefully her house didn't look like a home improvement center. She arranged everything in the cabinets in an orderly fashion because without cabinet doors, it was almost the same as anyone being able to see inside her underwear drawer.

She let Shackles into the yard and heard the sound of a car door closing. Matt and Hunter were early. Maybe they could help her. Suddenly her house had never looked so…inadequate.

But when Sarah glanced outside, she didn't see Matt and Hunter but the same vehicle that had dropped Hunter off last week. Joanne was making her way to the front door.

"Oh, crap."

Joanne. Early.

Okay, no problem. Sarah could handle this. She'd done most of the straightening, anyway. Even if her house needed a little dusting—okay, a lot of dusting—Joanne would probably not be pulling a white glove out of her purse.

Sarah was at the door before Joanne could try the doorbell and find out that it didn't ring, but crackled instead. Something else she had forgotten to mention to Matt. Plus, when it *had* worked, it was the strangest doorbell she'd ever heard. It played "Grandma Got Run Over by a Reindeer" year-round. One thing about her father was that he'd had a strange sense of humor. And horrible taste in music.

"Hi," Sarah said. "You must be Joanne. I'm Sarah Mcallister."

"Are Hunter and Matt here?" Joanne smiled pleasantly enough but she clearly didn't want to waste any time with the preliminaries.

"They'll be here at five. You're a little early. Please come in."

Joanne stepped inside. She was dressed in a

halter top dress that showed off her slender arms and teeny-weeny waist. Sarah tried not to notice that Joanne was immediately assessing the living quarters. Perhaps she didn't like the look of a home stuck in the middle of renovations. It was hard to entertain like this.

"We're—I'm in transition."

"I can see that. Hunter told me that he's been helping you renovate." She stepped into the kitchen, and got a nice view of everything in Sarah's cupboards.

She might be blushing. Her cans were showing. She wished they were prettier, or at least low sodium.

"He's been such a great help. Such a great kid." Compliment the kid and how could you lose?

"Most of the time." It seemed that Joanne wasn't having a proud-mommy moment.

"Would you like something to drink while you wait?" Sarah opened the refrigerator door. "I have water, milk and soda."

Joanne's lip curled up like she'd smelled a rat. "You buy *soda*?"

Might be a trick question, so Sarah answered with a question. "Um, don't you?"

"I won't have it in the house. I'm not naive and I know Hunter has it when he goes to a friend's house. But I won't allow it. I won't buy pizza, either, unless it's gluten-free. No candy, either, of course."

Sarah nodded in agreement but damn, no wonder they were both so thin. And no wonder Hunter was in a perpetually bad mood. She'd once tried a gluten-free diet for about a week, and wound up tearing everyone's head off at work. Her boss had begged her to give wheat another chance.

"Not even a little treat now and then?" Should she confess now or wait until Joanne hauled her into an interrogation room?

Joanne laughed. "Oh, relax. I don't expect everyone else to be the health nut that I am. Hunter grew up this way. Matt was always 'fun dad.' Always taking him to the fair and buying the cotton candy and the chili fries. I let it happen because I understood it had to be that way. Not seeing him for such long stretches made it a special occasion every time he did. I just made sure that I fed him healthy the rest of the time."

"Tough job, but someone's got to do it." Sarah had a strange and sharp longing for her own mother, who'd let her have junk food on occasion.

"Exactly."

There was too much silence, and Sarah rushed to fill it. "I think Hunter missed you."

Her eyes widened. "Really?"

"Sure. You know how kids are. They might act one way on the outside but the truth is that they love their parents. And a boy needs his mother, whether he'll admit to it or not."

"He needs his father, too."

"Wow. So true."

There was another dead silence.

Sarah heard Shackles scratching on the glass door, as was his custom when his highness was ready to come back inside. Thank God she had a dog!

"Excuse me, please."

She let Shackles inside and he trotted in like he owned the place. He stopped short when he noticed Joanne, gave her one big sniff, yipped once and then walked right past her. Good thing she wasn't an ax murderer.

"You have a dog. How cute."

"It's more like he has me."

"What's his name?"

"Shackles."

"That's a strange name for a dog."

"Well, yes. Yes, it is."

Was that a car door she heard slam outside? Oh, joy! It had to be Matt and Hunter. Sarah walked back to the kitchen, Joanne following.

"Sounds like they're here."

Matt walked through first, followed by Hunter bringing up the rear. Joanne stood just inside the entrance, smiling, though her arms were folded across her chest. A protective, closed-off stance. Not that Sarah was going to overanalyze or anything like that. She was going to stop doing that any day now. When Hunter stepped inside, there was an awkward moment during which Sarah could swear that she saw an angel on one of his shoulders and a devil on the other. He was clearly caught in that heartbreaking shift between child and man and he obviously didn't want to be too happy to see his mother. He shoved his hands into his jeans pockets and assumed an arrogant stance, his mouth set in a grim straight line.

But his shiny and wide eyes told Sarah another story. "Hey Jo—Mom," Hunter said.

This was where Sarah exited stage left. Another private family moment where she didn't belong.

She picked up Shackles and slipped out the back. She'd give Hunter and his parents some privacy. Although maybe it wasn't the desire to give them privacy that forced her outside so much as the unwelcome memory that flooded back to her as she'd watched the exchange. Her earliest memories of her father were fuzzy and faded, but the one last clear memory was of the last summer she'd spent with Dad. She'd been thirteen, at an awkward stage, and deeply resented being forced to spend the summer in California and leave all her friends behind. An entire summer! It was the last year in which she'd have no choice in the matter. Stone had been fifteen and had already made his choice. Mom had cried and behaved as though she'd lost a limb. She'd have to spend all summer without either kid. But for Sarah, that choice had meant she'd finally spend the summer with her brother for the first time in about three years.

It had been the one and only thing she'd looked forward to in coming for her visit to California. Unfortunately, at fifteen, Stone had been as ass. He'd had a large group of friends he never invited her to join, been learning how to drive a car and had about five different girlfriends he juggled at once.

Setting Shackles down now, she opened up her shed. She hadn't sketched at all this entire week. Like Matt, she'd been too caught up in work and the renovations. In feeding Hunter. But on a trip to the store this week she'd made a side stop at the local art supply store and bought acrylics and watercolors. She'd start painting this weekend.

Unless she could talk Matt into keeping her in bed all weekend, in which case she'd gladly come back to the painting at another time. Right now, she set up her easel with a new blank canvas and put the sketch of El Toro in line with the rest of the as-yet-unfinished work. It needed something. If only she could figure out what that something was. Matt thought it was people.

In so many ways, he was her diametric opposite, outgoing and gregarious while she was introverted and kept to herself. He'd drawn her out, though, and it wasn't just because of his appearance. Matt had something else going for him besides his incredible intellect and looks. An indefinable quality that she assumed was the reason she'd crushed on him for so long. He'd been larger than life to her. But now this was so much more than a simple crush. It was real and rare and she'd be lying if she didn't admit she was scared. Scared, sure, but excited about him, too. Alive.

Another scary thing? This blank canvas. There was nothing quite as intimidating as a wide-open space because she could go in any direction. Choose any medium she wanted. And also fail miserably. The point was to get started. Anywhere. Just draw. Because the beautiful thing about art, as all of her many teachers over the years had drilled in, was that everything could be fixed. It was never a lost cause. But as many times as Sarah told herself that simple and pure point, she didn't want to start anything until she was sure of her direction. It was always much easier to start with perfect than to come back later and fix a huge mess.

Or worse, start over.

This was her life. She was thirty years old and couldn't start all over now. She had a life in Fort Collins with people who respected her. Not an exciting life, but at least fully formed. Safe. Job, condo, friends. Mom was there, and she'd dedicated her entire life to Sarah. Been a great mother, even putting off her own career as a wannabe singer to take a job as a legal secretary so she could support the two of them after the divorce.

It was only right to go back to the home she'd always known, so why did she feel a hard pebble lodged in her throat every time she realized she was going to have to sell this house? She'd pushed herself into a corner and now she was in debt to Matt, too. She couldn't afford to stay. Matt expected her to sell and give him his portion, and she couldn't pay him back for the materials and his work otherwise.

Even if all else was out of the way, there was still Matt, unwilling to go that extra step with her. Either he didn't trust her, or he didn't trust himself. And she got it. Sex would change everything between them, but change wasn't always a bad thing. She'd been afraid when she'd first come to Fortune. But more than afraid, she'd been too tired. Tired of feeling shut down and half-alive.

Shackles trotted up to Sarah and sat on her foot.

"Okay, you're right. I'll get started." Sarah mixed some red acrylic paint, took her brush and drew a curvy line from the top of the canvas to the bottom. She had no idea what she was doing. It was a line. A beginning.

She looked down at Shackles. "Happy now?"

"Actually, yeah," Matt said from the entrance to the shed. "It has color."

She turned briefly to Matt, surprised she hadn't

sensed him first, and then went back to her canvas. "Everyone gone?"

"Yep." He took a few more steps and she sensed him, standing right behind her.

He was a warm and solid presence, and she wanted him so much that her longing spread like butter, scattering down her thighs and wrapping around the back of her knees. She'd never really met a man that made her feel both weak and strong at the same time.

"Joanne seems nice."

"Sorry I missed introductions, but she knows about you."

"What did you tell her?"

"That you're a good friend of mine."

Not sure how she felt about that too-accurate description, Sarah held her brush to the side and changed the subject. "I don't think we were supposed to feed him pizza. Or soda."

He shrugged. "Joanne has always lived on her own planet. I feel like a little of that now and then isn't going to kill him."

She met his eyes. "We agree. But on her own planet or not, she must have been very special to you at one time. First love and all."

"Yeah, I guess." He broke the gaze to check out the brush in her hand.

"That sounds so heartfelt," she teased.

"Don't really want to talk about her." He took the brush from her. "It's in the past."

And he'd probably talk about Sarah the same way someday. With any luck, with a little more feeling than he seemed to have for his ex. "It's in the past, but sometimes we need to talk about it to resolve it."

"Not this guy." His eyes told her the conversation was over.

And was she seriously going to feel threatened by Joanne? Okay, so she was skinny and pretty but that wasn't what bothered Sarah. What bothered her was that she and Matt had such a special past together, one which had brought a child into the world. A person. They'd forever be linked no matter how far away they lived from each other. She was a little bit envious of that. When she left Fortune, she and Matt would have nothing to tie them together other than a special friendship. She hoped. Even the house they were working on together, pouring so much blood, sweat and tears into, would be gone to some other owner.

Matt moved toward the canvas, brush in hand. "Teach me how to paint."

"Honestly?"

"Just the basics."

"If I was starting with the basics I'd probably go over the color wheel with you first."

"Yeah, skip that. I want to get on with it."

"Oh, do you?" She took the warm and rough hand that held the brush to position it. "First, don't hold it like it's a hammer."

She then took another brush from her supplies and demonstrated. "You want to hold it like this, and just brush a stroke across the canvas."

He grinned. "Did you say stroke?"

"What are you? Twelve?"

"Just don't say thrust or I won't be able to get through this lesson. I had no idea art was this sexy."

She laughed. He somehow got more laughs out of her than anyone in recent memory.

"It's not. Not usually."

"Maybe that's because you haven't been doing art the right way." He met her eyes. "With me."

Those edgy dark eyes were throwing off some smoldering heat and she was quickly wilting. "That's interesting, coming from someone who doesn't think we're a good idea."

"Didn't say that. Not recently."

"No. You just keep saying you're sorry."

He didn't speak, merely studied her lips.

"Um, so what do you want to draw? I always like to start with at least an idea," Sarah said.

"How about a plane?"

"Why am I not surprised." She took his brush and instead handed him her best fine camel hair one. "You'll need straight lines for that. And also a plan. You want it to be perfect, don't you?"

"I thought art was supposed to be spontaneous. Creative."

She chose to ignore that, even though, dammit, he was right. Maybe that's why her painting had suffered for years. She'd fallen straight out of creativity when forced to for her day job. No creativity allowed. But then again, letting go and trusting in the process had been difficult for years.

One of her teachers in college had told her, *You'd be extraordinary if you could just let go of the rules. You know them well, Sarah. Now is the time to play with them.* Easier said than done when those "rules" had been ingrained into her by every teacher she'd had for years. Not to mention the safety of rules in the real world. Guidelines. She'd let go of certain rules once before, after all, and it had nearly killed her spirit.

But letting go and giving in to her attraction for Matt felt freeing and not like something she wanted to hide. Like she could get back to at least a small part of who she used to be before everything had spiraled so out of control.

Admit it. He's different.

Matt was loyal to the core, and in him she recognized a kindred spirit. He'd screwed up bigtime. She'd screwed up, too. The only difference between them was that she hadn't come out of that dark and painful time with a living, breathing reminder. She understood him far better than he realized. And she wanted Matt to know that she wasn't going to become just one more item on his to-do list. He didn't need to fix her or rescue her because she could save herself.

She already had once before and she'd do it again.

Matt had been painting his lines for a few minutes and they weren't half-bad. It wasn't impressionism, far from it, but she'd seen fans of abstract art do a lot worse. It was definitely decent for his first effort. She wondered if he excelled at everything and if it was at all possible that she'd eventually grow to hate him for that.

She nudged him with her shoulder. "Not bad, Conner."

Instead of accepting her praise, Matt turned to her and painted her nose. Just a little flick of the wrist but nevertheless. Her nose.

"Hey!" She laughed and rubbed it off with her thumb.

"You look sweet with a red nose."

"I'm sure I do."

"But you'd look great in anything." He studied her lips.

Before she could think to stop him, he'd flicked another dot of paint on her mouth with the tip. Then he leaned down and kissed the spot. Licked it.

Holy hell. "Uh, Matt…that might be toxic. I'm not—"

He apparently didn't agree, because he dropped the brush and cut her words off by kissing her again. And again. Long and deep, blazing-hot kisses. In no time at all he had her pinned against one wall of the shed, one arm braced on each side.

When he broke off the kiss, she thought she might scream and curse at him.

He pressed his forehead to hers. "What are we doing, Sarah?"

"Whatever it is, I think we're headed in the right direction." Her hand went to his hip and she tugged him closer. "You know what I want."

"And would you like to hear what I want?"

Oh yes. If he was about to tell her how he liked it, favorite positions and personal fantasies, she only wished she had a notebook nearby to take notes. "Yes, please. All of it."

"I don't want to be someone you ever regret." His thumb traced her jawline and his big hand came to rest at the nape of her neck.

The raw honesty in those words went all the way to her heart. He couldn't know yet how many regrets she already had in her life. She didn't make rash and impulsive choices any longer.

"You won't be."

"How can you be sure?"

"Because I'm a grown-up. I know the score."

"The *score*?"

Uh-oh. The tone in his voice told her he didn't much like her word choice.

His thumb swept her lower lip. "Try again."

"I don't need you to fix my life, slay my dragons and all that. I rescue myself. I always have. And I promise I won't fall in love with you. Believe me, I know the difference between love and sex."

Damned if he didn't look disappointed, but then his gaze softened on her again. "I can't give you much right now, but I can give you this."

"This is all I need. Just you. More than ever." She reached up and pulled on his neck, trying to bring him close again. Being that he had the rock-solid strength of a building, he didn't budge.

He still studied her, almost as if he caught something in her eyes, too. "You don't know how glad I am to hear that. Because I've been watching you all week, and I swear I got hard every time you even looked at me."

Oh boy.

Finally, he allowed her tugging and he bent down and kissed her again, slowly and more deliberately. He stopped kissing her only to grab her wrist and pull her out of the shed. "Inside."

"Good idea," she said, following him inside to the much cooler home. "It's really hot today."

Another balmy June day and the California dry heat wave had continued with little relief in sight.

"It's about to get a lot hotter."

And she could hardly wait. She headed toward her bedroom, racing ahead of him now. She'd just passed the couch when she was summarily spun and tugged down by her waist onto the couch. She wound up splayed on top of an edgy and sexy Matt. Perfect.

"We spent our first night together right here," he said.

The unexpected romance behind those words sliced right through her. She straddled Matt and smiled as she slowly unclipped her hair. "I remember."

"And what I want to do to you right now is what I could only imagine doing that night." He reached to slowly pull off her blouse.

And this was where she stepped out of her head. She'd dreamed about peeling Matt's button-up Mcallister Charters shirt off more times than she could recall. Now she unbuttoned it carefully and deliberately, her eyes eating up all that beautiful and taut male skin. He shrugged out of his shirt and threw it on the ground, turning his full attention to her.

He unhooked her bra faster than she could and it fell to the ground. His mouth covered one breast, while his hand palmed the other. They were rough and callused, the hands of a man who worked with them. Incredibly turned on by that fact, her fingers roamed from his pecs down to his abs and settled near the waistband of his cargo pants. Still fascinated by her nipples, he licked and suckled till she whimpered. Instead of just trying to please her, it was almost as if he was paying tribute to her breasts. As if he obtained all his own pleasure from hers.

Wanting to get to him, she shifted her body and went to the front of his pants to tug desperately. She was no longer thinking, no longer worried or holding back, but simply more alive than she'd ever been before. He stopped her from going for his pants and went for her jeans instead, unzipping and opening up just enough to allow his big hand inside to reach her core. He stroked in slow and deliberate rhythmic movements. She squirmed and circled her hips in time with him, completely taken up in this moment. With him. Outside of herself. He stroked until she almost asked him to stop because she couldn't take that anymore. He stroked until she shuddered and moaned, coming apart for him.

Her last moan was swallowed by his long kiss. "So good."

He stood her up and pulled down her jeans and panties the rest of the way. "Step out."

She did and stood completely naked before him. Shivering even in this summer heat. He was still wearing everything but his shirt. Seemed unfair somehow.

"I want to touch you." She reached for him. "All of you."

"There will be plenty of time for that later." But he stood to pull off his cargo pants and then his underwear in one quick swoop.

Wow. A perfect male form…all hard angles and…hard everything. She stared, but he didn't let her do that for long. He pulled her back on top of him again and she used that opportunity to slide down the length of him. She licked from his neck to his abs, making her way south. The sound of a condom packet ripping open made her look up, and Matt handed it to her. She took her time and pleasure covering him, loving the way his entire body tensed like one hard coil beneath her.

The way he moaned beneath her touch… "I want inside you."

He positioned her hips where he wanted them and thrust inside her with a push that made them both moan. When he didn't move for a moment, she used the time to feel him pulsing inside her, closing her eyes to the intense pleasure he gave her. Then she realized that he was waiting for her cue and so she moved to take all of him. Rocking. Letting him in. The swaying motion of her hips seemed to propel him and he plunged into her faster. Over and over again.

"Sarah," he groaned. "You're so beautiful."

She did feel beautiful right now. Like a striking and stunning gazelle in the forest, running wild and free and uncontained. She didn't feel prickly and untouchable anymore. Over and over again he told her how gorgeous she was, how much he wanted her, the soft words a sharp contrast to the strong way his body pumped into hers, completely filling it.

"Matt," she breathed, saying his name over and over again.

"What do you want, babe? Tell me."

"Harder," she said, hoping that would send him over the edge and needing so much to give him the same pleasure he gave her.

As he drove into her, he reached between them and stroked her core again. Once. Twice. She shuddered and quivered, coming with a fierceness that shocked her. She was pulled under, boneless and unable to stand. Riding the crest with him, she felt him shudder under her soon after. They both gasped and moaned. Catching her breath, Sarah fought hard to recover the steady pattern of her breaths.

Not like this. Never like this.

She wasn't even sure she was still breathing, but by the sound of her heartbeat thudding in her ears she was very much alive.

CHAPTER TWENTY

MATT KNEW THAT the sex would be good between him and Sarah. He wanted her, she wanted him and they'd both had enough foreplay in the past week, hell, the past few months if he were being honest, to rev up the coldest of hearts. Still, he'd never thought it could be like this.

Not a sensation where his heart would leap out of his chest, the sharp thuds practically cracking his rib cage. Had he not known any better, he'd have to guess he was out of shape. But this had nothing to do with physical prowess and everything to do with something that came uncomfortably close to his heart. He forced himself to school the pattern of his breathing and pretend this kind of thing happened to him every time. *Yeah, sure, buddy.*

He skimmed down her spine to the small of her back, without a doubt the softest skin he'd ever touched. He rolled and tucked her under him. "You okay?"

Why not ask yourself that?

Because, hell, he already knew the answer.

Definitely *not* okay. Unless "okay" could fall under the same definition as shocked. Reeling.

"Uh-huh."

He fervently hoped she was lying, too.

"Hi," she said and her hands came up around his neck.

"Hi yourself." He kissed her gently, and then again not so gently. "Man, you're sweet. So fucking sweet."

"No, I'm not," she said, breaking off the kiss. "I'm tougher than I look."

He chuckled, having come up close and personal with tough more than once. "Not to me you're not."

"Well, I'm not a marshmallow."

"True. But you have a lot in common with a marshmallow. I want to eat you both." He watched as the color in her eyes shifted and darkened with heat.

She drew in a sharp breath. "Matt Conner, you are a very naughty man."

"Tell me something I don't know." He tugged on a lock of her hair, then leaned in and nuzzled her ear. "We both need a shower now. Cool off."

"Mmm." Suddenly she stilled under him. "Shackles!"

Matt turned to look and Shackles sat right outside the sliding glass door, panting from the heat but waiting for them patiently. This was a damn good dog, rescue or not. Matt pulled on his boxers and opened the sliding glass door to let him inside. The poor dog went straight for his water bowl.

"I feel awful," Sarah said. "I didn't even hear him scratching at the door."

"You were otherwise occupied."

She was sitting up on the couch, still as naked as on the day she'd been born. Those long, soft, curvy legs that he would have wrapped around his back next time. Nipples rosy pink, and still slightly wet from his tongue. Her hair wavy, wild and untamed. Just like he loved it.

Whoa. Maybe he should slow the three-alarm fire down. Or not.

"And I plan to keep us occupied for the rest of the night." With that he tugged her up off the couch and led her by the small of her back into the bathroom.

"Promises, promises."

He leaned in to turn on the showerhead and she copped a feel when he did, shoving her hand down his boxers and stroking him until he moaned.

"Do you like that?"

"I think you know how much."

He almost came again under her strokes, which would have been embarrassing. It had been a long time since anyone had touched him like this, possibly never, and he wasn't sure how much more he could take. The water lukewarm enough not to shock their systems, he pulled off his boxers and tugged her in after him. He took the brunt of the shower headfirst while she stood just under him getting some of the spray. Palming her ass, he tugged her to him and kissed her.

She kissed him back, deep and longing kisses which showed him more of the Sarah he'd wanted to see for months. The beautiful and sexy woman under the hot librarian look. But when she pulled back, her eyes were watery.

He jerked, and so did his heart. Those were tears in her eyes. "Hey, what's this?"

"Tell me you're not sorry about this. You said you didn't want to be my regret. But I don't want to be yours, either."

God, she hurt his heart as certainly as if she'd stuck a nail in it. "Hell, no, I'm not sorry. Never. You?"

"No!" she protested, another tear rolling down her face and mixing with the water spray. "I never thought I would be. I just don't want you to be."

He wasn't sure where this was coming from, but understood insecurity when he saw it rear its ugly face. Sarah had no reason to feel insecure about this thing between them. He was on board. He'd been through the flight check and was ready for takeoff. In other words, he was a complete idiot for her. He was pretty much jumping out of a plane without a parachute. But this was Sarah, and he'd die before he'd hurt a hair on her head.

Which meant if anyone got hurt in this scenario, it would obviously be him. And given his past, he shouldn't be surprised if that was exactly what happened.

"I'm not sorry, babe," he said, cupping her chin. "I'm so *not* sorry I'm going to show you how *not* sorry I am for the rest of the weekend. How's that?"

Her warm smile cut right through him.

Two hours later, Matt lay in Sarah's bed. Sated. Exhausted. She was snuggled next to him, one long leg between his thighs. He tried hard to remember the last time he'd felt this relaxed and came up with a big fat zero.

"What do you want for dinner?" he asked, his finger skimming the inside of her arm. Her skin was so soft his rough palm felt like sandpaper against it.

"You mean I get all this and dinner, too?"

"You get whatever you want, babe."

"Careful," she teased, coming up on one elbow.

She looked so beautiful, her fresh face pink from exertion. "I mean it."

"Okay," she said, her fingers tracing the Eagle with blood talons tattoo on his rib cage. "When did you get this done?"

"You don't want to know about that. I was drunk. Believe me, that's the only way I'd let some dude come at me with a needle."

She scrunched up her nose. "I can't picture you drunk."

"Why? Because I'm such a saint?"

"You're no saint and I know that better than anyone." She bent down and kissed his pecs. "I meant because you're always in such control."

He wanted her to keep thinking that way. Certainly didn't want her to think that he was still lying here wondering what the hell had just happened to him in the past few hours.

"It's the Air Force. There isn't much wiggle room in an F-16 at Mach speed."

"I can imagine. Important to be precise."

"Lives depend on that precision. A tenth of a centimeter off could be fatal."

"It had to have been difficult, the transition to such strict order and rules. You were a teenage father and that had to be tough."

"It wasn't all that different going from my father's house to boot camp."

Truthfully, he still didn't want her to know how rough, or how badly he'd screwed up. How much of that guilt he still carried with him, despite all the years that had passed. If she understood the half of it, she'd see him differently. Any woman would. This wasn't exactly his idea of pillow talk, either, but he supposed he owed Sarah an explanation. She was under the mistaken impression that he and Joanne had been some sort of young first love story.

"But it was rough, being a young dad." He ran a hand down his face with his free hand. The other one he kept around her, maybe hoping that he could physically keep her in place even if his words might chase her away. "Particularly since I didn't love Joanne."

"Never?"

"It was one date. One stupid lousy date fueled by alcohol and teenage hormones. Failed birth control. She wasn't even my girlfriend."

Her green eyes filled with something that looked a lot more like compassion than judgment. "Oh, babe. I'm sorry."

"I know it would have made a much better story had we been in love and just unable to keep our hands off each other. That it just hadn't worked out because of how young we both were. That's not my story. Of course, I asked her to marry me but she was the smart one. She knew she deserved better. That we both deserved better."

She didn't say anything, but pressed her face into his neck.

"The truth? I was never the angel everyone believed. I'd flown under the radar for years, getting supremely good at lying to everyone. School was easy for me and I excelled, so teachers and parents loved me. And I put up a good front. Hunter ruined that front. It showed everyone who I really was."

"Human?"

Now *he* didn't say anything. Far more than human, he'd been a piece of excrement during that time in his life.

Tired of spilling his guts, Matt flipped Sarah so that she was now under him. "Your turn."

"How am I supposed to do that with you on top?" She squirmed and her hand dove between them.

When her hand reached between his thighs, he went instantly hard. "Not *that* turn. Tell me your secrets."

"Oh. Don't have any." But her face grew pink.

"Nice try." Cupping each of her wrists, he pinned her down. "You're staying right here until you talk."

"Unfortunately for you, that's not exactly my idea of a threat. But what do you want to know?"

"First love."

He wasn't imagining it when her body grew tight under him. She closed her eyes as if she didn't want to look at him. "I wish I had a better story, too."

"Tell me." At the same time, his own gut churned and tensed.

"It's ugly."

He quirked an eyebrow and considered giving her a pass because telling him her secrets was one thing and opening up a vein another one.

"You know how some girls with daddy issues get all prickly and frigid about men?"

"Yeah?"

"That wasn't me. I went a little wild." Her finger idly traced the length of his arm.

Now he went up on an elbow. "How wild?"

Her voice got softer. "Um, quite a few...boy-friends."

"Look, you don't have to tell me this. You—"

"You might think you screwed up, but I was much worse. I was the smart but seriously stupid girl that thought sex meant love. And every time a guy would drop me I'd move on to the next one because I was sure love was waiting for me right around the corner. Like all those sappy love songs. But instead all I got was a lousy reputation that was ugly and hurtful."

"*God*. Sarah, you don't—"

"Now you know why I can tell the difference between love and sex. And it's different with you. I know you won't hurt me. Not like that."

"Never," he said and meant it.

And if she told him any more, there was a good chance he'd be so pissed at these boys that he'd need names and addresses from her next. He'd look the little geniuses up next time he was in the glorious state of Colorado. Teach them a thing or two about being a gentleman.

"But I did a one hundred and eighty in college. It was my mother who told me that I could reinvent myself if I wanted to, and I did. No more sex, casual or otherwise. I had one very long dry spell."

"How long?"

She closed her eyes. Opened them again. "Um, five years, give or take?"

Holy shit. They were far more alike than he would have ever realized.

"It's just that sex left me feeling a little dead inside. For a long time."

She slayed him. Again. But he reminded himself that she didn't need him to be her white knight. No, she'd done a fine job of that herself. Risen from the ashes and started over. In a way, he'd done the same with the Air Force.

"And how do you feel now?" Still hard from when she'd touched him, he pressed into her sweet flat stomach.

She responded, grinding into him. Not a shy and retiring lover, Sarah. No, far from it. She'd pretty much rocked this airman's world.

"I feel like I want to touch you. Everywhere. And I don't even know where to start." Her hands pushed against his chest. "Move."

Allowing her to move him, he rolled and lay flat on his back. Completely exposed, because dammit, he trusted her that much. More than he'd ever thought he could trust a woman again. She proceeded to touch, and lick, and otherwise slowly kill him while he pretended this was business as usual. Just two lonely and unattached friends who were intensely physically attracted to each other, casually enjoying the way their bodies could please each other. Nothing more to it than that.

And if he told himself that enough times, he might actually start to believe it.

CHAPTER TWENTY-ONE

SARAH ROLLED OVER in bed. She turned to reach for Matt, but he was no longer lying in the bed next to her as he had been all night. The bedroom door was open, daylight spilling through it as well as through small openings in the blinds. She reached for her phone to check the time. Nine o'clock and three text messages from Mom already.

She'd overslept. And something else was different. Oh yeah, that's right. She'd slept through the night for the first time in weeks without any difficult or confusing dreams. Relaxed. Completely satisfied. She reviewed Mom's messages and wondered if she could handle typing her response before the first cup of coffee. Deciding she couldn't, she set her phone back down on the nightstand and stretched under the soft cotton sheet. She wanted coffee, extra-strength. And a shower. And bacon. And Matt.

Mostly Matt. Wanted him holding her all night long again in his strong arms, telling her over and over again how much he wanted her. There were sounds in the kitchen, a pot rattling, something being poured, and she sat up in bed, rubbing her eyes. She grabbed her glasses from the nightstand and tried to focus. Matt appeared in the doorway, grinning, a coffee mug in his right hand. The only way this could be any better would be if he had a chocolate doughnut in his left hand. And was completely naked.

"Good morning, gorgeous." He handed her the coffee mug and took a seat on her side of the bed.

She was still undressed and pulled up the sheet to cover her breasts. Silly, she understood, but protective. She still felt a little...reserved, hard as it was to believe. Long-formed habits were hard to break, and she was still working on no longer being prickly. The orgasms were helping.

Matt was unfortunately fully dressed in a blue cotton T-shirt and khaki board shorts. She liked this casual Matt as much as she liked the put-together, in-charge-of-everything pilot. Maybe even more, because he looked so at ease. His honey-hued rumpled hair was a complete turn-on because it proved he'd just rolled out of bed with her. She kept telling herself that sleeping together wasn't an intimate act, and not to read too much into it since they already happened to live together purely out of circumstance.

She took the mug from him. "Why didn't you wake me?"

"I did," he said with a sly grin. "Don't tell me you already forgot."

"I didn't mean *that* way," she said, taking a sip of coffee.

Her face flushed as she briefly relived that moment at the crack of dawn when Matt had reached for her. It was true, he'd woken her out of a sound sleep. Then worn her out so much she'd fallen back asleep in his arms.

"You don't like waking up like that?" He pulled her into his arms.

"It's my new favorite way."

"I'll remember that."

"See that you do." She turned his words back on him.

His strong arms were wrapped around her and the man was so solid. Strong. A tornado couldn't move him. His unshaven jaw grazed her neck, and damned if she didn't feel limp with lust.

He wasn't asking or prying, as that wouldn't be his way, but she still wanted to tell him about the crying. She'd been mortified when the tears had rolled out of her in the shower. Not part of the plan, falling apart like that. Making him perhaps wonder if he'd just made love to an unhinged woman.

But then he'd been so loving…so sweet.

For the first time since she could remember she'd felt raw with emotion. The sensations… desire, happiness, longing, had been felt far too deeply, as if they'd been bottled up for so long they'd expanded and blown up in her face.

She sat up on the bed, clutching her mug, and leaned her back against him. "About the crying…"

"You don't have to say any more."

"I know," she said on a sigh. "But I want to."

"I'm listening, then." His jaw nuzzled her neck and he kissed her shoulder.

Her phone buzzed on the nightstand next to her. No doubt Mom again. She had the uncanny timing of an orchestra conductor.

"Do you have to get that?"

"No." She took a deep breath and went for it. "I think for the first time I'm letting myself feel… stuff…again. And it's a little overwhelming."

He didn't speak. No, he was a damned good listener, too.

"I want you to know that I'll never regret this time together." Her hands were trembling for some odd reason, and she fisted the mug tighter to still them.

"Goes double for me," he finally spoke. "And—"

Before he could say anything else, she cut him off. "I don't need you to say anything more."

God, she felt pathetic. A small part of her was back to being that stupid teenage girl begging an ex-boyfriend to take her back. To please love her. This was different. She wasn't lying to Matt when she said she understood the score. She remembered it far too well. But she'd also spent too many years living half a life, too afraid to let go and get hurt again. Matt made that easier than it had ever been. She understood above all else he would protect her. He'd proved it more than once. Their relationship had started with a friendship that had grown faster and deeper than she could have ever expected.

Matt took the mug from her and set it on the nightstand. He turned her to face him and met her eyes. "You're the strongest woman I know, babe."

Before she could protest he kissed her. When they came up for air, she opened her mouth to speak but he kissed her again. And then again and again.

And the rest of the morning was taken up by something far richer than coffee.

CHAPTER TWENTY-TWO

"...AWAKE?" CASSIE ASKED.

"Huh?" Apparently Sarah had missed some part of that sentence.

She was taking Emily's place at Magnum Aviation late Monday morning, since Emily was out on another chartered flight, this time bringing her father back from his Texas cattle ranch. Her sister-in-law to be, Emily—the pilot. Sarah loved that Emily was a kick-ass pilot, but she still didn't get the fascination with flying. She preferred her feet firmly planted on the ground, thank you very much.

"I said—did you have enough coffee this morning? You don't look like you're awake."

"No, I probably need another cup." Or five hundred.

Who needed to sleep when she had Matt lying next to her? She'd been completely sleep-deprived this weekend, and pretty happy about it, too. Meanwhile, she would swear her skin was more radiant. It had to be all the endorphins.

"Everything go okay with Hunter?"

"Yeah, he's back with his mother. Of course,

he'll be coming back this weekend. And every weekend after that."

"So she finally agreed to that? Poor Matt has been trying to get time with his son for months, now suddenly she's interested in dumping him off on the weekends."

"Guess it's the new boyfriend." Sarah shrugged.

She'd already judged Joanne harshly enough for the abandonment. But for all intents and purposes, at least she'd come back for her son. She got points from Sarah for that.

"And so how's the remodel progressing?" Cassie dumped more flight reports for filing in front of Sarah.

She so did not want to talk about the remodeling.

"Got the new kitchen cabinet doors up. They're beautiful."

No more cans showing. She thought back to Matt putting the last door up late last night. Remembered how he'd looked perched up on the ladder, using the power screwdriver he wouldn't let her touch. His powerful arms holding the door in place as he worked with it. Didn't need her help. Surprisingly enough, he was "good."

Oh, yes, he was.

She'd reached for him when he'd come down the ladder. Had said his name, and he'd turned to her in expectation. But then his eyes had registered the invitation in hers, heating in response.

He'd picked her up and carried her into the closest bedroom.

"Um, hello?" Cassie asked.

"I'm sorry. What?"

Cassie sighed. "Good grief, girl. You make me wish I still had hormones."

"I'm sorry, Cass. I've got a lot of things on my mind."

Like for instance the fact that she was falling for Matt Conner a little bit more every day and she had no idea what she could do about that. She was doing it again. Mixing up sex and love and being "that girl" again. This time the boy was a man. One who wouldn't make her feel dirty and used, of course he wouldn't. But that didn't change the fact that separating the two actions wouldn't be difficult. No, already she wanted so much more.

"I bet you wonder what your father would think about you selling the house."

One thing she'd never asked Cassie, but yes, Sarah did occasionally wonder. Not that it mattered anymore. She nodded, showing Cassie she was still with her, still listening. Not daydreaming again.

"For what it's worth, I don't think he would care. He'd want you to do whatever you want with it. He left it to you kids, and whether you sold it or kept it, the point is he would want you to be happy."

"Really?"

"I never met a more generous man than your daddy. And I mean that."

"Nice to know."

"Listen, honey." Cassie took a seat closer, a clear indication that she had some more motherly advice to impart.

Sarah got ready to hear more about how her father had helped Cassie through the years, how he'd given her advances on her paycheck the year her son was sick and she'd missed so much work.

"When you first came to Fortune, anyone could see how much you hurt inside, even if you had to grieve in your own way. Stone thought you were bitter."

"I was."

"But it was obvious to me that this town didn't feel safe to you. That you wanted to leave almost as soon as you got here."

"That's not true—"

"Shush now and listen. You might have felt like a fatherless girl, but you weren't. Never. I'm sorry, but in your case it doesn't count. Your father loved you. Even if he did it from a distance."

Sarah knew better than to argue with Cassie. "I know."

The loving-from-a-distance part? Yeah, that was the problem. It wasn't okay. But she now realized that maybe it wasn't all her father's fault. She'd played a big part in the gradual decline of their relationship. Maybe she'd even started it all, when she'd stopped coming to visit during summers once the choice had been given. When she'd stopped calling him on his birthday, Father's Day, Christmas.

Yes, she'd been angry and she'd had every right to be. Livid that he hadn't even asked why she didn't want to come back, just accepted it easily. Irritated that maybe it had just been easier not to have a difficult and hormonal teenage girl at home he could barely understand, much less try to help. Hurt that he'd picked Stone over her.

But none of it had been an excuse to be cruel.

"Did I tell you I found boxes in the attic? All my old clothes and drawings for him. Cards I'd sent."

"I'm not surprised," Cassie said. "He used to talk about you."

"What did he say?"

"I always knew he had a daughter. He said you were brilliant and an artist. Completely the opposite of him. But he was proud of you anyway. Believe it."

"I always thought I'd see him again."

"Honey, now, forgive me for saying this. I'm not one to criticize another woman, but...your mother should have done more."

Sarah also thought so, but felt too guilty to bring it up to Mom. "Like what?"

"I don't know, but it's the mother's job to be the

softness in a child's life. To smooth over rough edges between father and child. I've had to do it a million times with my children. There are some men of your father's generation who are too tough for their own good. They don't believe in showing any sign of weakness. I think it was hard for your dad to admit that he missed you."

Later that afternoon, Sarah heard Emily over the CTAF communicating with all other pilots in the area of her approach and plans to land. Another few minutes and Emily and her father stepped into the hangar. They were laughing. Smiling.

Mr. Parker bent down and kissed Emily's cheek, and they parted with a wave. There went an interesting man. CEO of Parker, Inc. and owner of several other businesses. Nevertheless he dressed like John Wayne. Same swagger, too.

And he clearly adored his daughter.

It was tough to watch, that easy connection they had as father and daughter. An investor in Mcallister Charters and owner of his own private jet, Mr. Parker occasionally dropped by Magnum for meetings. He had a strange mash-up of a Texas drawl and a Western accent, and he always made Cassie break out the belly laugh. A rare feat.

Emily breezed through the entrance to the offices. "Hello, all."

"How was it?" Sarah asked.

"The usual. Cattle, cattle, cattle. Wish my father could talk about something else. Anything else."

Sarah heard that often enough from Emily. "He seems happy today. In a good mood."

"One hundred head of new cattle," Emily said, pulling down her bun and shaking her hair out.

She wore the same Mcallister Charters uniform the other pilots did, though it certainly didn't look the same on Emily. Her long blond hair was usually tied up in a tight bun similar to the one Sarah wore. But Matt liked Sarah's hair best when it was down. And spilling all over his flat abs on the way to…

This time, Sarah pulled herself out of the daydream. "Cattle make him *that* happy?"

She kind of doubted it was all cattle making him proud, judging by the tender way he'd bent down to kiss his daughter's cheek. Anyone could see the pride shine in his eyes every time he came by the office to see his daughter, the pilot.

Emily shrugged and glanced in the direction of Stone's office. "Where's Stone?"

"Ground control to Major Thomas." Stone's voice came over the CTAF. "Pretty sure I left Matt Conner in my dust. He's slow but I hear he's worth waiting for, in case any eligible females are listening to this transmission. Over."

"I'm right behind you, shithead. Don't get cocky." Matt's voice.

Her big brother was without a doubt one of the single most annoying people she'd met in her lifetime, and working for the police department she'd met her share. Cocky. Bossy. And also, she really, really…loved him. He was her family, and she would miss him when she went back to Colorado. Miss watching the way he treated Emily, as if the sun rose and set on her. Without a doubt, he'd kill anyone who messed with her with his bare hands.

And sure enough, a few minutes later when Matt and Stone walked into the office, Emily practically jumped into Stone's arms. Sarah found herself smiling at them, no resentment left in her. They deserved to be happy.

"What are you smiling about?" Matt asked, coming up to her.

"Aw. Well. They're cute together."

"Yeah." He sighed. Ran a hand through his hair. "Rough day for me. Too many irritated and entitled passengers."

"I haven't had the best day myself. I forgot to order more coffee and so now we have to pay extra for an expedited order. Also, I may have misfiled some flight plans." She blew a breath out.

Matt tugged on a lock of her hair. "Do you know what I need? Ice cream."

"Ice cream?"

She hadn't had ice cream for a year. The problem with ice cream, as she saw it, was that it was hard to stop at one pint. It was one junk food far too dangerous to keep in her kitchen freezer, and she wasn't exactly a health nut.

"It's a sweet cream that's frozen with different kinds of flavor added. Has a bazillion calories, which I know you don't care about."

She slid him a look. "Thanks for the four-one-one on ice cream. And how do you know I don't care about a bazillion calories? Maybe I do."

"I can always work it off you later."

The absolute heat of those words hit her like a whip. Because they were no longer friends tied together by their mutual connection to Stone.

Now they were lovers.

And she was so out of her element. Wanting him more every day, while reminding herself she'd made a promise not to fall in love with him. Matt didn't make it easy. If she didn't watch herself, she'd wind up getting burned. When she left Fortune, Matt Conner would be fine. He'd rolled and glided through his life, not even letting a teenage pregnancy rock it. And he'd move on when Sarah left. She'd barely register as a blip on his radar.

But that was her future and this was the present. This moment was her "right now" and all she had. She resolved to enjoy it for as long as it lasted, swallowed her fear. She'd promised to live out loud again. To feel everything again, even if it hurt. Because, as it turned out, it hurt far worse to feel nothing at all.

"Okay, Airman. Lead the way."

CHAPTER TWENTY-THREE

THE LICK N SPOON was almost empty when they arrived, and after they'd chosen their ice cream, Matt led her to a booth, his hand on the small of her back.

Sarah had chosen Rocky Road and regretted it almost the moment she took her seat. She always chose Rocky Road. It was her go-to ice cream. No ice cream shop could ruin the chocolate, marshmallow and nut blend.

But it wouldn't have killed her to try something new. She'd promised herself to shift old patterns and beliefs, and to try something new for a change. Experiment.

Actually, Matt had what she wanted in his ice cream dish. It was a cherry, chocolate and vanilla combination. She pointed to it. "I should have ordered that."

He arched a brow. "Switch?"

"You would do that? That's sweet, Matt, but not fair. I don't want to take your ice cream. This is fine. I always—"

But he had already switched them. "I'm easy."

She did like a man who took charge. Didn't she? "Oh, thanks."

She took a bite of Matt's ice cream and had a mouth orgasm. "Hmm."

He grinned. "You had close to the same look on your face around midnight last night. That good, huh?"

"Yes," she squeaked out.

He didn't speak for a beat, eyes filled with amusement, his lips twitching.

"Glad to see you and Stone getting along now. I remember when you first came to town. You couldn't stand him."

"He wouldn't even let me in our father's house for a while."

"Well, he was angry you were trying to sell the aviation school to a contractor who was going to put in another strip mall."

She didn't want to think about the way she'd behaved. Hurt and angry, she'd thought Stone and their father had shared a special connection that left her outside in the cold. She'd felt like the outsider, like the relative who'd been summoned to the last will and testament reading to get her share. Not like a daughter who wanted to grieve her father. So she'd behaved in the way they'd expected of her, and on her mother's advice hired an attorney. If all her father had wanted her to have was his money, than why shouldn't she sell to the highest bidder?

Nothing had worked out as planned. Stone had decided not to leave Fortune, and hadn't wound up selling at all.

"I just wished I'd known my father was so sick. That's all."

"Stone realizes how wrong he was about that."

"He only did what our father wanted."

"But sometimes you have to make an executive decision. It was a bad call on his part."

True enough, and it was Matt who'd acted on her behalf as a go-between.

The first time she'd ever laid eyes on Matt Conner, it had been at the Airborne Bar & Grill where she'd discovered Stone hung out with his Air Force buddies. She'd driven there to confront him, hoping they could avoid litigation. Hoping to understand. On some level, she'd yearned for the connection, too. But like they were back to being children again, Sarah had allowed every action of Stone's to produce an equal and opposite reaction from her—most of them not at all positive.

She'd known better. Understood how to deal with difficult people, and even taken higher education courses on the issue. She'd believed she understood psychology and the human mind, understood how to handle hostility, but when it came to her big brother, all of her training flew out the window. She was back to being the same awkward thirteen-year-old girl from her last summer in Fortune. Her anger had ruled her life.

She had walked into Airborne Bar & Grill a few months ago and almost immediately wanted to turn around and run. The place had been hopping with testosterone. Not a female in sight. Several men had already zeroed in on her like their eyes were laser beams that could cut right through her pantsuit. Yes, pantsuit. She'd been overdressed for the occasion, her hair pulled up tight in her usual workplace bun, glasses on instead of the contacts she wore now.

"Excuse me," she'd said, as some force she might call her guts propelled her to the bar. "Have you seen Stone Mcallister?"

Conversation had pretty much stopped. Maybe because most of it, or what she could hear, had involved the F-bomb being tossed around like a comma.

Then Matt had stepped up to help. She'd noticed overt and clear sexual interest in his eyes—dilated pupils, check—and slightly parted lips, which flattered her and made her feel attractive for the first time in a long while. Someone had noticed her. Not just someone, but Matt Conner, a man who everyone noticed.

But all that had been pulled away from her with one simple word. That she was Stone's *sister*.

For the rest of the night, he treated her like he would a kid sister. This had irritated the hell out of her. Steering her in the other direction of any man who would talk to her. Making it clear every one of them understood that she was off-limits.

She and Matt had talked for hours late into the night. He was easy to talk to once you got past all the hormones he naturally stirred up in her and any living, breathing, heterosexual female. He'd listened to her sad story and said he'd put a bug in Stone's ear. But he'd also defended Stone as she might have expected. He'd tried to give her another side. The side of a son who'd only done what his father had asked. A son who was trying to save jobs at the airport, and save the aviation school that had mattered so much to their father.

And much as she'd protested them at the time, she had taken Matt's words to heart. Largely because of him, she'd swallowed her pride and given up the lawsuit. Since then, she and Stone had a friendlier relationship.

"Tell me what you're thinking." Matt interrupted her thoughts.

"I'm thinking about the first time we met."

He cleared his throat. "In my defense, how was I to know you were Stone's kid sister?"

"I'm not sure why you let it bother you in the first place."

"Fair enough." Matt licked his spoon. "But maybe you don't understand *The Bro Code*."

"Maybe?"

"Volume two of *The Bro Code*, page seven

hundred, paragraph six, line four says—'Thou will not make a move on your bro's kid sister.'"

It actually made her feel a little warm and toasty inside to think that she had been protected by the guys because of her brother. "Oh, Matt. You broke the bro code."

"I haven't finished. Subsection B clearly states—'unless big brother clears you first.'"

"Ah. So you've already been through clearance?"

"Say what you will about your brother—he's cocky, bossy and arrogant. However, he's also fiercely protective of the women in his life. And that includes you now. I like to think he knows I would take care of you. He knows I would never hurt you." Matt's eyes grew soft. "Besides, he couldn't have kept me away from you."

She felt a wave of tenderness kick her in the stomach, and she considered asking for that in writing. *I would never hurt you.* He wouldn't mean to. They were both grown-ups and consenting adults. She'd walked in with her eyes wide-open. And she'd never regret it.

Not a single day in her life.

Her throat clogged with affection for all he'd done to help her and Stone just talk to each other again. Handle it without the attorneys. *Fire the lawyers*, Matt had said.

Talk to your brother.
Talk to your sister.

Without Matt, without knowing she had someone on her side who would listen and understand, maybe she would have given up and left Fortune. Let the lawyers hammer it out while she waited in Fort Collins.

She set her ice cream aside and reached for Matt's hand. "Hey."

"Tell me." He squeezed her hand.

"Did I ever say thank you? For stepping in and talking to Stone. For understanding me even when I was being the B word."

His thumb traced her palm in gentle circles. "You don't need to say thank you."

But for the first time she was beginning to believe that maybe there were things left for her in Fortune. Reasons she might stay. "I want to. The truth is, I've been so busy mourning what I lost that I forgot to pay attention to what's still here. I do still have a brother, and he's about to have a beautiful wife. Maybe children down the road."

"I guarantee it, the way those two go at it."

"I'm going to be a sister-in-law and an aunt. Someday."

And I'm going to hate missing a second of it.

"He's a great guy, your brother. Got my ass out of a few jams. He's a smart-ass, sure, but he's loyal to the core."

"Sounds like someone else I know. No wonder you two are such good friends. You're so much alike."

"Please don't compare me to your brother. Not right now. I'm not feeling brotherly at the moment." His thumb swept her lips.

"I definitely prefer you this way." She licked his thumb just as her phone played "I Will Survive" in her purse. That would be Mom again, since Sarah hadn't responded to her calls.

Sarah pulled the phone out of her purse. "Sorry. I have to take this."

She stepped outside the ice cream parlor for privacy. Maybe Matt would think it was work-related or something. At the moment, she didn't want him to know that at thirty she was still not fully independent of her mother. Frankly, it was more like her mother wasn't independent of Sarah. And yes, there was a great deal of guilt tied to the situation. Sarah's. As much as it wasn't true, Mom often acted like Sarah was her only child. Mom had been chronically paranoid about Sarah's safety for years. She had given Mom good reason to be, but that was all in the past and had been for years.

"Hey, Mom. Sorry I haven't called. I've been so busy with the renovations. They're really coming along."

"Nice to hear, sweetheart. But I'm calling with some great news. Do you remember Brock Montgomery?"

The name rang a bell but she couldn't say that an image sprang to mind. "No. Why?"

"I'm surprised. He's only the former running back for the Sliders. He's getting a divorce!"

"Uh-huh. Why is that *good* news?"

"Sweetheart, we're talking about the most eligible soon-to-be bachelor in Fort Collins. He came into our office yesterday and he's buying some land just outside of town. To build a compound of sorts. Every secretary in the office and even some of the attorneys took out a photo of a niece, daughter or granddaughter. So I showed him your photo, of course. He actually smiled. I think the widest smile was for your photo, Sarah. Seriously. And best of all, he'll be around a lot until we get all the contracts done."

Sarah might have a fever. Either that or it was this oppressive heat wave. Or maybe having a mother who was insane.

"Mom," she breathed out. "Look, you don't have to do this."

"Show your picture around? Why not? Everyone else did."

"I'm coming back. You don't have to have me almost married off to get me to come home."

She sighed loudly. "I'm beginning to wonder. We lose a lot of them this way. California seduces people to the other side. The near perfect weather, the mountains for snow and skiing only a few hours away from the valley, so that you can have the best of both worlds. Wine country. San

Francisco an hour away, not to mention Hollywood and Disneyland to the south."

"Do you realize you sound like a travel brochure?" Sarah figured it was a side effect of working for attorneys who specialized in real estate deals. "I'm not here for the mountains, the weather or the wine. And Hollywood is a six-hour drive."

"Do you have your plane ticket yet?"

"Well, no. But I was waiting until I'm six weeks out. That's when you get the best prices."

"By my calculations you should buy your ticket any day now."

Dammit, she was right. It was time. "All right. I'll do that. Talk later."

Sarah hung up and the glass door to the parlor dinged behind her. Matt stood just outside the entrance, hands shoved in his pockets, that ready-for-anything grin on his face.

"We all set?"

"Yep," she said, moving toward his truck.

Sandy beaches. Mountains. Wine. Her brother. Emily. Cassie. Her father's house.

But if she were being honest, there was only one reason why she'd find a way to stay. He was a little over six feet tall, made love to her as if he'd like to make a career out of it and kicked her heart into overdrive every time he smiled.

CHAPTER TWENTY-FOUR

HUNTER HAD HIS phone back and life was almost back to normal.

That was the good news. The bad news was that he still couldn't use his phone to go online. Couldn't play "Call of Duty" or "Halo" online, tweet or Instagram. And in a bizarre twist of fate, it wasn't because of Joanne this time.

He'd spent the past week with Megan, meeting at The Drip for a few hours every day, walking to the nearby park where they each challenged themselves to all of the exercises listed on the exercise station, and then ran three laps around the empty baseball diamond. Because she wasn't giving up on this "go dark" challenge, he couldn't give it up, either.

He didn't lose to anyone, much less someone he wanted to impress.

Plus, he still didn't have any idea why she'd voluntarily taken this "go dark" challenge. And his curiosity was getting the best of him. He'd been digging all week and had come up with nothing. At first, Hunter thought maybe Megan had been cyberbullied. But he'd asked her and she'd denied it, unless she was lying. Then he'd asked his friends, lied to them and said he was still grounded, and wanted to know if anyone had been bullying Megan.

Nothing. No one was teasing or bullying her, or if they were none of his friends knew about it.

He was into the second week of this challenge—he was for sure counting the days it hadn't been his choice—when Megan suggested they ride bikes to Lake Anderson in town.

There were bicycle trails that led to one end of the lake, and Hunter led the way. He'd grown up here and knew the area well. Lake Anderson was a man-made lake connected to one of the largest dams in the country. He had friends with parents who had houses on the dock, and boats. Boats they couldn't use anymore since the lake had been closed off to boating because of the drought.

After a few miles, he walked his bicycle to the side of the lake shoreline and laid it down. Megan followed and did the same. For a while Hunter just stood there staring at the water. He couldn't remember the last time he'd even been here. Probably with Matt a few years ago. Joanne wasn't much into lakes.

"I have to go back to my father's house this weekend," Hunter said.

"Are you giving up?"

When she smiled like that at him, her long

blond hair all shiny and her face all pretty, he wanted to give up the stupid challenge if it would make her happy to win.

Almost. "Why would I do that? So you can win?"

She laughed. "So what's your dad like? Why do you live with your mom? Did you get to choose?"

Whoa. So many questions all hitting him at once. Megan had probably never asked him that many. And anyway, she sort of knew about Matt. It was a small enough community that people all around here had heard about Matt. He was kind of one of their "native sons" and everyone acted like he was some sort of hero.

"I didn't get to choose." Maybe she'd stop at one question.

"Do you like living with your mom?"

No such luck. "It's okay."

"Would it be better to live with your dad?"

"It would be better to be on my own."

"You don't mean that. Who would cook you dinner?"

"I know how to cook my own dinner, genius. Don't you?"

She shrugged. "My mom likes to cook dinner every night."

"That sounds bomb."

"Yeah. She's a good little wifey."

Somehow Megan made that sound like a bad thing, the way she said it between her teeth.

"I don't really care. When I'm a Marine I'll have to live off bugs and stuff."

"Ew." She threw a rock in the lake. "Why would you want to eat bugs?"

"I figure I'm ahead of the game if I can learn to live on that."

"Don't they give you those MREs to eat?" Her nose wrinkled like she smelled something gross.

"Sure, but what if I run out on a mission? Then I'm ahead of the game. I can eat bugs. And bugs are everywhere."

"You think of everything." Megan laughed a real nice belly laugh, like she thought Hunter was super funny. So he laughed, too.

"You're really cute, you know that?" Megan said.

"Yeah?" It's the first time a girl had ever come right out and said that to him.

At school, some girls followed him around and when he'd turn to say something, they'd run and hide in the girl's restroom. He didn't get it. Was he good-looking or not?

"You're better-looking than Justin Bieber, even."

Oh crap, he was going to throw up. All the girls loved the shit out of that dude. It was supposed to be a compliment, and maybe if he'd wanted to be a model it would have been. He sure hoped he looked tougher than the Biebs.

"Yeah. Thanks." What else could he say?

"Why don't you ever talk to me at school?"

"What?"

"When you see me at school, you never talk to me."

"I hardly ever see you."

"I'm always with Julie. She used to follow you around until you turn and then she would run into the closest classroom or bathroom. She'd pull me in with her."

"Why did she do that, anyway?"

"Duh. She had a humongous crush on you. But now she's dating Sam."

"I didn't know." Because, hello? He wasn't a freaking mind reader. Though he was beginning to wish he was, at least when it came to girls.

"Do you like her?"

"Not really." He shrugged. Julie was all right, he guessed, but he was beginning to like Megan. A lot. He didn't know why exactly, except that she was hella pretty and she *talked* to him. Most girls just stared at him, giggled and made him feel like a total weirdo.

"We better get back," Megan said, and picked up her bike.

They started the ride back to town but ten minutes into it Megan's tire blew. Hunter could have fixed it if he'd had a patch kit because Matt had taught him how one summer and he still remembered. But without a patch kit, he didn't know what to do.

"You can ride on my handlebars," he offered.

"No way. Call your mom for a ride back."

"She's at work."

"I don't want to call my mom. She's too busy."

"I thought she didn't work."

"She doesn't, but believe me, she's *busy*."

Hunter figured he was dealing with a language barrier again, also known as "girl speak," so he thought of the one person he knew who would come and not ask either one of them many questions.

Sarah picked up after the second ring. As Hunter expected, she agreed to come and pick him and Megan up and didn't ask him anything beyond where to find them. Not that he had anything to hide, but he didn't want any dumb questions later like whether Megan was his girlfriend and whether they'd thought about protection. Joanne was always jumping to conclusions that way, if she even so much as saw him standing within a foot of a girl.

He hung up. "Okay, so my dad's girlfriend is picking us up."

"Your dad has a girlfriend?"

"I'm not supposed to know that, so don't say anything when she comes. They don't want me to know they're banging."

"Parents are so stupid."

"Word."

"How did you find out about them?"

"I just know from hanging out with them last week when I was grounded from my life. I heard them talking, too, one night, and my dad sounds all soft and shit when he talks to her. It's not like he usually sounds."

"I hope you didn't hear any other sounds." Megan made a face.

"Nah, but I always turn the music way up in my earbuds at night just to be on the safe side." He'd freaking *die* if he heard Matt and Sarah moaning. Just tear out his eardrums and feed them to her dog.

"Smart."

"Anyway, Sarah's cool. You'll like her."

He liked Sarah, just not as much as he liked Megan.

Not even close.

CHAPTER TWENTY-FIVE

ON SUNDAY, MATT, Hunter and Sarah were invited to the Parker family ranch for a big outdoor barbecue. It was Father's Day, and Matt had never been much for the Hallmark holiday. And not only because for many years he'd been away for the celebration. Matt's father always said Father's Day was *his* day, and therefore a day he should be left alone to his own devices. Matt, who hadn't always been stateside anyway, usually humored him after a quick phone call to check in, even if he realized that his Father's Day probably meant a full day of TV sports interspersed with Oreo-cookie shoveling.

Emily and her family owned Fortune Valley Ranch. It was no longer a working ranch, its glory days forever ended when a freeway and eminent domain took much of their sprawling acres of land. Mr. Parker, CEO of Parker, Inc. and cattle rancher, had regrouped and taken the money to buy a working cattle ranch in Texas. Jean Parker, his mother and the family matriarch, an ever-resourceful spitfire of a woman, had made lemonade from lemons. With Emily's help, the family had created a place to hold town events, company parties, weddings and huge receptions. They had twenty acres of land left and put each one to good use. The family home, a sprawling Victorian, sat at the top of the hill. A red barn had been cleaned out and become a gift shop selling local arts and crafts. They still maintained a small petting zoo.

Matt drove his truck up to the main Victorian house sitting on the hill. He'd been here a couple of times in the recent past with Stone and knew that Sarah had, too.

"This is where we had our Sadie Hawkins Dance," Hunter said from the back passenger seat.

"How was it?" Sarah asked.

"So stupid. The girl who asked me bought us matching T-shirts that were pink. I had to wear it the rest of the night. Sucked."

Matt snorted. "Real men wear pink."

Sarah smiled and squeezed his hand.

The Parkers had several tables set up outside under a large canopied area. A little red-headed girl ran from table to table squealing with laughter. That would be Sierra, Emily's two-year-old niece and her sister Molly and Dylan's daughter. Dylan was helping Mr. Parker to man the grill while Molly chased her little girl around.

"Hey, you guys!" Emily met them at the crest of the hill. "Thanks for coming. Happy Father's Day, Matt."

Hugs followed because that was how Emily rolled. Matt introduced Hunter, and Emily even hugged him. "So great that you get to spend the day with your dad!"

"Yeah," Hunter said, shuffling his feet and looking at the ground. "I've been here before."

"Sadie Hawkins Dance, right?" Emily winked. "Have a seat, guys. We're almost ready to eat."

Matt found a place for him and Sarah at a table with Stone and Emily, but Hunter joined Molly and Dylan at their table. Their little girl, Sierra, appeared fascinated with Hunter. She wouldn't let him out of her sight, following him wherever he went. Eventually she tugged Hunter to the petting zoo nearby. Mr. Parker was talking cattle with his mother and her new boyfriend and old family friend, George Carver.

A versatile man, to be sure.

Toward the end of dinner, Emily crawled into Stone's lap. "Baby, we'll be married soon. When are you going to let me fly the Bonanza?"

Matt smirked. Stone wouldn't let anyone fly the Bonanza. It was his "pet" plane. The man was protective about his planes, and Matt could completely relate.

"We'll talk about it," Stone said.

"We sure will," Emily said with the smile of a woman who realized she had a man over a barrel.

"Great party, Em." Matt understood that second to Stone, this ranch was her heart.

Emily grinned. "Thanks. I love doing it. And the next family party I want to have here is a going-away one for you, Sarah."

Sarah cleared her throat. "You don't have to do that."

"I want to. Summers are busy here, but we can always fit family in. When are you leaving, anyway?"

Matt assumed Emily thought the question was an innocent one. She didn't realize that the question was loaded with meaning for him. He'd been wondering the same thing. Wondering if he had the right to ask. Wondering if he even wanted to know.

She squirmed visibly in her seat. "I've been waiting for fares to get lower before I buy my ticket."

"Wait," Stone interrupted. "Why would you fly commercial? We can get you there."

Matt had been wondering the same thing. He'd fly her himself if she insisted on leaving. Colorado would mean taking the Beechcraft, a bigger plane with more hours of fuel reserves. Emily regularly flew her father in that plane back and forth from Texas.

"I'm not sure I can afford that. I know chartered flights are more expensive." Sarah fiddled with her glass of iced tea.

"Are you kidding me?" Matt said. "I think we can work up a cut rate for you."

"Extremely low," Stone said. "Generous, even."

"How did I wind up here?" Sarah laughed. "In a family of pilots."

"You'll never fly commercial again," Matt said.

"Are you kidding me? No more waiting in the TSA lines taking off my shoes and occasionally getting a loving pat-down?" Sarah said.

Matt squeezed her hand under the table. "You're in the big leagues now."

"So when are you leaving?" Stone asked.

"Does next month work?" Sarah said.

"I'll check our schedule but I'm sure it won't be a problem," Stone said.

"You'll be back for the wedding, right?" Emily climbed off Stone's lap and went around pouring more tea in everyone's glasses.

"Of course I will."

"And would you go wedding dress hunting with me tomorrow? I want reinforcements for when Molly tries to get me to buy the sexy bride dress," Emily said, as she poured more tea in Matt's glass.

Matt wondered if Sarah realized that Joanne owned the only bridal shop in town. "Where are you going?"

"Joanne's, of course. Mostly because she'll have the fewest amount of erotic bride dresses. If any."

"I don't know what that is, but it sounds good." Stone grinned at his fiancée.

"Sure, I'll go. We can't have you dressed like a porno star on your wedding day," Sarah said, holding her glass out to accept more tea.

"Will someone please explain to me why that's a bad thing?" Stone asked as Emily ruffled his hair.

Then she leaned in and kissed him. When the kiss went on and on and stretched into next week, then Stone pulled her back into his lap, Matt looked away. He envied what those two had a little more each day. It would be nice to have that kind of trust with a woman, to know that they'd have each other's back.

After what he'd been through with Joanne, trust had taken a serious hit.

She'd once told him that he'd always be a part of Hunter's life, marriage or not. Military service or not. They'd work it out. But that's not exactly how it had wound up. There had been many times when he'd been stateside unexpectedly. When he'd tried to make arrangements to see Hunter, Joanne would check to make sure it fit into the carefully planned, intricately arranged schedule she had for their son. No one messed with "the schedule." His visits had to be booked and planned accordingly, and even though he'd once tried to explain that the United States Air Force did not operate on Hunter's nap schedule, she wouldn't listen to reason.

Of the five times he'd been able to secure a

Christmas-time leave, he'd only been able to see Hunter twice. The other times Joanne had plans with friends and family and they didn't include Matt.

Maybe it was time to trust someone again.

His gaze collided with Sarah's, who was also looking away from the display. She chewed on her lower lip, then licked it. He felt a grin tug at his lips.

Oh yeah. Do that again. I dare you.

What would everyone here do if Matt leaned over and kissed Sarah long and deep and hard like he wanted to right now? Stone might have given him the consenting-adults line, but it didn't mean he wanted to see any groping or fondling. Matt respected that. But maybe then Stone ought to stop with the PG-13 rated scenes because the slow torture was getting to Matt.

It was true that he had never been much into defining relationships or using labels. Then again, he'd never slept with a buddy's sister. Not that they'd done much sleeping. He didn't know how or when it had happened but he'd grown accustomed to having her in his bed every night. A tenderness washed over him every time she nestled her face into his neck and whispered good-night. There hadn't been many good nights with women in his life. Mostly a whole lot of goodbyes. And in another month, he'd have to say goodbye to

Sarah too, whether it was at an airport tarmac in Colorado or one in Fortune.

But both had zero appeal to him.

He glanced around and saw that Hunter and Sierra were still hanging behind the petting zoo pen, Mr. Parker was engaged in an intense discussion with his mother and her gentleman friend, Dylan and Molly were in a clinch, and Stone and Emily were still…doing what they always did.

He stood up and tugged on Sarah's hand. "I want to show you something."

He didn't meet with any resistance from her as he pulled her along and guided her a little farther up the slope of the hill to the barn. The Parker family had converted the old barn into a small gift shop in which they showcased local artists' work. Pottery, woodwork and some art, though not anything of the caliber he'd seen in Sarah's small shed. He flipped open the barn door and led her by the small of her back inside the poorly lit area. Only a small sliver of sunlight shone through the crossed barn windows.

Sarah walked along the aisles of pottery. She stopped in front of a large bowl and looked at the price tag. "Nice craftsmanship, but are they serious about this price?"

"Hey, it's art. Look at this." He stood by a sketch of El Toro, an amateur effort in his eyes compared to Sarah's.

"Oh. Maybe the artist is new and just getting started on landscapes."

He smiled at Sarah's kind critique. "It won an award."

"Really?" She met his eyes.

Now he could see the wheels turning. She'd told him that she couldn't sketch people anymore, or didn't want to. And he could understand why. For years she'd had a skewed view of her art. Her talent and abilities had been shut down and fixed to the barest necessities. He had a feeling that what she'd created in her shed so far was only the start of where she could go. Was it wrong of him to want her to rediscover that part of herself before she went back to Colorado?

"Well, art is so subjective." She shrugged. "It's not bad."

"It's not great. I think you need to put your work in here."

She shook her head. "Absolutely not. I don't want any favoritism from my sister-in-law-to-be. People will say she put my art in here because we're related."

He one-armed her and tugged her in close, holding on tight. "Damn, woman, why are you so stubborn? Your work is excellent. Everybody deserves to see it, and you deserve for it to be seen. What good is your art if you can't share it?"

He recognized by the shift in her eyes that he'd reached her on some level. Hit the bull's-eye. Fear kept her from doing what she wanted to do with the rest of her life, whether she could cop to it or not. Fear of failure, fear of getting too close to anyone and falling in love—not that he could blame her for that last one. He was a fairly healthy cynic himself. Still working on it.

Her hands went up against his chest. "I might just not be ready to share it."

"I hear a lot of excuses." He tugged on a lock of her hair. "Maybe you're afraid."

That lit up her eyes with the fierceness he loved to see. "I'm not afraid. What would I be afraid of, anyway?"

"That someone might see inside you."

At this, she went still. Wouldn't look at him for a minute.

Then she met his eyes, and hers were heated and challenging. "Is this one more thing you're trying to fix for me, Matt Conner?"

"I think we've reached the point where you can just call me Matt." He brought his hand up to the nape of her neck and pulled her in until they were sharing oxygen. Just one breath between them. "Or maybe just 'babe.' I'll respond to either."

He smiled against her lips and kissed her, enjoying her sweet taste, like iced tea on his tongue. Her lips were ridiculously soft and her tongue wet and warm and willing. It teased mercilessly with his. That now familiar rush of blood pumped through him, speeding up his heart rate and wreaking havoc with his head.

Both of them.

Man, he wanted her more and more each day. She was sweet and smart. Funny, even when she wasn't trying to be. Beautiful. And from the moment he'd first met her he'd thought…somewhat lonely. Or maybe that was him.

But she was also opinionated, insecure, prideful, stubborn and…his.

Uh-oh. Careful with that line of thinking, Airman.

No. *Not* his.

She broke off the kiss and stared at his lips, a little breathless. "Did you bring me in here to make out?"

"That depends."

"On what?"

"Whether or not you like that idea."

A small grin formed on her lips. "You know I do. I like kissing you."

"You like a lot more than kissing." He grabbed a fistful of her hair and tugged her closer, even if he had no business acting like a horny teenager hiding in a dark barn with his favorite girl.

"That's true. And I think you must know how long I've had a crush on you."

"Yeah?"

He didn't like the idea of being her crush. It

sounded weak and temporary, but he reminded himself it was all he could expect when he'd been the one to offer her so little.

This is all I can give you right now.

I won't fall in love with you.

She still had plans to go back to Fort Collins because this thing between them was temporary and he needed to remember that. She still had plans to sell her father's house, even if every day Matt found another reason to love it. Not just because it was a Craftsman classic but because the walls held history inside them. The history of a family, fragmented though it had been. He was sure if Sarah held on to it she'd realize she already had what she was searching for. It wouldn't matter how much they changed and updated, the foundation would remain. And it was a firm foundation. If only Sarah could see that.

"I've crushed hard on you, since the first time I met you at the bar, and you gave me that full-on smile that promised me heaven."

"Did I deliver?"

"Yes. You did. Finally." This time she reached up and kissed him.

Long. Deep. Hard. Hot. By the time she was done kissing him, her eyes were hooded with desire.

He was hard, his breaths coming sharp and uneven. "Let's get out of here before you make me do something crazy."

He took her hand and led her out of the barn even as his heart told him: *Too late, genius. Too late.*

CHAPTER TWENTY-SIX

"MOLLY, I'M SERIOUS! I'm not going with the mini-skirt." Emily wrestled it out of Molly's hands and put it back on the wedding boutique shop's "no way" rack.

"All right, fine. Be a country bumpkin if you want. I'm just trying to get you to stretch." Molly went back to the other side of the store, presumably to find something less outdated.

"Leave your sister alone," Jean Parker called after her. Mrs. Parker sat on the love seat the store provided for mothers and in-laws. "She has her own ideas."

What had seemed like two hours but was probably just fifteen minutes ago, Sarah had stepped into the extremely exclusive "by appointment only" wedding boutique with Emily and her family. She'd said a brief hello to Joanne for the second time in the same month. Today Joanne was dressed in a beautiful satiny pink dress that made her look like everyone's favorite bridesmaid. She was welcoming and kind, but quickly found one of her attendants to help their party. Then she'd gone back to the front of the store where she seemed to be going through paperwork.

Emily turned and held out a long sleek white dress with a sweetheart collar.

"This is more what I'm thinking."

"How lovely, Em." The woman would probably adore anything Emily chose. The love was clearly written all over her dim blue eyes.

Emily held up her phone and took a photo of the dress. "Joanne said I could take photos, since Rachel can't be here."

Emily's best friend Rachel was on ordered bed rest for her pregnancy.

"What do you think?" Emily asked Sarah.

She'd been standing behind the couch just to the right of Mrs. Parker. Now Sarah nodded in agreement. She had to. That dress said Emily Parker-Mcallister in a thousand little ways. Elegant and beautiful. Classy. Unique and modern but deeply traditional.

"Beautiful."

Beyond that, Sarah had nothing more to add. She'd been chewing on Matt's words about her art since yesterday and still wasn't sure how she felt about it. He'd challenged her on her fears and she wasn't used to that. She'd expected him to be like most men and be content to simply get laid, but no. That didn't seem to be enough for one Matt Conner. Why this annoyed her she wasn't quite sure.

"I don't know," Emily said, wrinkling her nose. "The dress has to be perfect."

"I see you're not asking too much of the dress," her grandmother said. "Only perfection."

"I don't want it to be too much over-the-top tradition. Just enough tradition, with a little bit of country."

"I don't see any country in that dress," Molly said, bringing over a couple of over-the-top dresses that looked like something a movie star would wear.

Not Emily's style at all.

"The sweetheart collar is a little bit country," Emily said, and went into the changing rooms.

Both Molly and the bridal attendant followed her in.

"Ever been through this before, dear?" Mrs. Parker turned to Sarah. "Picking a wedding dress?"

"Oh, no. Not me."

"Been through this once before." Mrs. Parker sighed, and when she brought the champagne flute to her lips, dozens of silver bracelets jangled and chimed on her wrist.

She was the most unconventionally dressed geriatric woman Sarah had ever met. No track suits with piping for Jean. She wore designer jeans with sparkly and glittery patterns on the back pockets like something you'd find in the junior section of a department store.

It was difficult not to like Mrs. Parker. "Molly's wedding?"

"That's right. Never made it to the wedding dress part with Emily's first engagement. Thank the good Lord for that! But this. Oh my, Sarah, dear, this here is the *real* thing."

"I know what you mean." From what she'd heard through the grapevine Emily had been through a disastrous breakup before meeting Stone.

He'd met her through, of all things, the aviation school, when Emily had decided to get her pilot's license. She'd probably not been planning on meeting the love of her life, either, and yet it had happened.

Sarah hadn't planned on falling for her brother's best friend, but some days she felt down and out for the count. Drowning. Matt made her toes curl and her heart all squishy.

"How about you, dear? Any prospects back home?" Mrs. Parker asked.

"Um," Sarah said. "No one special."

"Maybe we can take care of that. You're family now, and we take care of family."

"No." First Mom, and now Mrs. Parker was joining the fray. "That's okay."

"What about Matt Conner?" Mrs. Parker asked just as Emily stepped out and, with the bridal assistant's help, climbed on the pedestal in front of the floor-length mirror. "Oh. Emily! How beautiful."

"Thank you." Emily hoisted back the short train of the dress. "What about Matt?"

"I was just thinking that he's single, isn't he?" Mrs. Parker asked.

Emily met Sarah's gaze in the mirror and gave a sly grin. "I don't know. Is he?"

Sarah threw what she hoped was a casual look in Joanne's direction, but thankfully she still seemed preoccupied with whatever she was doing.

Matt was very much single and Emily knew that. She was obviously just as good at fishing expeditions as Sarah.

"Yes," Sarah squeaked out. "He is."

"Perfect!" Mrs. Parker sang out.

"Exactly," Emily said with too wide a grin.

"All right. Enough, ladies. This is not *Fiddler on the Roof*," Sarah said.

Emily broke into a rousing rendition of "Matchmaker, Matchmaker." Sarah used that moment to excuse herself from the teasing. She walked back to the front of the store. No sooner was she three feet away from her than Joanne turned to her, giving Sarah her full attention.

"Is everything all right?"

"Oh, of course!" Sarah ran her hand along the counter at the front of the store. "You have such a lovely store here."

"Thank you." Joanne had turned her full attention to Sarah, paperwork forgotten.

Sarah had to say *something*. She couldn't just walk in and out of this store and not talk to Joanne. Especially because she felt so guilty about all the earlier judgment. Woman to woman, she understood exactly where Joanne might have been at one time. But dear Lord, what to say. What to say.

We have a lot more in common than you would ever know. And I don't just mean Matt.

Joanne was still smiling. It might be a tiny bit pasted-on, but was nevertheless a smile. And she was waiting for Sarah to say something. Anything.

"I want to thank you for putting up with my son. I know it's got to be rough," Joanne finally said, probably tired of the awkward silence.

Finally! A safe topic of conversation. "It's fine. He's a great kid. Very smart."

"Thanks," Joanne said. "And I'm sorry about the sudden visit. It was an emergency, and I just… You know, sometimes I need a break."

"Of course you do!"

"And I probably overreacted." She looked at the ground briefly. "I know Matt thought so."

"He…he didn't say anything to me," Sarah lied.

If Sarah wasn't mistaken, Joanne wasn't really buying that.

She shook her head. "Anyway, I know Hunter

should spend more time with Matt. But it's just harder than I thought it would be. I'm used to doing things my way, you know, and it's hard not to be a control freak."

Sarah could imagine what it must have been like all those years with a daily physical reminder of Matt. Raising the son of a man who didn't love her. A man she'd quite possibly never loved, either. Sarah still recognized loneliness enough to see it reflected in Joanne's eyes.

"Hey, Sarah! Get over here. You have got to see this," Emily yelled.

Sarah walked back, and this time Joanne followed.

Emily went into a full-on belly laugh when Molly came out wearing a dress that combined the eighteenth century with the twenty-first. Or maybe whimsy coupled with just plain lunacy. It was scandalously short, hitting just below her thigh line, but had a high-necked Victorian collar.

"I can't believe you found that," Joanne said, shaking her head. "I thought I sent it back."

Molly carried a matching parasol with it. "I like this. Maybe Dylan and I should renew our wedding vows."

She paraded twice in front of Mrs. Parker. Molly bent down and pointed her ass in Mrs. Parker's direction, giving her a half moon.

Mrs. Parker laughed so hard she spilled her champagne.

CHAPTER TWENTY-SEVEN

"Thanks for putting up with my nutty family," Emily said as she and Sarah took a seat at The Drip.

Emily had dropped off everyone else but she wanted Sarah to join her for coffee.

"I love your grandmother, and Molly is hilarious."

"She loves to be the center of attention. I don't mind. I'm used to it."

"I guarantee when you walk out in that gown on your wedding day, no one will be able to take their eyes off you. You looked like a princess, even before the attendant put the tiara on your head."

"Yeah, I won't be getting the tiara." Emily rolled her eyes. "All I care about is making Stone's jaw drop. You know how hard that is to do."

She actually didn't know. "Maybe his jaw doesn't drop easily, but his eyes get soft every time you walk in the room."

"Speaking of eyes, I noticed the way Matt looked at you yesterday. Not to mention the way you two sneaked into the barn. Something's changed between you two. Am I right?"

Something had changed all right, and Sarah was afraid her heart was already involved. It had been from the minute he'd started trying to fix everything between her and Stone. And it had probably been her worst idea ever to have sex with the man, but damned if she still couldn't regret it.

"We're…having fun." That seemed like a safe enough admission. "A lot of fun."

"That's how it starts."

"Is that how it started with you and Stone?"

"You probably don't want to compare us. Our situation was different. It involved a list I made with stupid rules we broke."

"Intriguing."

"I used to think I could control my love life, like I controlled everything else. My best friend Rachel tried to tell me I was nuts. So did Molly, but for obvious reasons I wasn't listening to her. I thought I could just have 'fun' with Stone. Be a wild woman. But dangit all, I fell in love with the big guy."

"I can't fall in love with Matt." It was the first time she'd said it out loud.

"Why not?"

"Well, first, I told him I wouldn't. That was kind of our deal."

"Uh-oh."

"What do you mean, uh-oh?"

"It's just that…in my experience, it's not wise to make deals like that."

"I don't really believe in love, anyway. Not the real and lasting kind."

At Emily's crestfallen face, Sarah quickly recovered. "But I mean, with you and Stone…it's different." She hoped.

Besides, Matt might want to fall in love again, but he wouldn't fall for Sarah.

Because you're the one who told him you wouldn't fall in love. Didn't believe in love. Why would he hitch his wagon to your star?

"And also, we live in different states." Sarah was reaching now for excuses.

"The different-states thing could be remedied easily enough. You already have the house here. You could move."

"My mother…she's a little too dependent on me. I've told her I'm coming back, and she's been waiting."

"You and Matt could try the long-distance thing. He is a pilot."

"A relationship is complicated enough without adding in making it part of his job to come and see me."

Emily sighed. "It sounds like you know what you want, but I hate that you're leaving. We haven't had much of a chance to get to know each other, and I know that Stone would like that, too."

"So would I. But I have a life back in Fort Collins. A job and friends. I've dropped out of that for too long."

"Of course. I'm sure they miss you."

Sarah nodded. So much so that she'd only had two phone calls from her coworkers—one asking when she'd be back and the next to ask for a referral to another forensic artist. She'd bitten her tongue and given a referral to the best artist she knew, hoping she'd still have work when she got home. But the more time that passed, the less likely it became. On some level, she wondered if she were quietly burning bridges behind her so that she couldn't ever get back to that old life.

Sure, she loved Fort Collins. Loved the handful of friends she'd collected over the years, many of whom texted every other week and kept in touch. Loved her mother. She wasn't certain she loved the job any longer, or if she ever had. Life back home seemed set in stone whereas in Fortune it felt as though she could go in any direction. Start over. Starting over was scary, but at least here she had a start. A beginning.

"But we'll all miss you here, too."

"That's nice of you to say."

"It's true. And I don't only mean Matt. Stone and I will miss you. But as long as you come back for the wedding we can forgive you. And don't worry. I'll pick elegant bridesmaids dresses. I won't let Molly have any say at all."

"If you do, you'll have an interesting wedding. And I don't think the men would mind much, either."

"Right. And Molly would love to see Dylan salivating over her in a sexy dress. She was too pregnant when they got married to wear anything revealing."

"Frankly, I would even get a kick out of seeing my mother's face. She's always been pretty conservative."

"I'm glad she's coming. Stone wanted her to attend."

"She wouldn't miss Stone getting married and it's good to know he wants her there."

"You're both lucky to have your mother, and I totally get wanting to be close to her. I'm sure I'd be the same. I don't ever want to move away from Fortune and Granny. I'm so glad Stone decided to stay, because of course I would have gone anywhere with him."

Sarah patted Emily's hand instinctively. She'd lost her mother to cancer at age ten and been raised by her father and her grandmother, Jean. "What about your father?"

"What about him?"

"Wouldn't you miss him, too?"

"Daddy?" Emily grinned. "I would now. Miss him sitting next to me on the trips back and forth to the Texas cattle ranch, asking me if I'm sure I know what I'm doing. But you know, for a long time we didn't get along too well."

"Why not?"

She took a sip of her coffee and set it down. "He much preferred Molly over me."

Sarah nearly spit her coffee out. To say something so matter-of-fact, and yet so obviously painful, threw her for a loop. "I'm sure that's not true."

Emily laughed. "It's not that weird. He loves me the same, of course. But those two have a lot more in common. Wild, funny and unpredictable. Loud. I'm a lot more like Granny. Levelheaded. Grounded. I used to think that was boring, but it's just who I am."

Sarah respected Emily's grown-up attitude, and guessed that she didn't get there overnight. Sarah's attitude most of her life hadn't been so much grounded and levelheaded as angry and hostile. Most of her life she'd been in the same position as Emily, with an absentee father. She'd taken the attitude straight into her life and work, resulting in being thought of as a difficult person. Her coworkers and few girlfriends had advised her to loosen up, lose the bun and trade the glasses for contacts. Trade the pantsuits for dresses, and she might get asked out on a date sometime—even laid. She'd been told by her friends that she was pretty but unapproachable. Perhaps she'd even orchestrated that on purpose.

Her psychology textbooks would agree.

CHAPTER TWENTY-EIGHT

MATT HADN'T EXPECTED a turkey dinner with all the trimmings, but he also hadn't thought his father would order enough Chinese food to feed a party of ten. Joanne had agreed to let him bring Hunter over for dinner the day after Father's Day, to spend some time with Dad.

"I could have cooked," Matt said. "You didn't have to order all this food."

"This is great," Hunter said, in between bouts of shoveling food into his mouth. "Thanks, Grandpa."

It shouldn't surprise Matt that his son could eat in such large quantities. It seemed to be a Conner family trait. That and the brown eyes.

"So how have my boys been?" Matt's father asked, helping himself to fried rice. "And thank you for leaving me in peace on my day. I had a great time."

"That's so weird," Hunter said. "My mom makes a huge deal out of Mother's Day. I have to spend all day with her or I'm a bad son."

"Hunter, there's one thing I need to tell you right now about men and women. We're different."

"Gee, Dad," Matt said. "That's a great help."

"Let me finish, wiseass," Dad continued. "As the French say, *vive la différence*. You'll be glad someday, too. Do you have a girlfriend yet?"

Matt braced himself for the pants talk. If Dad started with Hunter keeping "it" in his pants, not only would he be embarrassed but so would Matt. "Dad," he warned.

Hunter stopped shoveling in the beef broccoli long enough to answer. "Nah, but my dad does."

Fantastic. Both sets of brown eyes turned on him.

Dad gave the biggest grin Matt had seen on him in some time. "Is that right?"

"No, that's not right." Matt shoveled in some Kung Pao chicken. If his mouth was full he didn't have to talk.

"If Sarah's not his girlfriend yet, he wants her to be," Hunter added helpfully. When Matt slid him a death stare, he lifted a shoulder.

"So there's a woman," Dad said.

"There's a woman." Hunter nodded.

Matt, mouth full, shook his head. This conversation would not happen. He hadn't talked to his father about a woman in roughly… Take Hunter's age and tack on another nine months. Now was not the time to try to explain what he felt for a certain long-legged brunette when he could hardly explain it to himself.

"I might have suspected it." Dad directed the comment to Hunter, ignoring Matt. "What's she like?"

"Super hot." And then, possibly at the frozen look Matt felt forming on his face, Hunter burst into peals of laughter.

Matt choked down his food. Coughed. Hit his chest. And also remembered not to speak on the basis of the whole Fifth Amendment thing. He now wondered how much Hunter had noticed. When it came to Sarah, it couldn't be about what Matt wanted. Even if he'd like her to stay and give them a real shot, there was the whole "I'm never falling in love with you" thing. Yeah, he hadn't forgotten. And he was not about to discuss his unique relationship with Sarah with either his teenage son or his father.

"Your dad has always been quite the ladies' man," his father added.

Now Matt would have to speak up. "Not true."

"The hell it isn't. We used to have the girls calling all the time. Your mother included," he said to Hunter.

Hunter smiled and kept on chewing.

"Dammit, Dad."

Matt didn't want to go there, back in time to when Joanne had called him incessantly after their one date. She'd had something important to tell him and it had to be in person. Matt had thought it could wait a week, since he'd been in the middle of finals with a heavy AP and honors course load. Turned out it couldn't wait. That significant, life-changing "thing" Joanne had to tell him about now sat across his Dad's kitchen table, eating Chinese food. Matt's mini-me.

"There's nothing wrong with that. You're lucky." Dad leaned over and spooned some more chow mein on his paper plate.

Cue one for the books. First time he'd ever heard his father talk about how lucky Matt was a ladies' man, or label Matt as one. He glanced over at Hunter and realized again how fortunate he'd actually been. Lucky that he had a son at all. Lucky that the kid didn't hate his guts after all the time he'd spent away from him. Lucky that maybe he didn't know, and hopefully he'd never know, that at one time Matt had been a scared-shitless teenager who didn't want a kid. Who wasn't ready for him.

On the way back to drop Hunter off at Joanne's, Matt used the car time to clear things up.

"Hey, thanks for putting up with Grandpa."

There was a small silence and then Matt spoke again. "And by the way, I'm not a ladies' man, no matter what he says."

"Grandpa's a funny guy. But I know you're not a ladies' man. Sarah wouldn't go for that type."

Matt had to bite his lip to keep from laughing. "Think so?"

"She's too smart for that."

Leave it to his son to realize that. Matt would have to agree. "You're pretty smart yourself."

"I do okay."

"Still thinking the Marines?"

Hunter nodded.

"I'll put you in touch with a buddy of mine."

Hunter's body actually swiveled in Matt's direction. "Yeah? Joanne won't like it. She'll probably give you a hard time."

"She doesn't have to know for now. But you need to promise me you won't enlist until you graduate. And until you, personally, are the one to tell your mother."

Hunter nodded.

"If the Marines are what you really want, I'll be the last person to discourage you. But make sure you're not joining up because you're running away from your life."

"I'm not."

Matt swallowed hard, not at all sure he wanted to ask the next question. "Is there really not...a girl?"

Hunter swiveled back to face the windshield. "No."

Or in other words: yes.

"Because if there was, that would be okay. I would just want to talk to you about some…some things you should know."

Hunter sighed. "I had this talk in the fifth grade. From my teachers, from my mom and from you, too."

"This is like phase two of the talk."

Matt gripped the steering wheel tighter. He didn't have anything prepared, but Hunter had made male appreciation comments about Sarah. His son was a man-child, with all the physical equipment he'd ever need but not the fully matured brain he'd eventually have. The brain he would need to make life-changing decisions. Matt would have to wing it. He pulled up to Joanne's curbside and turned to give Hunter his full attention.

Hunter rolled his eyes. "I'll let you know when I need the next phase."

"It kind of sounds like you already do. You noticed Sarah."

"Take it easy. She's too old for me."

Matt laughed. "Yeah. I know. It doesn't mean you're not looking at girls your own age that way. Wondering what you can get away with."

"You're wrong. I don't even know how to get a girl to like me."

That single heartbreakingly vulnerable statement hit Matt hard. Hunter might not have even realized that he was reaching out to Matt.

"Just be yourself."

"Everybody says that. What does that even mean?"

Matt took a deep breath. He didn't want to screw this up. "It means there's no 'getting' anyone to like you. It just happens. All you can do is talk to a girl. Get to know her. Be yourself, like you would be with any friend."

"Yeah? I fart in front of my friends."

"Okay, not exactly like when you're with your friends. And granted, a friendship with a girl *is* different. But it's also the same. In more ways than you would ever realize."

"Wait. So are you and Sarah still just friends?"

"No." Matt cleared his throat. "We're more than friends. I'd do anything for her."

"Yeah," Hunter said with a sharp nod. "That's how I am with my best friends."

"That's how it is with a girl. You have to respect and treat her right. Have your girl's back like you would your best buddy. Don't assume they're a different species just because…because sometimes it feels like they are."

"Yeah. Girls talk weird."

Joanne had now opened the front door of her home and stood waiting, arms folded across her chest.

"The talking thing. A subject for another time. We'll call that phase three, which, by the way, I'm still learning."

Hunter jumped out of the car and slammed the door. Shoulders hunched and hands shoved in his jeans pockets, he lumbered up the walkway to his home. He was probably six inches taller than the last time Matt had seen him and even all these months later, he was still getting used to the fact. Hunter towered over Joanne as he stepped past her.

Not a kid anymore, his son. In fact, he was only a year younger than Matt when his entire life shifted off course.

CHAPTER TWENTY-NINE

TODAY'S ASS-CRACK-OF-THE-MORNING flight to Lake Tahoe wasn't the norm, and Matt settled into the copilot's chair already resenting Stone.

"Move. Let me take over."

"Hell if I will." Stone adjusted his headset.

"Let's talk about your flight record versus mine."

"Never mind, Boy Wonder. Let's talk about the fact that I own this company."

"So it's like that," Matt grumbled, putting on his headset. Copiloting it would be.

This morning's chartered flight was for a larger passenger group than normal, and so, more for their image than anything else, Stone had decided they'd all put on a good show and both he and Matt would be the flight "crew."

Meaning Matt would mostly sit next to Stone and basically twiddle his thumbs, which pissed him off. "Is this necessary?"

"Just sit back and enjoy the ride," Stone said and communicated his position and plans for takeoff.

"Watch the mountains. You don't see those every day," Matt said. "Make sure you clear them."

"Yeah, thanks, genius."

Once they were airborne, Matt considered a short catnap. Closing his eyes for a few seconds couldn't hurt. He hadn't slept well the previous night. Again. Even if he was fully aware that Sarah didn't owe him a thing just because they'd had one weekend of mind-blowing sex, he couldn't help but want her in his bed every night.

And it was more than a little strange not dating a woman he was living with. A woman who made his eyes roll to the back of his head.

"So. You and Sarah," Stone said.

"Next subject."

Stone snorted. "Try again."

"Thought you didn't want to hear it."

"I don't," Stone said. "But Emily asked. Can you give me the G-rated version?"

"Let me help you out," Matt said. "There *is* no G-rated version."

Stone scowled. "Man, remind me to let you pilot next time we do this. You make one pissy copilot and a real pain in my ass."

"Remember that." Matt's conscience got the better of him and he relented. Sighed. "Okay, what do you want to know?"

"What Emily wants to know is if you're seriously interested in Sarah."

"Tell Emily I'm interested."

"Really?"

"Not that it matters. You know my track record with relationships."

Alexis had dropped him when he'd moved to Fortune from Texas to be closer to Hunter. What he'd thought was a fairly solid relationship with plenty of possibilities had turned out to be nothing at all. Frankly, he was sick of failure with the opposite sex and it had been easy enough to abstain because he hadn't been excited about anyone for months. And then he'd met Sarah. His best friend's sister. A woman with plans to leave, when long-distance had worked so well for him in the past. Another recipe for certain disaster and still he couldn't stay away.

After they'd arrived, disembarked all their passengers and wished them a pleasant day, Stone was forced to wait in another long queue to taxi down the runway.

"Man, I'm so fucking bored!" Stone yelled.

"Because you have the patience of a gnat."

Stone grunted and whipped out his phone. He cursed under his breath, then looked at Matt. "This isn't me saying this, but Emily says you need to tell Sarah you're interested and ask her to stay."

Matt counted to ten and chose his words carefully. "Tell your fiancée that I can handle my own love life."

Stone threw the phone at him. "You tell her."

Matt laughed and caught the phone. "I appreciate all the love-line help, but this is your sister we're talking about. My good friend, too. Maybe I'm not going to take a chance on losing our friendship."

"That makes me laugh. Want to know why? I didn't want to risk hurting Emily. Of course I did anyway, but then I fixed it." He lifted a shoulder. "Maybe you can do the same, if it should come to that."

While Matt wanted to believe so, they were comparing apples and oranges. Stone and Emily hadn't first had the kind of deep friendship that Matt thought he had with Sarah. Unlike him and Sarah, they hadn't circled each other for months. Flirting, playing, dancing around their desire for each other. Now that they'd given in to that desire, he was supposed to be good with that. It should be enough. And yet all he could think about was whether or not he could talk her into keeping the house. If she did, that single move would tell him a lot. It would show that she was ready to go to another level with him. And if that were the case, he was all over it. He just needed the green light.

The rest of Matt's day passed in a blur of flights to Oregon and Arizona. Matt finally got to call it a day around six o'clock. As he pulled up to Sarah's house he noticed a woman in the front yard holding a stake and a sign placard that read For Sale.

"Can I help you?" Matt asked.

The woman turned to him, giving him a smile probably required for graduation from real estate school. "Hi, I'm Jenny. The Realtor? I tried knocking on the door and no one answered. But I already talked to Sarah about putting up the sign. She said it was okay."

"Did she?"

He considered that for a moment, wondering why he thought in a million years that anything he wanted mattered. "We're not quite ready."

"And you are?" She squinted, as if trying to place him.

"Matt. I'm taking care of the remodel."

"That's okay. I know about the repairs. But since I'm in the neighborhood, I just thought—"

Matt took the sign and stake out of her hands. "I'll put this up when we're ready."

The finality of that seemed to register with Jenny. "Oh, but—"

"Thanks for coming by." He gave her his best charter pilot smile. And damn if he'd almost said *Thanks for flying with us.*

Jenny politely said goodbye and hopped into her gold Mercedes-Benz. Matt watched her drive away, telling himself that he didn't need the additional pressure of the sign going up. That's the only reason he wouldn't let the Realtor put it up. It wasn't because he didn't want the house to be sold. It would be sold, and he had to wrap his mind around that fact once and for all. No matter how attached he'd become to it.

He walked inside the house and once again endured Shackles's assault. He picked up the creature who for some reason seemed to adore him no questions asked, and gave him a rub. The shower was going, which meant Sarah would be in there. Naked. Wet and naked.

One of his favorite combinations.

He pressed his ear to the door and heard Sarah singing the theme from *Titanic*. Off-key.

Actually, there was no reason he couldn't enjoy their time together, whatever little was left of it. It was what he'd signed up for at the start of all this. He was crazy to want more, anyway.

He was going to forgive her for selling this house.

Just as long as when he walked into that bathroom, she wasn't quite done showering. He went for the door which, thank you, baby Jesus, was not locked. He walked inside and shut the door closed again, then pulled off his shirt and kicked off his shoes, pants and underwear.

CHAPTER THIRTY

SARAH SANG HER heart out as she belted out the theme song for *Titanic*. Boy, it was truly amazing how awesome she sounded in the shower. Might be the acoustics in here. She wondered whether if she stood on the bow of a ship, the wind blowing in her hair, she could look half as good as Kate Winslet had. Deciding it was all a pipe dream, she massaged the sudsy shampoo in her hair that had promised to tame her unruly waves.

The shower curtain flipped open. "Don't quit your day job."

"Gah!" Sarah screamed and lost her footing but before she could slip and fall, Matt's strong arms righted her and held her in place.

"Whoa, there."

"Matt?" she said, opening one eye.

"Were you expecting someone else?"

She wiped the suds out of her eyes and stared at Matt. He was naked and in the shower. Shower. With her. Naked. She shouldn't complain, but, dammit, her heart had briefly reconsidered the song's pledge to go on and on.

"Warn me next time. Slam the door or ring a bell. Something."

"I'm sorry, but I was enjoying your moving rendition from *Titanic*. Do you always sing water-related songs in the shower? 'Singing in the Rain', 'Michael Row Your Boat Ashore', that kind of thing?"

She slapped his shoulder. "You almost gave me a heart attack."

"My plan was to give you an orgasm."

"Oh, um—" Before she could say another word, Matt had led her back under the shower head and started rinsing the shampoo out of her hair.

She closed her eyes under the warm water, and luxuriated in the incredible feel of his hands in her hair, fingers gently massaging. Stroking. She was no stranger to his talented hands—she just hadn't thought that talent would extend to shampoo rinses. But oh yes, this was amazing, and she moaned, feeling strangely beautiful when she did. She might not be Kate Winslet, but right now she was one of those shampoo commercial models. The ones with the long dark hair that was shiny and straight.

"Oh God, you're so good at this." *Too*, she might have added, but she didn't want to give him a bigger ego.

"Keep singing," Matt said as he leaned in and briefly nuzzled her ear.

"No. I know I'm not any good. I sing for myself."

"I like it," he said. "Sing for me."

"No." Damn him anyway, and his incredible fingers, which were massaging her in tiny little circles now. She moaned again.

"You have to fight me on everything." He stopped massaging. "Please."

She tried, but her breath hitched when one of his hands dropped to her nipple and tweaked it.

"Yes? What will your heart do?" He grinned at her, the wicked man. His hand slipped down between her thighs and she forgot the words. As in, every word. Ever.

Matt's fingers were exploring every inch of her folds and pressing in all the right places. She opened her legs for him, her hips helplessly gyrating under his touch. The warm shower water pounded in her ears, mixed with the uneven sound of her own heavy breaths coming shorter and faster. Matt swallowed one of her moans with a long and deep kiss. The two of them were wet and slippery and this moment in time might be the single most erotic moment of her life.

"Matt," she gasped, "You…you better stop. Please. I can't… I'm going to…"

"Do it," he said, his voice sounding husky near her ear. "I want you to."

Sarah didn't know what to think or feel anymore. She only knew that she wanted to fight this overwhelming feeling and loss of control. To hold back a moment and stop everything. Stop this emotional monsoon that was Matt. But then he sunk his teeth into her earlobe and she quite possibly sunk her nails into his back. Every random worry and thought was wiped away as in the next second she came completely apart. Her tense legs liquefied under her and she would have fallen to the floor if not for Matt.

But she didn't fall because he was right here holding her up like he'd done far too many times already.

"Mmm. Okay?" He nuzzled her wet hair as he held her tightly in his arms.

She could feel the hard length of him pressing into her, but he was asking whether or not she was okay. He was somehow tender with her even when he teased her mercilessly. How did he do that? Manage to make her feel sexy in a shower? Manage to get her to let go the way he did every time?

She'd been fooled many times before into thinking that sex was love. *Am I doing it again?*

No. She wouldn't. Couldn't.

"I'm fine," she murmured against his neck and laughed a little at how she'd been the opposite of fine a few seconds ago.

Truthfully, she wasn't sure she'd ever be fine again.

Matt shut off the shower and stepped out. He toweled off, then tried to dry Sarah.

She took the towel from him and did it herself. He quirked an eyebrow but she just smiled. "I can do it."

She did, and wrapped a towel around protectively. It was the harsh light in this bathroom, she told herself. Not the most flattering to her body. Matt's body, on the other hand… The lighting didn't hurt his looks and she found herself staring as he draped a towel around his hips. The bulge underneath the towel could not be hidden.

He caught her staring. "You want to help me with that?"

Hoping she didn't look too eager, Sarah nodded. "Please."

Matt chuckled and tugged on her hand. They wound up in his bedroom this time, where he managed to take her towel off in one swift move. She didn't resist, but just stood there underneath his heated gaze. He removed his towel, and then they were once again just two lonely people who were physically bare to each other.

"You're so beautiful." Matt stroked almost reverently down her stomach and to her thighs.

She wanted to believe him but also correct him. She didn't feel beautiful. Women like Emily were beautiful. The women in fashion magazines were beautiful. And perhaps girls who hadn't grown up like Sarah had, angry and bitter. That kind of bitterness eventually made it to the outside. But none of that was any longer the point. The glorious and amazing point was that Matt, somehow against all odds, found Sarah beautiful. She believed him. Those weren't just words to him. Not Matt.

Maybe someday she'd believe it, too. For now that was good enough for her.

Well, that and the way Matt lowered her onto his bed and then wedged his big body between her legs. He kissed her over and over again. Long and deep kisses that left her panting. He had such a handle on this kissing thing that she could subsist on those alone. But there was always more with Matt. Much more in his bag of tricks. He pushed her arms up over her head and urged her to grab hold of the bottom of the headboard. Then he slid down the length of her body, licking as he went. Down the column of her neck to her shoulder, spending time on each nipple sucking and licking as if he were not in a hurry to get anywhere else. As if he had all the time in the world.

She, on the other hand, was in a hurry as she wriggled and squirmed underneath him. Letting go of the headboard with one hand, she placed it on his hip and tried to get him to move where she wanted him to be. Where she needed him to be.

"Patience." He guided her arm back up into place.

"You're killing me here." She tightened her legs around his body and arched toward him.

He groaned and ignored that, sliding farther

down her body to lick her bellybutton. "Good to know."

She moaned. "That isn't helping the not-killing me thing."

"Neither will this," he said and put his tongue and lips on her core.

Sarah gasped and froze. "Matt…please…you really don't have to…"

But he wasn't listening. Instead his tongue teased her as she slowly lost her mind, or what little was left of it. So this was it. This was what it felt like when the last barrier of physical intimacy had been ripped away between two people. Gone. Her body whipped into frenzy, Sarah felt her heart come along too in leaps and quivers. She wanted this man so much. Sarah gripped the headboard until she heard it creak. She fisted the sheets. Lowering her arms, she curled her fingers into his hair, trying not to pull and hoping he would still have most of his hair by the time he was done with her.

A wave of intense pleasure rolled over her with a fierceness that shook her body. She shuddered and came right out of herself, crying out his name. Matt slid up her body, holding her tight as her breathing slowed and she came back down to earth again to rejoin the mere mortals.

When she opened her eyes to take a good look at him, he was propped up on one elbow, smiling down at her. It didn't help the situation. She'd been gasping and panting like a fool who'd just met the Stairmaster, feeling sweaty and flushed, damp hair plastered to her cheeks.

His fingers lightly swept some of the stray hairs off her cheek as he studied her. "You look sweet. As sweet as you taste."

She couldn't help but laugh. Wrecked as she felt, she somehow looked sweet. To him. It wrecked her all over again. He did that to her.

"And I think you liked that."

"Whatever gave you that idea?" She grinned, batting eyelashes at him.

She'd never batted eyelashes in her life. Good-bye prickly, hello bag of feathers. Apparently there was a first time for everything.

"Probably when you said, 'More, Matt. Please.' You're so polite. Always with the please."

She narrowed her eyes at him. "Would you prefer orders, Airman?"

"That depends," he said, rolling her on top of him. "I take my orders from superior officers."

She bent her head and licked from his neck to his abs, her long hair leaving a trail as she went. He tasted salty, and sweaty, and one hundred percent all man. His body tensed, and the hard length under her left no doubt to his physical state. She rose on her knees and stroked him until he groaned and thrust into her hand.

"Get in me," she ordered with a small smile.

"And I take orders from sexy women, too." He

reached over and ripped open a condom with his teeth, which he handed to her.

His hands grasped her hips firmly where he needed her and he thrust into her with a force that made her moan. She took her cues from him, meeting him stroke for stroke, and together they found and moved in a rhythm all their own. Moving above him, her hips gyrating in time with his, she felt fully desired and more powerful than she ever had. She'd been missing this…for too long.

Her body tightened as she rode a peak and this time said his name on a sigh. He continued to thrust into her and held on tight through the release as intense waves of pleasure rocked her world. It was only a moment later, eyes half-mast, when she realized they had ridden this one together.

She rolled off him and he tucked her under his arm. "You slay me each and every time."

For once in her life, the feeling was quite mutual.

CHAPTER THIRTY-ONE

HUNTER FINALLY HAD this parental-unit thing down. Now that he had managed the parents, life was hella easier. Matt was way cooler than Hunter had remembered, and as for Joanne, life was simpler when he kept her completely in the dark. Like a mushroom.

She seemed happier now that she had her special time with Chuck. Hunter had apologized to the guy for the meme, and Chuck had surprised Hunter by actually being pretty cool. For a minor league player.

Before work Joanne made Hunter bacon and eggs, which was so unusual for a weekday that he wondered if he'd forgotten his own birthday.

She set a plate in front of him. "What would you think if Chuck and I made it permanent?"

Hunter took a bite of bacon and considered what Joanne was really saying. Grown-ups always had some secret meaning to every freaking thing they ever said. This could be a trap.

"Permanent?"

"You know. As in Chuck and I get married."

"You're getting *married*?"

"No, not yet. But what would you think about that?"

"I think that would be great. And if you have to move with him, you know, for the baseball stuff, I can always live with Matt and his girlfriend."

Oh, crap. He hadn't meant to say that out loud. Joanne's eyes got dark and small like they did when she was über-pissed.

"Why? Would you rather live with them than me?"

Hunter shoved more food in his mouth and pretended he couldn't chew fast enough to talk. He shook his head.

But Joanne waited him out for more, eyes about to pop out of her head.

Finally he had to stop chewing. "I'm just saying."

Sometimes he really would like to live with Matt and Sarah and it wasn't because of the food. If Matt was cool, Sarah was like the head designer of cool. The CEO. As far as he could tell, she'd never told anyone about the time she'd picked him and Megan up by the lake. The last thing he wanted was to sic Joanne on her.

Joanne went fists on hips. "You're my son, Hunter."

"Like I don't know that?"

"Sure, it's easy for her to be your friend. I don't get to do that. You only have one mother."

"Take a chill pill. I hardly know her. She's not going to be my new Mommy or anything."

Joanne shook her head. She looked like one of those Mylar balloons, hours after the party when he and his friends had pounded all the air out of it. "I'm sorry. That wasn't fair."

Huh? What?

"I really do like Sarah. She's nice and I do appreciate that she's been kind to you."

Hunter didn't speak.

"You and I...we've got to work on our communication. If you would just talk to me more, tell me when stuff is bothering you, and when you think I'm being unfair. Well, maybe that might help."

"Huh. Okay." Hunter wondered if now might be a good time to bring up the Marines.

Probably best not to push his luck. But the formerly rough waters looked smooth for sailing. Tomorrow he'd ask about the Gold's Gym membership, even if he'd already had a decent start on getting in Marine shape, thanks to Megan.

"Do you...have a girlfriend yet?" Joanne wiped the surface of the counter for the bazillionth time, not looking at him.

"No!"

Girlfriend or not, he wasn't going to discuss Megan with his mother. He'd already heard more than he'd ever want to hear from her about "being prepared" and "lasting consequences."

How sometimes all the preparation in the world didn't work. Yeah, yeah, yeah. He got it. He'd been one hell of a surprise to both Joanne and Matt. And he'd decided a long time ago that he'd never be as stupid as his parents.

Joanne finally left for work and Hunter showered and got ready to bike over to The Drip and meet Megan. Week three of this challenge and he didn't know what was going on in the world unless he flipped on the TV. Then all he heard was a bunch of old men yelling at each other. Getting all red in the face. Pointing fingers. Political shit. He liked to hand pick his news. How did people live before the internet? He had no idea who the current top scorer was in online "Halo" or "Call of Duty".

Last week, he'd been watching a movie and recognized an actor he'd seen before but couldn't remember the name of the movie. He couldn't use Google to search his name and find out. His friends still couldn't believe he was "going dark" by choice. He was working toward becoming a Marine with his first big and uncomfortable challenge. In the desert he would not have access to his phone or contact with the rest of the world for weeks at a time. He should have thought of it sooner. It was good training, and he had Megan to thank for it. Not to mention all the push-ups he'd logged at the exercise stations. He was up to one hundred now.

Now all he needed to do was find out why Megan had made the challenge. Unless maybe, as Trent believed, she was only doing this because she had a crush on Hunter. She'd figured out a way to monopolize his time and Hunter was so slow on the uptake that he hadn't caught on to it yet. But he didn't believe that. Megan had something else going on, and just didn't trust Hunter enough to tell him yet.

No sooner had Hunter locked his bicycle outside The Drip than Megan met him with their coffees.

"Here." She handed over his usual caramel macchiato.

It was iced like he liked it with plenty of caramel dripping down the sides. As usual Megan had put a straw in for him, only leaving the top part with paper so he could easily slip it off. She was super sweet like that.

Hunter fished a five-dollar bill out of his pants pocket and handed it to Megan.

She put out her hand to stop him. "No. It's my treat."

"Why?"

"To celebrate. Because you won."

He must not have heard Megan right. "Wait. I won? What did I win?"

"The challenge, dummy! You win because I give up."

"No way. You're gonna *let* me win? Just like that?"

"It's a long story, but I have to check on something and I need to go online to do it."

So the challenge was over and he'd won. Why didn't he feel like a winner? Probably because it was too easy. Megan was giving up on him.

"That's bullshit. I don't want to win like this."

"Sooner or later, one of us had to win. Might as well be now." She whipped out her phone and took a seat at one of the outdoor umbrella tables.

"This better be important." He took a seat next to her and tried to look over her shoulder. "Important enough to lose."

"I don't know why you care." She was flipping through Facebook. "Oh wow. It's true. My friend Lily changed her status from 'single' to 'it's complicated' because she had one date with Peter. *One* date!"

Great. So Megan had given up for something really important and life-changing. Good to know. "You never told me why *you* were doing this challenge."

She put her phone away. "You never asked."

"I thought—you mean all I had to do was ask?"

She slid him a look full of words, but didn't say one of them out loud. *Dayum.* Girls were a mystery wrapped in an enigma all right. He was going to have to ask Matt to give up all he had on phase three.

"Okay. I'm asking. Why?"

She squirmed in her seat and wouldn't look at him. "Because I like you. Okay?"

"Sure. I like you, too."

"No. I mean—I like you like…a lot."

He didn't say anything to that, wondering if they were talking about the same thing. With girls, one never knew. She probably liked him as a really good friend. There was like and there was *like*. He was about to ask for a Webster's Dictionary definition but she started crying.

Shit. Why would a girl tell him she liked him and start crying? He'd done something wrong, obviously. "Oh, hey, hey. Why are you crying?"

"Because I'm so stupid."

"You're not stupid." *I am. The first pretty girl tells me that she likes me and I can't say a freaking word.*

And it was weird, but even though another tear slipped out of Megan's watery eyes, Hunter didn't scoot away. Instead, his arm moved like it wasn't even a part of his body and settled around her quivering shoulders.

"When I heard that you'd gone dark, I figured maybe we could do it together. So you wouldn't be so alone and all. I was trying to figure out how to tell you that, and then I saw you online."

"Yeah, I remember that."

"Stupid, huh? Why would anybody do that on purpose?"

"It's a challenge, and you did it. You didn't even have to. It was really nice of you to do that."

"Well, I wanted to help you. And you want to be a Marine. I'm pretty patriotic too, you know."

"Yeah, and that's…you know, that's great."

This had worked out pretty well for him because he really liked Megan. More than he ever thought he could like a girl. Should he kiss her now right in front of The Drip? Or maybe he should wait until she stopped crying, because if someone walked out they might think his kiss had made her cry. Maybe then he'd get arrested or something and what would that do to his military career?

Plus, Joanne would be pissed and he didn't think Matt would be thrilled about it either.

This was his first kiss and he wanted to know what the hell he was doing. How was he to know he'd have a chance this soon? He should have been more like a Marine and planned better. Anticipated. Instead he just sat there and kept his arm around her shoulders, hugging her a little bit. Megan scooted closer to him, turned her face and pressed it into his neck, which made him extremely grateful that he'd hit the shower this morning. He thought he smelled pretty good, and dang, so did she.

"Do you want to kiss me?" Megan asked against his neck.

Holy shit, how did he ever get this freaking lucky? "Yeah, but you're crying."

Megan pulled back and reached into her backpack. She pulled out a packet of tissues and a mirror and set them on the table. She sniffed a couple of times into one of the tissues, and then grabbed her mirror. Holding the mirror, she rubbed at her eyes with another tissue. The makeup she wore on her eyes wiped off and all he could see were brilliant blue eyes the color of the ocean.

This was a lot of planning and effort for one simple kiss. He hoped he could deliver the goods.

She finally turned to him, smiling. Ready. He leaned in. She leaned in. They met in the middle and kissed. It was a sweet kiss. Megan's lips were soft and smooth. His first thought was that she tasted like caramel. And he really loved caramel.

CHAPTER THIRTY-TWO

HUNTER HAD JUST killed his second Nazi when he noticed Trent online again.

Jarhead2018: Hey. Not grounded anymore?

StarWarz: Yep. Was going crazy.

Jarhead2018: Me too, but it was a good challenge. I might do it again.

StarWarz: Sure, I would too if I got a girlfriend out of it.

Jarhead2018: Megan? Yeah, she's cool. I guess she's my girlfriend.

StarWarz: Dude, she's so hawt. I would totally tap that.

Jarhead2018: Calm down asswipe.

StarWarz: Ha! Okay, I get it. You already totally have.

Jarhead2018: Shut. Up.

StarWarz: What does that mean? Yeah? No?

Jarhead2018: It means shut up.

StarWarz: I'm just saying hurry up before she hooks up with some other guy. I mean, Megan is pretty hot, so you know. She's been around. Tommy told me.

What the hell?

Jarhead2018: Don't talk about her.

StarWarz: Okay dude, but if she asks, are you going to say no?

Jarhead2018: Am I stupid?

It wasn't like Hunter didn't think about sex 24/7. Wondered what it would be like, and whether or not he'd be any good at it. Wondered what it even meant to be good at it. The problem was that his parents had drilled it into him that if he had sex he better be ready to be a daddy. And he'd better be a grown-up. His mother had never put it any other way. Want sex? You better be ready for a baby because accidents happened. He'd then sat through fifth grade class and found out all about how to have sex and avoid having a kid. But because his mother had also signed off on the class, she sat him down afterward and explained all about the failure rates of birth control.

As a result, Hunter felt like he knew more about sex than most of his friends and classmates. He didn't giggle about it and make disgusting jokes about blow jobs like Trent did. It wasn't this big and taboo secret to him. Sex was something he figured he'd do someday soon when he was a grown-up. He wouldn't use just one birth control. Not two either but three. Maybe every single one of them. A little over two years and counting. If he could go to war at eighteen, he was sure in hell going to have sex. And he'd be good at it, too. Whatever that meant.

Hunter wrapped up this round of killings. In a minute, he had to get ready for Joanne to pick him up and take him over to Matt's for the weekend. His cell phone dinged and he grabbed it, wondering if Matt was texting to ask what he wanted for dinner. But instead of a text from Matt there was an anonymous text from a number he didn't recognize. A photo of Megan popped up. Her school picture, but someone had made a meme out of it.

Text scrolled across the top of the photo: Head Ho of Fortune Valley High.

Jarhead2018: Did you do this? I'll kill you!

StarWarz: Do what? What happened?

Jarhead2018: The photo of Megan! Don't play dumb.

StarWarz: Dude, I have no idea. What photo?

Jarhead2018: You better not be lying.

Trent had made the meme of Chuck, so it made sense he'd make this one, too. Only problem was, Trent had created the one of Chuck to make Hunter laugh. And Trent had to know this one wouldn't make Hunter laugh at all. Plus Trent was not a genius who would send it anonymously. And he couldn't have sent it from his own phone, either, since Hunter would recognize the number.

A closer look showed that he wasn't the only one who'd received this text. There was a string of numbers in a group text. *Shit!* He recognized Megan's number in the bunch. Had she seen it yet? If she had, this would suck so hard.

Hunter texted Megan separately: Hey.

I can't talk right now.

Why not? You busy?

Yeah. You know how busy I am. I'm the head ho.

Crap!

That's BS. You're not.

Everyone is going to believe it.

I don't.

You will. Goodbye. And it was a nice kiss.

Wait. You going somewhere?

She didn't respond, nor did she to the next ten text messages he sent. Hunter threw the phone down, wondering how he could get ahold of the coward who sent that text. But he had bigger problems right now. If Megan wouldn't respond to his texts, he was going to have to find her.

He left the house before Joanne got home from work, grabbing his bicycle. She definitely wouldn't understand the need for a slight delay in going over to Matt's house. And if she figured out it had anything to do with a girl, she would ask so many questions he'd be sitting in his room answering them until next year.

When he biked over to Megan's house she wasn't home, but her little sister said she went to the lake. The lake was going to take him at least thirty more minutes on a bicycle. Which meant either way he looked at this, he was going to be late. Whatever. This was important. If nothing else, Matt would understand. Hadn't he told him that he had to have a girl's back? He headed toward the lake, and finally arrived as the sun started its slip down the horizon.

When he climbed off his bike and walked it toward the dock at the lake, he found Megan sitting there, her feet dangling in the water. Shoulders shaking. Great. Hunter ambled over, hands stuck in his pockets, wondering if his arm would magically make its way around Megan's shoulders or if he would have to force it to this time.

Hunter squatted next to her. "Hey."

"You found me." Megan glanced up at him with red-rimmed eyes. "I really didn't think you would."

"Why wouldn't you answer my texts?"

"Sorry." She went back to looking at the water, and not him.

"It's okay." Megan had to be embarrassed about the photo, even if she had nothing to be ashamed of.

"I don't know why people think I'm a ho. I

made out with Tommy once and when I broke up with him he started talking crap about me. I thought Julie was my friend, but she got jealous when she heard about me and you. Remember I told you she likes you? I bet she sent the stupid picture."

"I don't care what she thinks, and believe me, she's probably going to get grounded for sending that photo."

"Yeah, but I'm going to have to tell my parents about it and they'll freak out and probably ground *me*."

Hunter thought about his mom, and how much it must have hurt to see that photo of the guy she was crazy about. That Hunter had anything to do with it had probably made it a thousand times worse. It would be like Hunter finding out that Trent, his best friend, had sent the meme of Megan.

Matt was right in that this was just not funny.

"You didn't do anything wrong."

She nodded, a tear slipping down her cheek. "But I don't know if they'll believe me."

He understood that. "Well, okay, then we can handle this."

"We?"

"Yeah, of course I'm going to help you. I mean, you're my girlfriend."

"I am?" She smiled and wow, she had a great smile.

"Yeah, I mean, but only if you want to be."

"Yeah, I'd like that." A light breeze kicked up and she shivered next to him.

"You can't stay here all night. It gets hella cold near the water." Hunter shrugged out of his navy blue Windbreaker and laid it on Megan's shoulders.

"That's all right." She shrugged into the jacket. "I just want to stay here a little bit longer and look at the water."

What was he going to do? Tell Megan she should hurry up and look because he needed to get home before his own shit hit the fan? She would just tell him to go.

But he couldn't leave her all alone.

SARAH WALKED TO the sliding glass door where Shackles waited patiently to be let out again. This time she followed him outside and opened up the shed. Her favorite place these days. Good memories here. She'd been painting minutes before she and Matt made love for the first time. There'd been a shift in everything since that day.

And she'd rediscovered a part of herself that for years she'd stuffed down.

She was fully capable of loving someone, even if she'd tried hard not to. It turned out that the man had to be someone who she could fully trust with her body. Her mind. And until Matt, she'd never found a man so deserving of her trust. Who would give her his undivided loyalty and always have her back. That he would be her brother's best friend, a man she'd learned also had an over-the-top loyalty to his friends and family, shouldn't surprise her.

Sarah couldn't get Matt's words out of her head. *You could do this*. It had been too many years since anyone had believed in her. Since she'd even considered making a living with her art. She understood that most artists had to supplement their income in other ways, and she thought she'd done that well enough with the forensic sketching. But she hadn't pictured that it would slowly drain all the passion from her art. All the creativity. That she would no longer find the time, or crave it. That she'd doubt her abilities more and more each day, raising the standard to a place she could never hope to reach. Because maybe on some level she'd long ago decided she didn't deserve to be happy.

But Matt believed she could do it, and it filled her with a small amount of hope that maybe she could find more time to do not just the work she had to do, but the work she loved to do.

Sarah fished out the canvas from where she had it hidden in the back for privacy. It was her first effort at people in too long. Real people, not just the alleged criminals she'd never laid eyes on but nevertheless had to put a face to. If she were going to start drawing people again, she'd decided to start with two of her favorite people in the world. She'd sketched out their profiles in pencil first, and would later add in the colors.

She spent the next several quiet minutes adding depth to Matt's eyes. Then did the same with Hunter's. Putting pencil to paper had driven home how much Hunter looked like Matt. Same eyes and lips. Same hairline. Only Hunter's jawline was not as pronounced as Matt's, at least not yet. And he had his mother's Patrician-like nose.

Sarah worked until she lost too much natural light. The sun began to set which meant Matt was at least an hour late. Shackles nudged her leg, wanting back inside.

"All right." Sarah put down the brush. "I'm sure you're hungry."

No sooner had Sarah stepped in the house, than Matt flew through the front door, worry etched in every angle of his face.

"Hunter is missing."

"What do you mean, *missing*?" Sarah asked.

Joanne had come in right behind Matt, which suddenly lent the situation a heightened level of concern. She was also obviously worried, her normal pasted-on smile for Sarah gone. Matt walked right past Sarah without another word, and straight to the spare bedroom Hunter had been staying in.

"Missing, as in not home when I came to pick him up to bring him over. His bicycle is gone, too," Joanne said.

It sounded as though Matt were in the bedroom turning everything upside down. Shackles had followed him in the room and yipped for his attention.

"Did you call his friends?" Sarah asked.

"No, sorry, I didn't think of that. Of course I called! His friend's *parents*. Because his friends might want to cover for him. But none of them had seen Hunter." Joanne's eyes followed Matt as he came out of the room. "Anything?"

Matt shook his head.

"I'm sorry, but have either of you thought this could be a big misunderstanding?" Sarah wasn't a parent, but she was well acquainted with her mother, who had overreacted to everything for years.

"It's not a misunderstanding. He knew he was supposed to come over here today and exactly when I'd be bringing him."

"Did you look at some of the places where he might hang out?" Sarah asked.

"We went to The Drip and the movie theater. All the fast food places within walking distance," Matt said. "The high school track."

"How about the lake?" Sarah asked.

"The *lake*?" Joanne asked. "Why would he be at the lake?"

Two sets of eyes were trained on Sarah at once. Matt's always intelligent eyes were curious, attentive. Riveted to hers.

"I-isn't that one of the places he usually hangs out?" Sarah tried to keep her voice even. Calm.

Hard to do when she felt like the sole target of a firing squad. She'd done nothing wrong, but a twinge of doubt slid down her spine. She should have probably told Matt about the day she'd picked up Hunter and his friend at the lake, but it hadn't seemed important at the time. Instead it had felt like maybe Hunter had reached out to her, and she'd felt good about that simple act.

"No," Joanne said, drawing the single word out several syllables.

Matt wasn't speaking, his eyebrows knit together. He was waiting patiently for more. Sarah heard him loud and clear, even if he hadn't said a single word. *Tell me.*

"That's where I picked him up about a week ago. Him and his friend Megan, when her bike broke down, and they needed a ride home. Matt was on a flight at the time. He said you were at work, Joanne, and he didn't want to bother you."

"Megan who? Who the hell is Megan?" Joanne screeched. "There's a girl? Why do I not know this? Did you hear that, Matt? I wonder if he already has her pregnant."

"Calm down," Matt spit out.

His attention became riveted to Sarah, as if they were the only two people in the room. "Why didn't you tell *me*?"

"That he was with a girl? They were riding

bikes together, just friends, I thought. Innocent and harmless. It didn't seem important. And… and he asked me not to say anything." That sounded so incredibly stupid right now. At the time it seemed a small and harmless way to bond with Hunter.

"And you listened to him," Matt said, a flicker of anger in his eyes.

And as many times as she'd frustrated him and pissed him off, this was different. It was cold.

She fixed her eyes on Matt's. "I think you know I have a unique experience when it comes to this kind of thing, and that's not who Hunter is."

"He's a teenage boy. Other than that, you don't know who he is."

"Okay, maybe I don't," Sarah said, voice shaking. Matt was right, of course, and she hated that. "But maybe *you* don't know who he is, either. You seemed convinced he's just like you. He might look like you, but at least give him a chance before you're judge, jury and executioner."

But Matt simply shook his head. "He's *my* responsibility, Sarah. Not yours. You know better than anyone that I'm doing my damnedest to raise him and keep him from making the huge mistakes I did. I can't have you interfering and undermining me. Keeping important information from me. Keeping *anything* from me when it comes to him."

"Matt, I—"

"No." He pulled away, dragging a hand through his hair. "I don't want to hear it right now."

Joanne cleared her throat. "If you two will excuse me?"

Both Sarah and Matt turned, as if they'd almost forgotten Joanne was still in the room.

"I suggest we take a drive to the lake," Joanne said from the front door.

Matt wouldn't look at Sarah, and she felt the darkness of that, as if the sun had set one evening in one sudden and swift moment. Not slipped down the mountain crest slowly, but disappeared in an instant. Within seconds both he and Joanne were out the door to find their son.

Shackles, who had been following Matt from room to room, now barked at the door. Then he sat, and looked from Sarah to the door and back again. As if to ask *Are you going after him, or should I?*

Ha! "Neither one of us is going after him."

Shackles whined.

Sarah ignored that and went around the house opening up all the windows. The heat wave finally gone, nights had grown noticeably cooler, and the twilight air drifted through her open windows cooling off both the house and her temper. She'd been in a lot of arguments with Matt, but this one cut the deepest. He'd made it clear that she'd disappointed him. And most of all, that she had no role or place in his life. His biggest job was that of a single father, and he didn't need her help. Didn't want or need it.

But worse than all that was the fact that for the first time in a long while, she'd proved she was still too anxious to be loved and wanted. Again. She'd become too needy and let her emotions rule the day. And here she thought she'd been past all that ridiculous neediness and desperation.

But no. Not fully past it. She'd been the one to promise not to fall in love, but she'd done that, too. Fallen for someone who might not be ready to share every facet of his life with her. And now she wanted to hide. Burrow deep under the bed-covers and hibernate. Some bears hibernated in the winter. Why couldn't she hibernate the rest of this summer? Instead, she blinked the tears out of her eyes and glanced around the room, noting its physical perfection. No more nail holes in the wall. Matt had removed every one of them from her nail gun near-disaster. The walls were painted, windows framed and blinds back up in place.

In the kitchen, the new cabinet doors were up. New flooring: check. Everything in Dad's house was as perfect as it could ever be, considering perfect was an illusion.

Even if her heart hurt, and despite his obvious flaws, she couldn't get around the truth. She'd fallen hard for Matt. She loved the way he was so devoted to his son. Loved that he'd do anything for those he loved. Including her, at one time. But real love required tough decisions. Sacrifice. And tonight, they'd both let each other down. What's more, Matt was right. Life with the father of a teenage boy was never going to be easy or simple. It would mean coming in second all the time. Not like he hadn't warned her but unfortunately her heart had other ideas.

Sarah's phone buzzed and her heart jumped, hoping it was Matt calling to apologize. Instead, she recognized the number of the Realtor she'd been speaking to for a while.

"Hi, Jenny."

"Hey, Sarah. I dropped by the other day to put up the sign like we discussed—"

Sarah had forgotten to call her to postpone the listing for the third time. "I forgot to call you, but I'm going to need a little more time." Like possibly forever.

"I understand. That's what your…um, your… the gentleman I ran into outside said."

"Who, Matt?"

"Yes, Matt Conner! Thank you. That *was* him. I hardly recognized him and I've been trying to place him since that day. We went to school together, you know. A long time ago and I don't think he knew I was alive. Anyway, I'm not sure what he has to do with any of this but he didn't seem happy I was there."

"Why? What did he say?"

"He said you weren't ready, and he didn't look too happy."

Sarah didn't speak for a moment. The wheels were turning, as she wondered whether she'd disappointed Matt first. He might have been under the mistaken impression that she'd recently talked to Jenny, when that had in fact been weeks ago. The message he'd received loud and clear was that nothing had changed between them. She still had plans to sell and move. But the reality was that she'd been too busy falling in love with him, as she'd promised not to do, to remember a conversation she'd had with her Realtor a while ago. Staying here had nothing to do with the house, and everything to do with Matt.

"Sarah? The listing won't go up on the MLS for another couple of weeks, but I was in the neighborhood. I brought the sign with me so I figured I'd put it up while I was there."

"You brought the *sign*?"

"Yes, we talked about this."

Sarah needed more time. To talk to Mom. Quit her job in Fort Collins. Sell her condo. Spend more time with her art. Tell Matt she'd accidentally fallen in love with him.

"I promise to call you next week. You have my undying oath that I will never, and I do mean *never* sell this house through any other real estate agent. Even after your contract expires. Amen and all that."

"But…" Jenny let the word sit alone, the sentence unfinished.

Sarah took in a deep breath. "There's a teeny, tiny, miniscule possibility that I might not… ever…sell."

"I thought you had to sell."

"Yes, true. There is that. You have that going for you, so don't give up!"

Jenny sighed. Poor woman had probably heard it all by now. Buyers backing out because the price was too high, sellers backing out because the price was too low. Greed did crazy things to people, and Sarah got that. But this wasn't about greed. She had a real reason to stay, one grounded in reality. This was her father's house, dammit, and it was perfect now. She just. Couldn't. Leave. There was so much to do. She'd come here in hopes of changing her life, but never thought it would mean staying. Starting over. Never thought it would mean falling in love with a man harder than she'd ever fallen before. Which meant that she had a million reasons to stay now, and only one reason to go.

"Sarah…do you happen to know if Matt's single?" Jenny asked.

"Yes, and he absolutely is not."

She hung up with Jenny, then dialed Emily. "Hey, can you take me to Fort Collins tonight?"

CHAPTER THIRTY-THREE

MATT FORCED HIMSELF to drive calmly to the lake, not easy to do with the scene that had just played out. He gripped the steering wheel tighter as Sarah's words played on repeat in his head.

Give him a chance before you're judge, jury and executioner.

Had he done that? Maybe he'd been so focused on Hunter not making the same mistakes, that he'd failed to see his son. Whether or not he had, it hurt that Sarah would keep this, hell, *anything* from him. But then again, she already had one foot out the door. She'd proved that already. It was patently clear that all she wanted from him was physical, and that should work out fine since it was all he could give her. Too bad it wasn't okay with him. Not okay at all.

As they approached one of the docks, Matt switched his headlights on and chose not to respond to Joanne's incessant chatter.

But when she took a breath, he used it to say something it had taken far too long to say. "Don't worry, we'll find him. It will be okay."

"I hope so. He's been so difficult lately. Maybe it's because of me and Chuck. Maybe I shouldn't have—"

"No. You deserve to be happy. We both do."

She didn't reply and there was a long beat of silence between them.

Matt broke the silence. "I wish I'd been around more, for both of you, and I'm sorry that I wasn't. Just because you and I were never in love doesn't mean that we couldn't have been better friends. For Hunter's sake."

"I thought we did pretty good. Better than most."

"Maybe. You did a great job raising him. None of this is your fault. It's called…being a teenager."

"Yeah." She sighed. "I guess we both know a little about that."

His gaze scanned the horizon for any kind of figure as he drove slowly and methodically around the lakeside. It wasn't long before he spied two lone figures walking over the crest of a hill toward them. One tall, the other markedly smaller. He'd recognize his son's long lean form anywhere. Walking his bicycle, leaning forward like he might against a strong wind.

"Let me handle this," Matt said to Joanne, then left the truck running and walked toward Hunter. "Everything okay?"

"Megan needs a ride home," Hunter said.

Megan walked her bicycle, just behind Hunter.

She was dressed in jeans and a Warriors T-shirt. Pale blonde hair up in a ponytail. The only exceptional note about her being the fact her face and eyes were fairly puffy as though she'd spent some time crying.

Bad breakup? Bad news? No. That was you, asshole, not your son.

"No problem." Matt took the bike and picked it up by the handlebars. He took a moment to access the situation from Megan's perspective. "You okay?"

She glanced up at him and gave him a crooked smile. "Yeah. Thanks for the ride, Mr. Conner. I really appreciate it. It started to get dark and Hunter didn't want me to stay by myself."

Matt set the bicycle down, opened up his tailgate and both he and Hunter hauled the ten-speed in. Hunter threw his own in next to it. A few minutes later they had dropped off Megan at her parents' home in a gated community of Fortune, and Hunter hopped out of the backseat to pull her bicycle out. He walked Megan to her doorstep.

When he climbed back in the truck, a gaping silence filled the inside of Matt's cab.

Joanne was the first to speak. "Is Megan your girlfriend? I only learned about her today when Sarah told us she'd given you two a ride from the lake."

"I asked her not to say anything about that." Hunter scowled.

Matt pulled out onto the quiet residential street. "And she didn't. Until no one could find you tonight."

Joanne swiveled in her seat to face Hunter. "What makes you think it's okay to ask another adult to keep secrets from your own mother?"

"It's not a secret! But if I'd told you anything about Megan, you would have freaked out. She and I were just friends."

"Well, you don't have to be someone's girlfriend to get pregnant, Mister!"

"Stop." Matt spoke through a clenched jaw, calling on every one of his steel nerves.

He'd been in far more stressful situations and he could handle this one with his damned hands tied behind his back. That's what he told himself as he drove Joanne back to her house, along with the fact that Sarah was right and both he and Joanne had overreacted to the situation. They'd done that based on their own unpleasant experiences, without realizing that Hunter would make his own choices. Not that Hunter didn't owe them an explanation, but Sarah had been correct in that they should have at least heard him out first.

Trust was a two-way street. He could only speak for himself, but he hadn't trusted Hunter enough.

"I missed my flight," Joanne went on. "So I hope you're happy."

"That doesn't mean Hunter isn't spending the weekend with me." Matt spoke firmly.

He was finished being on Joanne's time schedule. Guilt notwithstanding, he was also done being her on-call babysitter. He was beginning to want a lot more time with Hunter and weekends weren't going to be enough.

Joanne didn't speak for a long moment, only slid him a surprised look.

When Matt parked in front of her home, she hopped out of the truck and opened the passenger door for Hunter. "Let's go inside and talk."

Matt didn't say a word. He simply stared straight ahead and waited for Hunter to make the call. He found he would be okay with either outcome, but Hunter had to know that he had options. Two parents who were there for him full time. Not one full-time and one part-time parent. Not one who stood by happy to take whatever scraps Hunter would give him of his time. Matt hoped he'd proved that he wanted to share his life with Hunter.

Hunter didn't move and his eyes shifted between Matt and Joanne.

It killed Matt to see Hunter so obviously torn, but Matt wasn't willing to make it easy for either one of them anymore. He wasn't dropping back or out or running any longer. It would have to be up to Hunter to decide.

"I promise to listen this time," Joanne said quietly from the curb. "Remember I told you that we needed to work on our communication? This is what I meant. If you'll start being honest with me, I'll meet you halfway."

Pained by the vulnerability in Joanne's voice, Matt didn't speak. He would have to trust his son to do the right thing now, too.

"Um," Hunter finally said. "I guess I'll go with Mom tonight and I'll see you tomorrow, Dad."

"Sounds good. See you tomorrow," Matt said. "Count on it."

CHAPTER THIRTY-FOUR

MATT DROVE THE rest of the way to Sarah's house
and it wasn't until he pulled onto her street that he
realized he'd forgotten all about dinner. The cold
pizza sat in the backseat of his truck, untouched.

Sarah.

One more person he hadn't trusted enough. Oh
yeah, this was bad. So bad.

Speaking of overreacting. He could be an ass.
Too many years of being alone, guarded and un-
trusting. No woman had ever had the patience to
stick it out for long. He'd have to call this mistake
part of the perils of being relationship-obtuse. Of
being the single dad of a teenager trying to manage life, and…deeply loving a woman.

The realization astounded him.

A little slow on the uptake, aren't we?

This wasn't part of the master plan, but had
anything in his life ever gone according to a plan?
Other than the missions he flew on behalf of the
United States Air Force, he'd have to say exactly
zip. Never planned on having a son at the age
of seventeen and yet it had been one of the best
things to ever happen to him. Hadn't planned on

going into the Air Force, either, but he'd met his best friends in the entire world there. Stone. Levi.

And hadn't planned on falling for Sarah Mcallister, but she'd somehow entranced him with her pantsuits and her hair clips and her...heart.

He loved the way she so obviously adored Stone and Emily. Had even made room in her home and her heart for Hunter, simply because she was a loving and brave woman, who despite feeling hurt and abandoned by both family and so-called friends in her past, had been willing to take a chance. On all of them. The entire town of Fortune. She'd slowly let go of the bitterness so that anyone watching could see inside her heart.

Matt picked up Shackles near the front door and after the dog had tongued him a couple of times, Matt headed to Sarah's bedroom door, not planning a damned thing he would say. This had to come from his heart. And with any luck, he wasn't too late for the best thing to happen to him in a long time.

The bedroom door was closed and when he tried it, empty. No Sarah.

She wasn't in the shed, either, but instead there was a sketch on her canvas which managed to both sucker punch him and take his breath away. He stepped closer, and picked up the canvas.

The landscape of El Toro she'd started was no longer a landscape. She'd taken his advice and added people. Not just any people, but Matt and Hunter, standing side by side at the foot of the hillside. She had Hunter's teenage "too cool to be bothered" expression dialed. His own rather muted and aloof look surprised him, and it killed him to think that's what she saw in his eyes. Distance. A protective layer she didn't think she'd reached because he hadn't let her know that she had. Hell, hadn't even fully realized it himself until tonight.

Idiot.

She was so talented that even he, knowing next to nothing about art, could see it. And whether she stayed in Fortune or went back to Fort Collins, as a real friend, he wasn't going to be able to let her resume a life sketching criminals. Too big a waste of talent.

He reached for his phone and dialed Sarah, who didn't pick up her phone. Considered leaving a message, then hung up because he'd likely see her before she listened to it.

He dialed Stone next. "Hey. Have you heard from Sarah?"

"They got there all right. Emily checked in with me a few minutes ago."

"Got where all right? Where did they go? Wedding stuff?"

There was a long pause on the other end of the line. "Fort Collins."

Matt nearly dropped the phone. "Colorado?"

"Yeah. I thought you of all people would know. Don't you two basically live together?"

The long pause was on Matt's end this time.

Stone snorted. "What the hell did you do?"

Emily would be back, that much was certain. But Matt wasn't so sure about Sarah anymore. Once back in Fort Collins and her life there, she might decide to stay. She'd already called the damned Realtor, which should tell him something. He could give up on this whole thing between them right now and get back to his mundane and boring life.

But he wasn't going to do that.

"Nothing. But I'm an ass."

"Ah, you poor sucker." Stone laughed into the phone. "Now you know what it's like. Finally. Is it something you can fix?"

Matt pinched the bridge of his nose. The reality was that Sarah was far more important to him than he'd let her know. Yet. He could wait until she got back, *if* she returned, and tell her once and for all how he felt about her.

Or he could do something he'd never done before and shock the hell out of both of them.

"Matt?" Stone was still on the other end of the line, no doubt waiting for an answer.

"Yeah. I can fix this, but I'm going to need a plane."

SARAH HAD ONE more reason to be impressed with Emily Parker.

First, she could fly a plane and the girl didn't

even look scared while doing it. But more significantly, she was the kind of friend who came running when called. No questions asked. Sarah had no idea what she'd interrupted on a Friday night—and didn't want to know—but Emily had shown up to the house within minutes. Driven Sarah to the airport, filed a flight report and flown both of them to a small regional airport outside of Fort Collins.

It wasn't until after they'd landed that Emily asked her first question about the trip. "Are you coming back with me, or is Matt going to hate me for this?"

"He won't hate you. I have something to do, and I felt like I needed to do it in person."

Emily took her pilot's headset off. "Does this have to do with another man?"

"It has to do with living my life full tilt. Like you do. And like my brother always has. I just realized we don't do any favors when we're less than honest with the people we love."

"Gotcha! I'm so totally on board with this."

"And I have to do this if I'm going to be able to stay in Fortune with a clear conscience."

Emily gave a wide smile. "If? You're thinking about staying?"

Sarah nodded and Emily, who was such a hugger, reached across the pilot seat and squeezed Sarah.

"Now don't get too excited. I still have a lot to

figure out. I don't know where I'll go from here, but the truth? I love Matt with all my heart. I just haven't told him that yet."

"This is so great! I *knew* you two were a good match. I don't want to brag, but I saw it right away. It took you a while."

Sarah would go ahead and let Emily believe that, despite the fact that Sarah hadn't really stopped thinking about Matt since he'd first approached her at the bar and given her the "ready for anything" smile.

"As long as this has a happy ending, I don't care what you put me through," Emily said.

"It has a happy ending." She hoped.

"Should I wait for you here?" Emily asked, as together they walked off the airport tarmac.

"I'm sure my mom would love to see you again."

Besides, Sarah needed reinforcements. Support. It was a good thing Sarah brought Emily along too, because once they took an Uber from the airport to Mom's house, she wasn't home.

"Hello there," Mom's next door neighbor called out. "She's at her friend Patty's house. I think they're having a wedding shower for Patty's daughter."

"Thanks, Mrs. Rivers."

So Sarah would crash a wedding shower. Why not? The timing wasn't perfect, and for the first time Sarah considered maybe she should have called ahead first. She could have prepared Mom for the seriousness of this talk. The Uber driver took them to Patty's house on the other side of town, and when Sarah spotted Mom's car parked nearby she let the driver go.

"This is fun," Emily said. "I've never crashed a shower before. Maybe I'll get some good ideas for mine."

Sarah walked toward the sounds of the booming music. The closer they got to the house, the louder the music became. It was Justin Timberlake's "SexyBack" coming through what sounded like surround-sound woofers. Five or six or possibly ten loud knocks later and the door was finally opened by a wild-haired woman with a flushed face.

"We're bringing sexy back!"

Sarah did a double take, then swore under her breath. *"Mom?"*

"Sarah!" Mom grabbed her in a bear hug and squeezed. "You're back!"

Then she practically shoved her aside to grab Emily. "Anyone else here? Stone?"

"We came alone," Sarah shouted to be heard over the loud music.

Mom waved them inside, past the group of women in the living room ogling at a gyrating Channing Tatum look-alike taking his pants off.

"I don't think I can have a shower like this," Emily stared, wide-eyed.

No. Stone would have the guy's nuts on a platter.

Inside the relative quiet of a back bedroom filled with Elvis memorabilia, Mom shut the door and turned to Sarah. "So how was your trip?"

Somehow she'd stepped into the twilight zone. Her mother was wearing jeans and a bright red top with a plunging neckline.

Where to begin? "What the hell is going on?"

"It's Tutti's wedding shower. And we never thought she'd get married, you know? Because of the irritable bowel. You know, all that uncontrollable farting. But now that she stopped eating wheat, no more gas! Patty just went all out. The Channing Tatum look-alike just sort of happened."

"I can see why that sort of 'happened' but isn't this a little much?" *Especially for you*, Sarah wanted to add. What about her raging blood pressure? Male strippers could not be good for a sixty-year-old's blood pressure.

"Not at all. Tutti deserves it. You should see the cake from the erotica bakery. What a hoot! Plus it's chocolate."

Emily giggled behind her hand.

"Okay, who are you and what you have done with my mother?"

CHAPTER THIRTY-FIVE

SARAH'S MOTHER SMILED and patted her hair, done in a new style, which made her look a little like a Cher retrospective. Every gray hair dyed. And were those hair extensions?

"All right, so maybe I've had a little too much to drink."

"A *little*?"

"It's the mimosas. They taste like sparkling orange juice. I can't resist." She patted Emily's lap. "Would you like one, honey?"

"No thanks. I'm flying."

Mom thought that was hilarious, apparently, given by the way she slapped her knee and snorted. "How many people can say that?"

"I need to talk to you. I'm staying in Fortune for good," Sarah said.

"Then why are you here?"

"I wanted to tell you in person."

Mom frowned. "Honey, have you checked the price of gasoline lately?"

"Emily offered and this is important!" Sarah took a seat in a blue velvet chair, and removed the large gold lamé Elvis-shaped pillow.

"Okay," Emily said, "I'm going to go out there and see about that chocolate cake." She shut the bedroom door.

"You're not coming home. Just as I suspected. I knew it. It's because of Matt, isn't it? And I've got all these great possibilities lined up for you right here in Fort Collins. I really hadn't thought of you as the girl who chases the guy anymore. You're too pretty for that."

"I'm not chasing him."

"But you're moving to Fortune because of him."

"Not *just* because of him."

Mom cocked her head, but didn't say a word.

"Okay, maybe it's mostly because of him, but there's a lot more to it."

"Has he *asked* you to stay?"

"No, not exactly, but that doesn't matter."

"Oh, Sarah." Mom sighed and tsk-tsked.

"Look, you've got to stop thinking of me as that teenager that messed up. I'm grateful for everything you did for me back then, believe me, but something happened today that made me realize that sometimes we just get stuck in old patterns. We get an opinion about who we are, what we deserve, and it's tough to move past that."

"But—"

Sarah held up her hand. "It's even harder when the people we love can't trust us to make better decisions. I've been making better choices for years now, but sometimes I think you still see me as that promiscuous teenage girl."

"Shhhhhh. My Lord, Sarah, do you want everyone to hear?"

"Over that music? I don't think so." Sarah shook her head. "It was a long time ago, and I'm not that person anymore. I made a mistake because I so desperately wanted someone to love. But it's been many years since I confused love and sex."

"But I don't see what any of this has to do with you staying in Fortune. It's the weather, isn't it? California weather wins again!"

"Let's talk about why I *wouldn't* stay. The only reason I wouldn't stay in Fortune is because of you. I always felt so guilty about wanting my own life, even about wanting to spend time with my father. I don't blame you for this, because it was my decision, but there were times it felt like calling my father, visiting him, would be disloyal to you."

"Honey—"

"Let me finish. You don't need me here like you think you do. Like I thought you did."

"Just because I'm having fun here today doesn't mean—"

"I'm glad you have a life and friends. That's how it should be. I'm a grown woman, and I happen to be in love with a man who has a teenage son."

"I never thought I'd see you settle. You've waited this long for the right one, why throw in the towel now?"

"Because I'm not settling! He's the best man I know and he's the right one. For me."

"Don't kid yourself. He might be perfect in every other way, or at least you think so now. But the teenager is a deal breaker. He's going to come first. Always. He needs his father, especially now."

"I know that, and he's a great kid. I love him too, as a matter of fact."

"I don't think you realize what you're getting yourself into, sweetie. He already has a child. He's not going to care about your eggs."

"*I* don't even care about my eggs!"

Mom wagged her finger. "You say that now. But this is going to cause you both a lot of grief. Believe me, the teenage years aren't easy. And the kid already has a mother."

"I'm not trying to be his mother. I only want to be a part of his life."

"The bond that Matt and his ex have over their son is unbreakable."

Mom said this with a straight face.

"You mean like yours and my father's bond? Like that?"

Her upper lip curled. "We're not the best example."

Sarah opened her mouth, then closed it. Why

was she arguing with her mother over this? The whole thing was pointless.

Mom, as always, filled the silence. "What do you love about him? And you better not tell me it's the color of his eyes."

Surprisingly, for a woman who prized color, it wasn't color that drew her to Matt's eyes. That honor would go to how expressive they were. His eyes could tell her in a matter of seconds whether he was pissed, happy, exhausted, confused, irritated…or horny. And if she'd thought she'd seen flashes of love and tenderness in them too, she only hoped she hadn't fooled herself into finding what she wanted to. The important thing is that he was worth risking her heart. More than worth it.

"I love the way he cares for his son. The way he takes care of his friends. I know he'd do anything for me. When I was so angry with Stone over the estate, Matt wouldn't let me get away without trying to work it out with Stone. He's kind and even sweet at times, but he's also strong. He won't back down from a fight and… I kind of love that." Yes, she'd been surprised by that herself.

"Oh…well then," Mom said, momentarily speechless.

The door opened and Patty poked her head in. "Tutti's getting a lap dance! You *have* to come and see this. Her face is turning purple. I'm not kidding. Hi, Sarah. Welcome back, hon. We missed you."

Mom stood up. "Come and get your own lap dance."

"No, thanks."

"But it's Channing Tatum!"

"That man out there is *not* Channing Tatum."

"Oh, who cares! Close enough."

Sarah sighed. She wasn't in a position to argue with a room full of women who were acting like this was more of a bachelorette party than a wedding shower. And frankly, she'd said what she wanted to say.

Sarah followed Mom out of the bedroom where she spotted Emily, trying to get away from Channing Tatum's look-alike. When he attempted to hump Emily's leg, she ran around the living room, bumping into chairs, couches and women. She finally landed, stomach down, sprawled over Tutti's lap.

Sarah pulled a shaken Emily back to her feet. "Congrats, Tutti. Great party, but we've got to run."

"So soon?" Mom said from behind Sarah. "But we still have the penis cake to cut."

Penis cake. Two words Sarah never thought she'd hear come out of Mom's mouth together.

"Wow. Sorry to miss that, but yeah. Stone is waiting for this one." Sarah patted Emily's shoulder. "You know how it is."

"I hope you can make it to my wedding shower, Mrs. Mcallister. It's not going to be anything like this," Emily huffed, shoving hairs back into her ponytail holder.

"Darling, you know I will!" Mom hugged Emily. Then she grabbed Sarah and stage whispered into her ear, "Don't forget what I said!"

From the safety of the great outdoors, as the loud music continued to reverberate through the middle-class suburban home, Sarah used her phone to order an Uber. She'd done enough to scare her future sister-in-law from the Mcallister genes forever. Sarah might be worried if she didn't already know how much Emily loved Stone.

"Sorry about my nutty Mom. She's usually not so…" Sarah searched for the right word. "Unhinged?"

"That's okay. I don't feel so alone anymore. You *have* met Molly."

"Yes, and I wouldn't be too shocked if you also wind up with a penis cake."

Emily laughed. "Penis cake aside, did you get what you really wanted today?"

Sarah nodded. But the day wasn't over. She had a lot to work out with Matt. Find some way of paying him back for all the materials and work he'd done to her now perfect house. Because Sarah wasn't going to live anywhere else but Fortune.

CHAPTER THIRTY-SIX

So far Matt was zero for two.

There weren't many flower arrangements left at Rosies and Posies because apparently there'd been a run earlier in the day. No one special occasion, except to hear the owner tell it, Jedd had stayed out too late and was in the doghouse with his wife; Dylan had come by because it was Molly's birthday day after tomorrow; and poor sap Jimmy was still dealing with Trish, his fiancée and the town's current Bridezilla. The owner said he regularly came in and ordered a dozen red roses, then threw them at her before she'd let him in the house. So unfortunately all that left was a rather sad-looking something with lilies, which reminded Matt of a funeral arrangement.

Not going there.

Plan B was chocolate, and he loaded up on the stuff. He'd never done anything remotely like this attempt at romantic. Over the top. A grand gesture to show Sarah how much she meant to him. Twelve years of the military life had pretty much obliterated the romantic out of him, had it ever been present at all.

But hell, he was trying.

Never in a million years did he think he'd be in this position. He'd seen plenty of his buddies beg after a fight, some of them married. Some of them not. Matt never had. Never been married and never cared enough to beg. But so help him God, he would drop to his knees if he had to. Ask her to come back to Fortune and give him another chance.

He'd asked Stone not to say a word as he attempted to surprise Sarah. He was coming for his woman. In a plane. What else said "I love you" better than that? He planned to tell her that whether here in Fort Collins or at home in Fortune, he wanted them to be together. They'd work it out long-distance if they had to. He had access to a plane. If there was anything else he could do to show how much he loved her, it had better be chocolate-covered because otherwise he had nothing. But when he arrived at the address of Sarah and Stone's mother, no one answered the door. So he did what any other poor sap in his place would do.

He sat on the front stoop and waited. And waited.

Eventually a sedan pulled up and out of it came Mrs. Mcallister.

"Thanks for the ride! It was a blast." She proceeded to move unsteadily up the walkway. Stopped in her tracks when she saw him. "Holy crap on a cracker. What are you doing here?"

He stood, knowing the answer before the question was out of his mouth. "Sarah isn't with you?"

"No."

Of course not, because this was going right along with the kind of day he was having. She took another step and almost tripped, recovering. That's when he realized Mrs. Mcallister had had a few. Hence the ride home, he imagined.

He took her elbow and guided her to the front door. "You okay?"

"I'm fine," she said, handing him her keys. "I saw Sarah here earlier with Emily. I think she's already on her way back."

Super. Grand gesture right out the window. He opened up the front door for her and stood aside as she walked past him. "Must have just missed her."

"You people sure do like to fly, don't you?"

"Yes, ma'am, I guess we do."

"Did you really fly all the way here just to see Sarah? Did you think she wasn't coming back?" She gave him a boy-you-must-be-stupid look he'd always treasure.

"I hoped she would, but I've learned not to take anything for granted anymore."

"Touché. Nice work, young man. Too bad your timing is off."

Story of his life. She didn't know the half of it. "If you're okay, I'll just head back now."

"Wait a minute." She flipped another lamp

on, plopped down on the couch and studied him. "Don't you want to know why Sarah was here?"

"You mean you're going to tell me?"

"You know what? I am. She came to tell me that she's going to stay in Fortune, and a lot of other nonsense you don't need to hear about. I guess she thought the news might be easier for me to digest in person. Plus she apparently has planes and pilots at her disposal 24/7."

Matt didn't speak. The news was good for him, best he'd had all day.

She sighed. "I thought I was competing with a place all this time. Fortune, California, land of great weather and beautiful people. Her father's house. But it isn't so much a place that's keeping her there anymore. Is it?"

Was he supposed to answer that? "I hope not."

"You should know my daughter loves you very much. There was a stripper and a penis cake at the party and she didn't even notice either one."

"Excuse me?"

"He looked just like Channing Tatum! And the cake was very tasty even if a little…obscene." She waved her arm. "But never mind all that. You have a teenage son?"

"I do. He's a good kid, and he adores Sarah."

"Seems to be mutual. But listen up. You need to put her, any woman you love, first. You're a father, I get it. A good one, from what I hear. But if you want this to work, she has to be first with you. Always."

"I know."

"Sarah seems a little confused about that. She seems to have accepted coming in second, which is something I never thought I'd see my daughter do. That's how I knew it must be love. You should set her straight on that. If my late husband and I had done that from the start, maybe we would have still been together."

"Good advice. Anything else?" He really wanted to get going and resisted taking a glance at his watch.

"Just don't hurt her, because if you do? Let's just say that I fly commercial and I will get there just the same."

He nodded sharply. "Fully understood."

"And one more thing? When you get back and you two laugh about this mix-up, you can also tell her that I was obviously wrong. About everything. I'll see you two for Stone and Emily's wedding shower. I'll bring the cake."

When Sarah got home in the late evening, Matt was still gone. Shackles was dying to go outside and when she let him out, he ran to the grass and unloaded.

"I'm so sorry, Shack. No one should have to hold it that long. I'm going to get you that doggy door tomorrow."

This house would be hers, finally really *hers*, simply because she'd laid claim to it. She'd work it out somehow, sell her condo in Fort Collins and everything she owned if that's what it took to keep it. Eventually she'd pay Matt back for all the materials and his labor. She would insist, even if she realized he wouldn't want to accept.

But that's how this whole journey had begun. Matt trying to help her, insisting on doing the work without pay. All she'd wanted from him was a little physical comfort. A reminder she was still alive. She'd had no idea or plan to fall in love this hard and fast.

So much had changed. Now she'd paint the walls of her home a different color. Put in dog doors and weird shag carpeting if that was what she wanted. It wasn't her father's house anymore.

Hers. At last.

But it had now been several hours since Matt and Joanne had left looking for Hunter with no updates. Had they not found him? If something happened to either him or the girl, Sarah could never forgive herself. Despite the fact that she didn't know how Matt would feel about her right now, and knowing Hunter was still none of her concern, she had to know. She grabbed her phone and texted Matt.

Is Hunter okay?

He replied: He's fine.

Oh thank God. Sarah took a breath.

You were right. Matt texted. Trust. I should have had more.

Where are you?

You wouldn't believe me if I told you. Just know I'll be back in a couple of hours. We'll talk then.

A couple of hours? And forgive her if "we'll talk then" sounded ominous.

It's going to be okay. She had a beautiful home, her brother and Emily, and her art. Even if her heart might crack in half without Matt, she'd survive.

Because she was nothing if not a survivor.

The important thing is that she'd managed to love someone completely. Trusting every part of herself, risking it all. Knowing it was worth it. She headed back to her shed. This had become her "happy place" and for once art no longer took on the ominous tone it had for years. She would no longer draw the faces of people she saw in her nightmares. Every day she looked forward to spending hours in here, often losing track of time. She went to work adding hues of chocolate brown to Matt's eyes and the honey tinge to his light brown hair. It wasn't half bad, even if this landscape had become something unplanned, exactly as Matt had suggested. And why not take a piece of art and make something completely new out of it? It didn't need a name, label or category to fit neatly into. It just had to be hers.

Maybe she would talk to Emily, as Matt had suggested, about selling some of her artwork at the barn. No special favors, of course, and she'd insist on a healthy contingency for Emily's family. But this one was for Matt. For Matt and Hunter. Sarah found a good stopping place, then placed her brushes in the acrylic solution jar. She walked back inside with Shackles and found Matt standing in the kitchen, staring at the new cabinet doors.

Shackles yipped and attacked Matt's ankles. Sarah stared at him because he seemed so lost, standing there alone, bending down briefly to pet Shack. Her heart leaped in her chest as she briefly wondered if it was fair to love someone this much.

"This wasn't how it was supposed to go." He looked disappointed, hands on hips and eyes half-mast.

Sarah's heart dropped to her toes. "Matt—I'm really sorry about the things I said before."

Still studying the cabinets, he slowly shook his head. "I wanted these for you. Sure, they're beautiful even at first glance. But if you get closer, that's when you see all the different hues of red that blend perfectly with the brown. You almost can't see them at first, but once you do the effect is…devastating."

He sees color the same way I do, Sarah thought,

but in the next moment she wondered why on earth they were discussing kitchen cabinets when they each had so much to say to each other. When she had so much to say to him.

"Matt. I know I said I wouldn't fall for you, but I didn't keep my end of that deal. And I'm sorry if I hurt you. You trusted me and I let you down."

"You didn't. No, you're probably the one person who's never let me down. I know why you didn't tell me, but you can't keep things from me from now on. We can't keep anything from each other."

She nodded, and her eyes became watery.

Then he cracked a sheepish smile, ran a hand down his face. "I'm such an idiot."

Sarah went for it. Now or never. She ran and jumped into his arms. He caught her easily and she had a good feeling that he always would.

"But you're my idiot."

"I've been waiting for this all day," he said, his hands tightening around the legs she had wrapped around his back.

"Where were you?"

When he told her the entire story, even adding Mom's veiled threat, she would have laughed if her heart wasn't so full. He'd come for her. But their two planes had nearly passed each other. A story for the grandkids, she thought.

"I was going for a grand gesture."

She wiggled in his arms, planting a kiss on his lips. "Message received."

"Let's get one thing straight. I'm not normally a grand gesture kind of guy, but I'm willing to try again. Maybe I'll have better luck next time. Remind me later, but there are several boxes of melted chocolate in my truck. Rosies and Posies was all out of flowers."

Sarah barely smothered another laugh. "The plane was more than enough."

He pulled her closer. "Look, babe. I know it's complicated. It's not easy for you and me. We're both from fractured families and doing the best we can. I get it. But the only thing that really matters is what we have here. You and me. Right now. It's the only thing that matters."

Yes, oh yes. "You and me. Me and you. This combination works for me."

"And I don't think you should sell this house. Don't argue. Just hear me out first."

"But—"

"No buts, Sarah. This is a beautiful house and no one deserves it more than you do."

"I agree. I'm not selling."

He looked a bit stunned. "Seriously? This has to be the shortest argument we've ever had."

"Here's to more of those!"

"There's one more thing I want you to do."

"Anything."

His big hand palmed her neck and he pulled her mouth close to his. "Don't ever let me put you second. I love you, Sarah. You're first with me. Always. You're it for me. Do you get me?"

She nodded, her eyes watery. "I love you, too. So much."

"You better."

"But we need to have a talk about how I can pay you back for all the—"

He shut her up with a kiss.

This was actually her favorite way of him shutting her up. "It's just that—"

He gave her another kiss. This one harder, longer. Deeper. If he kept this up she would soon forget her own name, much less all the money she owed him. When she came up for air he was carrying her into the bedroom.

"Oh, this is a good idea, but still. I'm going to pay you back. I mean it."

He plopped her down on the bed, shut the bedroom door and started unbuttoning his shirt. Her brain stopped working. There was something about a house and money but beyond that she had zip. "I—"

"I'll tell you what," he said, discarding his shirt on the floor. "How about I live here with you for the rest of my life? Will that do it? Can we call it even?"

Her heart slammed against her rib cage. Forever with Matt. She couldn't imagine anything better. And finally, for the first time in years, she was ready to risk it all.

"You've got yourself a deal."

EPILOGUE

September

BUTTERFLIES HAD TAKEN up residence in Sarah's stomach. Hell, it seemed like they were throwing a housewarming party in there. *Okay, calm down. You've got this. No worries.* And true enough, she was ready for all this.

Maybe.

Two months ago when she'd approached the owners of the Pandemonium Art Gallery in Fortune about a small showing, she certainly hadn't expected…all of this. She'd thought maybe a small event with a few of the locals. Some wine, some cheese, maybe a little panel discussion with the other artists on art and its many mediums. She wanted to start small so that if she bombed, not many would hear about it.

But events never stayed small when Emily Parker soon-to-be-Mcallister heard about them. She'd amassed such a large contingency of friends and family that it seemed as if the entire town had come out. The crowd of people spilled in as the doors opened and the married couple that owned the gallery warmly welcomed everyone inside. Sarah moved from where she stood in front of her paintings. She didn't want anyone to think they had to compliment her work because she was standing there, but it would be even worse if they insulted her baby right in front of her. How could she not haul off and slug them? Not even slightly at ease, she moved quickly through the crowd. She immediately caught Emily's eye as she headed toward Sarah, Stone behind her.

"This is so exciting!" Emily said and grabbed Sarah in a bear hug.

"Hey, sis," Stone said.

"Thanks for coming." Sarah wrung her hands together.

What should she do now? Walk around and praise the other artists' paintings? Should she mingle or hang out with her friends and acquaintances? Realistically, she understood Matt was right and that if she wanted to be an artist, her work would eventually have to be seen. But while she loved spending hours in the room addition Matt had recently built for her so that she no longer had to use the garden shed, she didn't care as much for all the schmoozing. Her art was so intensely personal and private that it made her ache a little inside to see it hanging up on the walls being judged. No, not judged. Appreciated.

There, that's better.

"Where's Matt?" Stone asked.

"On his way."

Sarah glanced at the time. He was actually a little late, but he'd gone to pick up Hunter, who at the last minute had insisted on being here, too. It was sweet that Hunter had been so supportive all along, but realistically, all she wanted, all she needed, was Matt. Only he seemed to soothe her frazzled nerves.

"See you in a bit. We're going to go stand in front of your paintings and pretend we know what we're talking about." Emily tugged Stone in the other direction.

Sarah continued to walk, scan the crowd, and greet friends and locals she recognized, stopping long enough to appreciate every artist and their work. There was so much talent in this one small room that she felt honored to be here among her peers.

She would have known Matt stood behind her even before she turned around. That magnetic pull to him still hadn't stopped, and she doubted it ever would now.

"Hey, beautiful."

She spun around to find Matt, her solid wall of strength.

"I want to get out of here." She could only be this honest with Matt, who understood. Who got her, time and time again.

"But you're not," he said calmly. "You're staying right here and taking the praise."

She laughed. "You're an incurable optimist. But I will stay. It helps that you're here."

He pulled out a dozen red roses from behind his back. "Got luckier this time, because I planned."

"Thank you. They're beautiful." She took them and went into his arms, such a safe and warm place to be.

"Hey, Sarah."

This was from Hunter, dressed as she never saw him: slacks and a button-up shirt. Not even looking pissy about it, either. "Hey, so glad you're here."

"This is way cool. Someone did a painting of a huge spider. And then someone else attached a string to a cup. Is that art?"

"Anything can be art," Sarah said. "As long as it makes you think."

"Huh. Mission accomplished." Hunter wandered off in the direction of the door another artist had painted black, after one of his favorite songs.

"Maybe my art is boring," Sarah said. "Maybe I should—"

Matt pulled her in for a kiss. "Shut up, babe. I love your stuff. Especially *Woman in the Garden*."

One of her favorites, also, and had taken the better part of two long months. Inspired by one of her personal favorites, Van Gogh, the painting of a woman alone in a garden of sunflowers was a fair effort at impressionism. She hoped.

Matt grabbed her hand and tugged her toward her paintings.

"Wait. I don't want to." Sarah almost dug in her heels. "What if—"

"Shhh," Matt said, squeezing her hand.

As she was pulled along by Matt, she heard voices drifting toward them. Several people stood in front of her paintings.

"I like the way the artist uses the medium to emphasize and express her happiness. Contentment." Emily's soft voice.

"I like the way your lips look when you talk. Which is pretty much always." This was from Stone, right before he grabbed Emily and kissed her full on the lips.

Sarah stifled a laugh and glanced up at Matt who had a sexy grin on his face. In the past months he'd seemed to get more attractive to her every day, even when she doubted that were possible or feasible. More than likely, she grew more relaxed every day about what they had together. Waking up next to Matt every morning in a house which would soon belong to both of them equally was no wish or dream. It was her new reality, and better than any of her fantasies.

After advising the Fort Collins PD that she would no longer be available as a forensic sketch artist, Sarah had put her condo up for sale. She'd tried to pay Matt back at least for the materials, but he'd refused. So instead she'd paid down her loans, put some savings aside for the roof replacement looming, and set up a college fund for Hunter. And then, just to be difficult and stubborn, she'd deposited a good chunk of money into a separate account for Matt to do with as he pleased. Speechless, he hadn't been able to complain. Much.

So this is what starting over looks like.

Sarah was in brand-new territory. She might be walking on a high wire with no net, but it was worth it. She was happier than she'd ever been, spending days at the airport, part owner of a business she fully intended to continue to be a part of. She might not be crazy about flying, but she loved the heck out of the pilots. All three of them. Make that four, if she counted James Mcallister, because even if he was no longer among them, she did love her father. Always had, and now she understood that he'd known it.

A long time ago, Sarah's mother had told Sarah to start over with a clean slate. Leave the ugly past in her rearview mirror. Start over. Once, she'd run from her past, but now she ran toward her future. That future was with Matt at her side.

"Hey!" The tornado that was Molly Parker approached, Dylan in tow. "I haven't seen the ring yet. Let me see."

Before Sarah could lift up her left hand, Molly had already pulled it up. "Oh my God! It's blinding me. Congratulations!"

"Thank you," Sarah said, and admired the shimmering diamond solitaire for possibly the millionth time.

Matt's arm snaked protectively around her waist and he pulled her close.

He'd proposed a month ago, using far too much of the money she'd deposited into his account to buy her the ring. Stubborn man. She would have given him hell for spending so much money on her, but she'd been crying too hard to argue at the time. With Stone's help, Matt had arranged for the proposal to take place at the Airborne Bar & Grill, the very first place they'd ever laid eyes on each other. Surrounded by her family and friends, all that had come out of her mouth was *yesyesyesyes*.

"When's the wedding date?" Molly asked.

"Working on it," Matt said, bringing up their joined hands to his lips. "As far as I'm concerned we can elope."

"Right," Stone said. "You should hurry before she changes her mind."

There was laughter among her group of friends as Matt made a move to shove Stone, and Emily giggled and got between them.

"Sorry, you can't kill him. I'm going to marry him."

Sarah gazed at the faces of the friends and family she loved. She couldn't even remember the last time she'd felt alone, or had thought there was nothing left for her in Fortune. Everything she'd ever wanted was right here. Right now.

And she couldn't think of any other place on earth she'd rather be.

* * * * *

If you enjoyed this story, don't miss
Stone and Emily in book one of
Heatherly Bell's
HEROES OF FORTUNE VALLEY *series:*

BREAKING EMILY'S RULES

Available now!

Get 2 Free Books,
Plus 2 Free Gifts—
just for trying the Reader Service!

Get 2 Free Books,

Plus 2 Free Gifts—

HARLEQUIN *Presents*

just for trying the *Reader Service!*

Get 2 Free Books,
Plus 2 Free Gifts—
just for trying the Reader Service!

HW17

Get 2 Free Books,
Plus 2 Free Gifts—
just for trying the Reader Service!